Tempest in Tulum

A Sports Romance

Cher Terais

Aggrandis Group, LLC

Also by Cher Terais

A Wanderlust Romance

Bali Blue

Mess on the Mara

Stay even more connected by scanning the the QR Code below to get bonus content for Cher Terais's books. Discover the fun things like:

The soundtrack to this book and the others;

Inspiration boards and visuals for each book;

Free downloadables, short stories and more!

https://linktr.ee/Cher_Terais

The trip doesn't stop here! The Booked Club community and podcast are COMING SOON!

Sign up for my mailing list for all the deets: https://bit.ly/cherteraismailinglist

Tempest in Tulum
A Sports Romance

Cher Terais

Aggrandis Group, LLC

Book Cover by Cher Terais

Illustrations by Cher Terais

1st edition 2024

www.cherterais.com

E-book ISBN: 978-1-7378260-5-7

Paperback ISBN: 978-1-7378260-8-8

Hardcover ISBN: 978-1-7378260-9-5

Author's Note

DEAR READER,

Thank you for giving *Tempest in Tulum a chance*. As with all of my stories, it is a reflection of real struggles, emotions, and growth. In this note, I want to acknowledge the three central themes that shape this story, as well as any trigger warnings that might affect some readers.

Themes:

1. **Healing and Growth**: The story centers on healing, both in body and soul. Delia and Okiyo, in their unique ways, face the broken parts of themselves and come out stronger. Through their journeys, we see that growth is not linear; it's filled with setbacks, resilience, and the hope of finding solace.

2. **Family and Belonging**: There's an unspoken power in being surrounded by those who see the truest version of us, even when we try to hide. Family—by blood or by

bond—plays a critical role. Our relationships shape us, push us forward, and allow us to rediscover our purpose.

3. **Survival and Connection**: At its core, this story is about survival, but also about the connections that keep us going. Okiyo and Delia learn that they don't have to bear their burdens alone, and in their vulnerability, they find strength, acceptance, and love.

Trigger Warning: The theme of sexual assault is present in this book. Although I did not experience it in the exact way that Iya did, I have faced it, as so many others have—women, men, girls, and boys. I know what it feels like to be afraid, to feel voiceless, and to wonder if anyone will listen. Through Delia's eyes, I wanted to tell a story about the aftershocks of such violation—not just on the survivor but on those who care about them. In writing this, I aimed to treat the subject with sensitivity, to show that while pain ripples out, so can love, understanding, and healing. To everyone who has ever felt like their voice was silenced, I want to tell you that you are heard. Your experiences are valid, your pain is understood, and your journey matters.

Thank you for letting me share this story with you.

With love and gratitude,

Cher Terais

"Love can be a storm—a holy tempest that sweeps you up, tosses you around, and leaves you breathless. But in that chaos, sometimes, you may find exactly who you were destined to be all along."

Cher Terais

Prologue – Delia

(10 Years Ago)

THE NIGHT THAT PROMISED inspiration and ambition became the haunting memory that shattered innocence amidst the splendor of my greatest dream. We stepped into the lobby of the new Rosemore hotel, an architectural masterpiece that loomed above Atlanta's city line like a goliath. The grand opening event here tonight was one I've eagerly awaited – a chance to mingle with famous architects from around the world and network with the best in the industry. A dream come true for a young, ambitious architectural student like me.

When Mr. Brooks, my Spatial Design professor extended the coveted invitation to me, I couldn't believe it. Every one of us in the freshmen class of the College of Architecture at GA Tech wanted an invite. But knew events such as the opening of the tallest skyscraper in Atlanta was reserved for seniors. Not just any seniors either.

Only those seniors at the top of the class and being targeted by some of the top Architectural firms around the world would get invited to this prestigious event. Yet, here I was. A 1ˢᵗ year student; a world of possibilities being placed at my feet. And I couldn't dream of sharing this experience with anyone other than my little sister.

Iya strained her neck as she marveled at the glittering chandeliers overhead. I smiled down at her, equally in awe of the space. I was extremely pleased with my decision to bring her along. My *mom* wholeheartedly disagreed. She openly chided me for inviting Iya before first running it by her and my dad.

"Iya is too young to be at a grand opening of anything," she'd fussed. "Especially a trendy hotel downtown, Delia. You should have asked us first before getting her hopes all up. I would never agree to my thirteen year old going to a formal event where no other children are invited. Hell, you're barely even nineteen. You shouldn't even be there."

And that was the end of the conversation. Except, it wasn't. I begged and pleaded for a week straight, while Iya walked around looking like a sick puppy until mom and dad finally acquiesced. But not before a terse, "You better have her home before 10PM," edict from my mom.

That big grin on Iya's face told me I'd been right to beg to let her come with me. I was exploding with excitement too. This was an amazing opportunity and was a major step in the direction of me being the world famous architect I'd dreamed of. I kept my cool though.

Once Iya and I arrived, I could see why my mom was concerned. This was definitely an event for the grown and sexy of Atlanta's elite. Yeah, I'd definitely have to contain myself. For starters, I didn't need my baby sister looking at me like I was lame, geeking out over a building. Secondly, we were both going to have to fit in like we were old enough to be here.

I playfully mushed Iya's forehead before linking arms with her to lead us across the illuminated marble floors into the elegant lobby filled with an elite mix of patrons decked out in black tie and cocktail gowns.

Though still hesitant, Mom helped Iya and I find the perfect dresses for the event and even let me wear her gold strappy Giuseppe heels. They matched my strapless body contouring gown to perfection. Iya was in an age-appropriate skater dress. I still had to keep telling her to pull it down because even though she was only thirteen, she had the longest legs, toned from years of cheerleading since the age of five. That and her Atlanta born and bred body was beginning to fill in.

A clothing challenge my mom struggled with for me too growing up. Finding age appropriate clothes for girls with bodies that presented as grown women too early in stores filled with skinny jeans, halter tops and booty shorts was damn near impossible.

Not even straight legged baggy boyfriend jeans could hide our god given curves. Begotten naturally from hers truly, our Mama.

The air in the lobby was infused with the heady fragrance of freshly cut flowers. It was the architecture that took my breath away though. Every inch of the space was a masterpiece—a harmonious blend of old and new. The sleek, clean lines juxtaposed with high, vaulted ceilings gave the lobby an expansive grandeur, while intricate arches hinted at classical influence.

The marbled floors reflected the light, giving the space an ethereal glow, and water features flowed gracefully, adding a touch of serenity to the bold design. It was as if the past and future had been perfectly fused into a symphony of stone, glass, and water, speaking a language only architecture lovers could truly understand. Only a genius architect could pull off such a feat. And he was the reason I could have kissed Mr. Brooks for extending the invite to me.

"It's like a fairytale, Delia," Iya's soft words mirrored my thoughts. "I'm so glad you let me come with you."

"I wouldn't have had it any other way, Chica." I playfully niggled her arm with the knuckle of my index finger. "Now you get to tell Mom and Dad how worth it this was for them to let you come!" I rolled my eyes in mock exasperation at my parent's concern. Iya beamed and nodded, agreeing the fight I'd put up to get mom to agree was worth it.

Mr. Brooks spotted me and immediately waved us over. He was mingling with a couple of guys, two of which I recognized as graduating seniors. Suresh smiled. I smiled back and waved as Iya and I sidled up. The other guy, everyone called him Jordy if I'd remembered correctly, just stood there. Arms crossed, face a mask as he looked me up and down then gave Iya a lingering stare before boredly giving his attention back to Mr. Brooks.

His energy kind of threw me off, but I'd been around spoiled, privileged pricks all my life. I guess by all rights, Iya and I could have been perceived as privileged pricks too, with real estate moguls for parents. But since I can remember, my mom would not let us forget our roots.

We, both Iya and I, became accustomed to dealing with the snobs and elite attitudes of our peers from the first days of private school and at the many functions we'd been dragged to by our parents.

Rather than label him a snob, I didn't really know the dude, I shrugged Jordy's cold reception off as him feeling a way about me being invited to a party on an invitation that should have been reserved for a graduating senior. Bringing my little sister, likely didn't help. His disdainful gaze lingered on Iya a bit too long still. That, he would not get a pass for.

Before I could check his ass with the words I'd been biting back, my attention was pulled away by Professor Brooks.

"Delia, glad you could make it." He gently pulled me into the group of my peers by the shoulder as I looked back at Iya, winking to make sure she was ok. "Look right over there, dear." He pointed towards the front of the room. Leaning in, he whispered on an excited breath, "Foster Yurman is waiting to talk to you."

Even in four inch heels, I had to stand on my tippees and angle around the crowd to see where Brooks was pointing. As soon as I spotted him, I felt the professors gentle nudge in Yurman's direction.

I was nervous to say the least. Iya and I'd barely just gotten there. I absolutely had an introduction prepared in my head. But it wasn't every day that a girl got to meet her idol. I was halfway across the room before I paused to turn back and search for Iya. She was pushing through the throng of people but was only a few paces behind. I stopped and reached out my hand to her and pulled her forward through the crowd.

Iya's hand now in mine, I turn again towards Mr. Yurman. Not realizing he'd spotted me first, I almost barreled right into the man. A bit disoriented, I looked up at him in awe. He smiled down at me before he looked seemingly right over the crowd to nod at Professor Brooks as if to let him know I'd made it over to him.

He was tall. Handsome and debonair in a swarthy way. He as effortlessly suave as his architectural designs in a dark grey tailored suit, pristine white shirt with top button undone and no tie. At a black tie affair in his honor, in a room of buttoned up suits and sequined dresses, he looked the most distinguished. He was smooth.

"You must be Ms. Delia Aguillen?" he asked, extending his hand for a shake. He peered around me, noticing Iya for the first time then extended his hand to her as well.

She looked like she was about to do a pee-pee dance, not at all thrilled about having to wait while I talked with Yurman. She was ready for the part of the evening where we got the tour—the hotel, the storefronts and model condos that filled the space of the full building. I wanted to see those things too, but not more than this opportunity to speak with *the* Foster Yurman. When she asked if she could go to the restroom, I quickly nodded yes, promptly turning back to Mr. Yurman.

"Delia Aguillen-McGhee," I stammered nervously. Finally taking his still offered hand and shaking it firmly. "Our mother would kill me if I left the McGhee off. But please call me Delia."

Foster smiled, his eyes twinkling. "Well, Delia, it's a pleasure. I've heard quite a lot about you from the faculty at Georgia Tech. According to Mr. Brooks, you're quite the prodigy."

I felt my heart skip a beat. Foster Yurman knew about me? I tried to keep my excitement in check, but I couldn't help the smile that spread across my face. "Well I just have wanted to be an architect since I can remember. "Mr. Brooks has been such a mentor to me.

He's been pushing me to think outside the box ever since my first class with him."

Foster nodded, clearly interested. "That's what good mentors do. You know, he mentioned you had quite a unique take on some of my recent projects."

"Well, I think architecture should be more than just buildings," I blurted, my excitement rising. "It should evoke an emotion—like the hotel you designed in London. When my family visited, I couldn't believe how you merged sleek modern elements with historical features. The glass atrium that drew in natural light while maintaining the structure's original elegance? It was... *breathtaking*. And your use of symmetry to create a sense of balance in the garden courtyard—it was a perfect harmony between nature and structure."

His eyebrows raised, a look of genuine surprise and delight crossing his face. "You visited the London project?"

"Yes. I begged my mom to take me."

"I'm flattered you paid that much attention to the details. That was precisely the goal—to keep the spirit of history alive while inviting in the energy of the new."

"Oh, absolutely! And honestly, seeing it in person only fueled my desire to be an architect even more. I've wanted this since I was a kid. Experiencing your work firsthand was... I don't know, like finally seeing what I'd always imagined but didn't have the words to describe. It all just clicked."

"Your passion for design is quite refreshing, Delia." His smile was genuine and I could feel my heart swell at his words. "You remind me of myself at your age—full of ideas and excitement for what could be. It's rare to find someone who truly sees what lies beneath the surface."

My breath caught for a moment, feeling seen in a way I hadn't expected. "Thank you, Mr. Yurman. That means so much coming from you. I want to design spaces that matter, places that people want to come back to. Spaces that make people feel—like your work does."

He gave me a warm smile, clearly impressed. "I think you will, Delia. You're already on your way."

I glanced around then, realizing that at least half an hour had passed and Iya hadn't returned from the restroom. My excitement turned to concern as I looked toward the direction she'd gone.

"Is something wrong?" he asked, noticing my sudden distraction.

"Ummm, It's just my sister's been gone for a while. She was excited for the tour, but I hope she didn't get lost." I laughed nervously, trying to keep it light.

"Ah, siblings. They're always a handful," Foster said with a knowing smile. "Why don't you go check on her? But before you do, let me give you my card. I'd love to see some of your work someday."

My eyes widened as he handed me his card. I took it, trying to suppress the ecstatic rush of excitement. "Thank you, Mr. Yurman. I'd be honored."

He gave me an encouraging nod before turning back to his next obligation, and I slipped the card into my purse, already feeling like I'd just taken the first step toward my dreams.

Ugh... Where was this girl? Let me go find her. I begrudgingly went in search of Iya. I decided to start looking by the restrooms since that's where she was *supposed* to be going.

The crowd had grown in the time I was in conversation with Foster. Champagne was flowing freely. Some of the attendees were already showing visible signs of overindulging. Easy to tell when you *and* your little sister were perhaps the only two people in the room who were not old enough to drink. Note to self, *definitely* should have listened to mom.

Another five minutes later, I made it to the corridor where the restrooms were located. Unlike the lobby, it was a dimly lit ghost town over here. I heard a door swing open in the distance down the hall. It appeared to be Jordy stepping into the hallway and adjusting his pants before quickly walking in the opposite direction towards the exit.

I'd gotten closer to the spot where I'd first seen him. *Odd.* The men's restroom was on the other side of the hall. I looked up. Just as I thought, the ladies sign was above this door. Confused, I looked back down the hall in the direction Jordy had just left. A sense of dread came over me.

"Iya, where are you?" I hissed under my breath. I entered the ladies room. It was huge. All the stall doors were closed. They were the kind of stalls that you see in high-end restrooms, doors from floor to ceiling, giving the utmost privacy in each luxurious stall. I didn't see her and was preparing to turn and walk out until I heard her sob.

My heart began pounding in my chest as I started beating on and opening each door. Panic surged through me after not seeing her in the first three stalls. Something was terribly wrong.

"Iya!" I yelled this time, my voice growing more desperate with each passing moment. "Where are you?"

Finally, I spotted her–a glimpse of her skater dress in the back corner of the last stall. But as I rush over, my relief turns to horror. Iya is huddled in the corner, her dress ripped and tears streamed down her face. My breath caught as I took in the blood marring her thighs.

"Iya, what happened?" I asked, my voice trembling with fear. Guilt already setting in.

She looked up at me, her eyes filled with tears. "Delia, I-I didn't know what to do. I tried to fight him off, but..."

Chapter 1 – Okiyo

(Present Day)

PERHAPS IT WAS THE break-in at this very restaurant before it opened just shy of two years ago that had me on edge. Or maybe my sense of vigilance tonight was because the media was now fully aware that Andra Bainswright was the newly recognized— very beautiful, very American daughter of the Kenyan billionaire, Leboo Baijan. My boss.

Both he and his younger daughter, Mackena, had flown in to celebrate Andra and her partner's foray into Michelin Star success with their restaurant's recent win. The fact that both Andra and Chef Kobe Abara, the owners of this swanky dive and the reason for this party tonight were also becoming media darlings, added to my heightened sense of alert.

This was hardly my type of affair. Room full of half-drunk people, loud music, and sappy speeches. I was not on duty tonight but here as an invited guest of the hosts. *We* were all back here in Atlanta to celebrate the success of Gastrafrique.

All of those things gave me reason to be protective and to ensure that my men who *were* on duty tonight stayed on point. These highly publicized affairs always brought out the crazies seeking their fifteen moments of fame.

Even though I was here as an invited guest, old habits tended to die hard. I did the necessary and was social, whilst still combing the crowd for interlopers, scanning for the slightest hint of trouble.

At the drop of an earring back, I or any member of my highly trusted security team, blended seamlessly into the background, would take them out before the next beat of the heavy bass of the song playing on the overhead speakers.

I caught the woman of the hour, standing hand in hand with her love, Kobe having a very private moment on the patio of the open restaurant space. She was safe. I turned my attention to her father, who too was having hushed conversations.

I groaned inwardly at the gleam in his eye. It was a bit too intense as he gazed at the upturned mouth of the elegant beauty he talked to in intimate conversation. They were too close. And the fact that the beauty was not his wife, who was back home in Kenya and refused to come, but the mother of his secret—well not secret anymore— love child would stir that scandal up all over again. This time it would make world news.

I made my way over and gently whispered in Leboo's ear, "Too close, ol' boy." He immediately understood, nodding in apology at

Evelyn Bainswright, stepping back slightly before letting her know he'd need to prepare to make his way to the front of the room to give his congratulations speech to the guests of honor.

Those of us in the billionaire's inner circle knew that Evelyn was and might still be the love of his life. It was my job to ensure that it stayed in the circle. Once Leboo moved to the front of the restaurant, I nodded at the beauty before politely moving on as well. No immediate threats here anymore.

Relaxing a bit, I nodded sociably at Mackena, who'd been on the arm of one of the architects of the very space we were standing in. She danced too close, laughed too hard, and hung on to his every word. She'd certainly be making an ass out of the dim-witted fiancé waiting on her in the wings back in Kenya. I was tired of watching the sad bloke die from the thousand cuts dished out by Mackena... If the media got wind of this, it would spare *mans* from further embarrassment. I chuckled inwardly and kept it moving.

I leaned against one of the intricately carved wooden columns that served as support and cultural décor. I looked out over the room. Women giggling with their dates, some arguing. Groups dancing. They were all so blissfully ignorant to threats against their persons or their pockets ever lurking. They looked so happy and full of themselves as though nothing could ever rain on their parades.

A wisp of red dress beyond the crowd caught my attention. Alarm bells vibrated in my chest rather than my head. Her beauty gut punched me. I couldn't break my gaze from her.

To the casual observer, her full attention was rapt on the overeager young man vying for her attention. I recognized there was something else quite different going on. She pulled it off masterfully, and through narrowed eyes I spied the subtle, graceful movements she barely made.

The classic feint. A defensive countermeasure I was all too familiar with accomplishing. I was mesmerized to see someone, especially as beautiful as she, pulling it off so effortlessly. Watching her in action was like watching a maestro's masterful *concierto*. His hand reached for hers. She swayed left giggling ever so demurely at whatever nonsense spewed from his lips. His hand grasping air, never realizing his move was thwarted. I was impressed.

I continued to watch. He leaned closer to whisper in her ear. She spins, grasping the elegant stem of a champagne flute from a passing waiter. *The Ghost Step.* I almost shouted bravo at her stealthy move and awareness of her surroundings. Because how else would she have known the waiter with the champagne tray was approaching from her rear.

I actually did chuckle out loud when her clumsy mate reached to grab a glass too, nearly knocking the waiter's tray out of his hand. She feints left again, *ever so slightly*, moving one index finger up to steady the tray while her other hand imperceptibly moves to the waiter's elbow to steady him, saving the tray before it teeters and crashes.

She had my full attention. She was average height, appearing much taller than she was, feet clad in impossibly high stiletto heels. Yet she moved as gracefully as a dancer. A less nimble woman would have stumbled in the haste of helping the waiter save his tray. The alarm bells were now ringing higher in my head. My eyes narrowed at her keen instincts. She was trained in her movements. *Trained in what though?*

I was busy pondering these thoughts when Andra sidled up. She paused, lips slowly spreading into a knowing smile as she mouthed, "She's gorgeous. Don't think I've ever seen you show this much attention towards a woman." She tilted her head in the direction of the lady in red. When I followed Andra's eyes, the lady in red was gone. Andra giggled again before saying, "She went that way," pointing towards a back corner of the room where there was an opening to a hallway. She looked up at me, eyebrows shrugging as if asking if I would pursue. Before my response, she winked, leaving me to stare in the direction she'd just pointed me in.

As if compelled, I headed in the direction of the opening.

I glanced down the hallway. Empty. Yet, subtle notes of Bond No. 5 perfume lingered. It had a rich, heady scent. An equally heady feeling had my feet moving of their own accord in search of her. Had to be hers. I inched down the hall towards the restrooms.

God man! What are you doing? Following a woman, even one as comely as her, not my style. Attachments nor entanglements were either. I blew out a deep breath, shaking the tingly feelings away. I straightened my suit jacket, preparing to just do a cursory security sweep of the hall before going to the men's room to get a hold of myself and stop this silly pursuit. *Pursuit.* Why in bloody hell *was I* pursuing some strange woman in a red dress? How cliché—

I heard the rush of air before I saw a fist coming directly towards my face. I ducked.

She appeared stunned that she'd missed. Her eyes narrowed. Stunning me even more when she advanced on me.

The corridor was narrow. One step in my direction and she was in striking distance. A swift upward swing of her knee aimed square at my manhood. Instinctually, I pushed down, one hand stacked on top of the other, blocking what could have been a crushing blow.

Why the hell was she attacking me? I was surprised, but curiously amused. Down right, *bloody* impressed at her boldness.

She quickly stepped back, firmly planting her feet unphased by my groin block moving out of my strike distance. As if I would *even* raise a hand to a woman. I was pondering that exact thought when she dropped low and did a spin to sweep my ankles. *Bloody fucking impressive!* Red had exacted a perfect low roundhouse kick. Ahhh… now I knew where her nimbleness came from. She was trained in the martial arts. That also meant she was breaking the Bushido Code of restraint. So again, *why the bloody hell was she attacking me?* We'd not had the pleasure of meeting. I jumped, evading her low ankle sweep.

Only countering her moves, I marveled at her skill and agility in those heels. Her beauty alone was a weapon and threatened to disarm me. Seemed we both were breaking codes tonight. I was a man of no entanglements, yet her heady scent, long elegant neck and exquisite frame that was contorting every-which-way but in my bed had my groin tightening. This spit fire of a woman had me on full alert, but in the most ungentlemanly of ways.

Then a quick flash of light. *Fuck.* She connected. It didn't hurt, but stunned me enough to make me reset my feet and firm my stance in preparation for her next onslaught. And in seconds she did, but this time, the heel of her dainty shoe caught in the hem of her gown.

She stumbled at the very moment I was reaching to grab her by the shoulders to stop her assault. Instead of grabbing her sexy sleek shoulders, however,, the mission changed from stopping her attack to stopping her from an embarrassing fall.

It didn't quite go as I'd planned. *It went better.* She ended up pressed between a hard wall and my chest with one of my hands gently pressed around the base of her throat.

We both froze. The only sound was our collective, heavy breaths. The only movement was the rise and fall of our heaving chests. Her breasts pushed into me with every intake of air. Though my hand was positioned around her neck and her head was pinned to the wall, I applied no pressure. She could have easily shifted out of my grasp. She didn't. I also did not step back when I realized her defenses were down.

This woman had launched a silent attack on me. Unprovoked. Yet all I could think about was how I wanted to lean down and kiss her so roughly and thoroughly that her lips would be bruised and swollen.

She looked up. Brown flecked eyes pierced mine and I was lost in the depths of her orbs. We studied each other like two wary animals. Competitors in the ring, sizing each other up. Just us, lost in each other, trapped in our singular thoughts about what the fuck this was and why. A deep clearing of a throat at the end of the hall caught both our attentions.

I stepped back slowly as Gin, one of my guys, moved a bit closer.

"Everything alright, boss?" He asked as he slowly stalked closer, not wanting to interrupt, but also not wanting to leave me vulnerable if Red was a threat.

I straightened my jacket, preparing to take my leave but not before staring into her eyes once more. Without breaking eye contact with her, I answered my *man*s. "Everything is good."

She took the distraction as her opportunity to get out of here. She pulled up the hem of her skirt, turned and rushed to the door of the women's restroom, disappearing inside.

I moved to follow Gin back to the party, looking back down the hallway once more to find it empty.

Chapter 2 – Delia

*W*HAT THE FUCK WAS *that, Delia?* I chastised myself between an upper cut and jab to the body bag I was pummeling. *How the fuck did I let—* KICK*— a rando hem me up in a hallway and damn near choke slam—* KNEE. KNEE. RIGHT HOOK *—my silly ass?*

I continued to strike, kick, punch and curse the bag trying to figure out for the life of me how this motherfucker had gotten the best of me. And I didn't mean in a fight. *Who was I kidding? What fight?* I'd attacked an absolute stranger.

The better part of me felt guilty for attacking him. *But why wouldn't I?* He'd followed me down a dark hallway, passing the men's restroom completely by. My thoughts went back to that night ten years ago when I didn't protect my little sister. I was triggered. I just knew he was up to some debauchery. He was the same Tom Ford clad, handsome guy that I'd caught one too many times staring at me from across the room. Handsome men can be weirdos too.

I didn't know who he was at the time of our— *interaction*. But what warm thighed woman could forget his broad, athletic frame. Or the serious, no nonsense eyes of a man who was totally sure of himself. And the glistening black waves of his low-cut Caesar, perfectly tapered into a precisely cut beard. *Sheesh and Dios mio at the same damn time.*

Under different circumstances, I'd want to lose my fingers in that thick mass of gently waving hair as I pulled him in for a kiss. *But* fuck all of that. I didn't care how fine he was. Fight or flight kicked in. So I swung on him.

What made the entire ordeal worse, I went back into the party hell bent on telling my boss, Rhiyan, that some strange man had followed me to the restroom. This was a work event for us. When I found her, she was chatting it up with the exact motherfucker I was about to tell on.

I tried to slink back into the crowd unseen but she saw me and called me over— *loudly*— causing him and her husband to turn around. All eyes on me. *Fuck.* He and I locked eyes again and damn if there wasn't a mischievous smirk playing at the corners of his lips as he recognized me.

Turned out, my stalker was head of the security detail that apparently wasn't announced in the memo about this party. And he said nothing. Just reached out a perfect gentleman's hand. Which

I stared at for way too long, focused on the thick veins that meandered across the smooth darkness of his skin.

When I finally gave him mine to shake back, he grasped it gently, quietly stating in a deep, rich, British accent, "Pleased to meet you, Ms. Aguillen-McGhee. Your boss has spoken ever so highly of you." He didn't say a word about our silent fight—*correction*—my silent attack on him.

The whole ordeal had me in the gym at the ass crack of dawn punching this body bag as if I were exercising demons. I tried to tell myself that I needed to punch this bag until I had a clear understanding of how this man had thrown not a single punch, yet was able to pin me against a wall by my neck. He might as well have choke-slammed me, because I was rendered totally incapacitated.

By the time I was ten minutes into my *'exorcism by punching bag'*, My utter embarrassment had subsided. Now I was trying to rid my body of the memory of his long, thick dick that pressed into my belly while he had my ass pinned between a literal wall and his hard place.

I should have been fighting for my virtue, but that chest, that beard and the *'good girl'* he spoke with just his eyes, had my panties puddling. Way to go, Delia... You let a hard dick and good cologne hit you with a flawless victory.

I reset and kicked the bag harder, rocking the whole of my wash-n-go into my face and back again from the force. I quickly pirouetted into a back spin roundhouse and connected with the bag. And from the sound that came from the other side, the bag had connected with a body other than mine.

"Umph," I heard his wince before he thudded to the ground. I grabbed the bag to quickly stop its swaying, then peered around it to find Rudy glaring up at me incredulously through greasy black unkempt hair that always seemed to be stuck to his sweat shined forehead. It baffled me how he was always sweating, but never worked out anymore at the gym he came to every day.

He was sprawled on the floor holding his chest after I'd unintentionally winded him. I was on a roll with hitting folks who didn't deserve it lately. I brushed the thought of Rudy's greasiness and the look of *ick* that was no doubt on my face away and reached down to help him up.

I was resetting in front of the bag preparing to take more of my aggression out on it, pausing to reprimand Rudy as I remembered this wasn't the first time he'd stepped behind my bag and ended up on his ass.

"I thought I told you to quit walking behind my bag." I didn't wait on his response before I started another round of combo punches and kicks.

"Shit, Deelz! I was hugging the damn wall trying to stay out your damn way, but you wilding out! The fuck wrong with you?" He questioned, still looking pained. He continued to mutter under his breath, "Fighting that bag like it said something about ya' mama."

I ignored his weak attempt at a joke. He sighed, then took a deep breath before pushing himself to stand fully upright. *And he was still in the damn way.*

I swear Rudy got on my nerves. If it wasn't for the fact that he had the inside scoop on the fight circuit, I would not be caught dead consorting with his grimy ass. Everything about him screamed shady.

He gave zero fucks about interrupting my workout and just leaned back, arms crossed. he was waiting on me to acknowledge him by the way he stared at me, lips pulled back in a shit eating grin as if he was bursting at the seams to share something.

When I paid him no attention, he whistled. "That round house looked spectacular though."

I kept hitting the bag.

"I told you all those damn squats were going to pay off big time. And not just because your ass poking out in them little ass tights either!"

That did it. Attention paid.

"Shut the fuck up," I seethed, walking past him, throwing a cutting look at his laughing face as I stalked by to grab a towel off the counter. He'd broken my concentration.

Rudy was my trainer at one point but I'd long outgrown his abilities. I would have stopped fooling with him a long time ago if it weren't for his connections to the fight club— a seedy world of street fighting I otherwise wouldn't be welcomed in. No way they'd let the daughter of one of the wealthiest, real estate families in Atlanta anywhere near those secret fight locations.

Most of these bouts were in run down warehouses across the city and surrounding metro area. All kinds of illegal activities went on. Everything from gambling to illegal ass selling. The fight scene was where the dope boy, the entertainer, and businessman or woman mingled as one.

On the scene, wealthy movers and shakers could be entertained while getting high on whatever their vice of choice. Mostly they got high on the brutality of bare knuckled, anything goes brawls that happened inside the fighting cage. Drug dealers, petty hustlers and your everyday run of the mill gamblers alike were all looking for a payday.

They couldn't know my identity, just like my family and close circle couldn't know my nighttime activities. Anonymity was my only friend here. I was in it to exercise my demons. Not to win. Just give and take—*mostly take*— a few blows and make it out of the cage with all of my teeth and ribs intact. Bruises were ok, though. Just not on my face.

I was finished with my impromptu, unscheduled workout. The glowing pink numbers on my watch read 5:26 AM. I was about to head to the locker room and grab my bag so I could rush the few blocks to my Centennial Yards loft apartment to shower and dress for work, when Rudy grasped my arm.

He pulled up short, releasing me, when my eyes snapped down at his offending hand.

Rolling his eyes at my disdain for him grabbing me, he tugged me around to face him. He quickly got down to business when he had my full attention. "We got an in."

I knew exactly what he was talking about. My eyes were back on his.

"When?" My only response.

"Endyra accepted your challenge."

"When?" I asked a bit more impatiently through tight lips.

"Friday night."

I gave him a quick nod before looking at his hand still clutching my arm. My tight eyed stare was his cue to release me and I continued to the locker room.

Though it didn't show on the outside, my heart thudded against my chest at the news Rudy shared. Endyra was one of the best female mixed martial artists above and underground in the Southeast and she had declined my offer three times before. Her and her squad didn't think I was on the same level as her. Not until I'd beat my last three opponents in mildly brutal knockouts in the cage.

That had gotten Endyra's attention. Either accept my challenge or be looked at as scared to face an underdog. Exactly what I wanted her to think of me. She was undefeated. Me? Not so much. Her name and title preceded her. Mine? Not at all. And I planned to keep it that way.

See the thing about fighting, the longer you practice, the better you get; even if unintentional. I wasn't in it to win but I wasn't not going to train either. Apparently, when you are good at it, it gets harder to pretend you're not. I didn't want to win. Winning caused attention and I didn't want attention.

The other thing about fighting is that most people have a reason, some big *why* for doing it. But when your sole reason is finding a release from years of unresolved guilt, you have to be highly selective about the matches that you take on.

I was in it solely for the pain. A self-punishment of sorts. I guess I could have inflicted it on myself... heard some people got the same release from cutting. But that wasn't for me. I welcomed the sting of hard punches, the explosion of a thousand tiny blood vessels rupturing under my skin, rendered by someone else. It was my ritualistic means of atonement for the guilt that shadowed my every waking moment.

Over time, the punches of weaker opponents weren't enough. I'd had to find better fighters and fights. But not too much. Endyra was the not too much fighter. Let the streets tell it, she was going to fuck me up. Good. I was here for all of it.

Chapter 3 – Okiyo

I N A SHORT TWO year span, I'd witnessed the Baijan family face a media spectacle. When the world discovered the billionaire had fathered an illegitimate child with an American woman thirty plus years ago, the gossip columns ran with it.

It was quite the scandal in Kenya. The story did break in the United States but was just a blip in the news cycle. But when Leboo's love child, Andra Bainswright, and her best friend now lover, Kobe became media darlings with a hit reality TV show and were in the running for a Michelin Star, the hate mail and threats skyrocketed.

Security needs in Kenya had died down a bit, but were ramping up here in Atlanta with this new Michelin madness going on. It had been a week since I'd arrived here with Leboo and Mackena. Typically, my team and I provided security for the family back in Kenya. Soon a detail of my men would be escorting Leboo and Mackena back to Nairobi, but I'd be staying on here for a little while longer. I'd been asked to stay and solidify the security plans for the restaurant here in Atlanta and the new locations that were soon to follow.

I'd left plenty of security with the family tonight, leaving me with much time on my hands. And instead of thinking about the minx of a woman who'd attacked me the other night, seemingly for no reason, I decided to use this time to feed my peculiar appetites. Appetites much more suitable to my nature. I needed to rid myself of the singed memory of her pebbled nipples against my chest when I'd finally restrained and pinned her to that wall.

Atlanta was not a new city to me. I'd been here a time or two when I lived completely in the shadows chasing boogie men, *and sometimes boogie women*, that the world didn't know were lurking. I knew exactly where to go to find that thing I sought tonight.

The thing I really wanted was not likely to be found on the surface of Atlanta's urban yet southern hospitable streets. Atlanta was a typical major city that pulsed with vibrant life and culture. The sheer volume of brown people in its middle, upper middle and super rich classes were a stark contrast to where I was raised in London as a boy.

My family was from Kenya. Atlanta had a similar vibe as the beat of Nairobi, the capital, where I was born and now called home. Atlanta also had an underbelly that I knew very well.

If you knew the right rocks to turn over, you could definitely find any trouble that you sought. I was in search of dark energy tonight. *Demon time,* as some of my younger security guys may refer to it if they were privy to my personal affairs.

My first thought was to find a willing beauty to find release in for a few hours tonight. But that wouldn't do. Not the release I craved. Even if it were, I doubted that if she wasn't *red dress* from the other night or an identical twin, the release wouldn't be worth it. Plus, the women of Atlanta, though beautiful and lush as they were, their southern hospitality and charm were at odds with my sexual appetites.

I leaned towards fleeting, unencumbered encounters. My desires lay in the thrill of anonymity and the transient connections of one-night stands. I treated all women with respect, of course. But my bed partner needed to understand that respect or not, I didn't need to know her name. Nor would there be any trading of numbers... And yet, deep earthy eyes, set wide above a delicate nose and full lips painted the same deep red as the gown she'd worn, pervaded my senses. Delia was her name.

I was pleasantly shocked to discover that the executive assistant of *the* very vice president at 3W, the architectural firm and developer of the building that Gastrafrique was located in, was my beautiful attacker. I'd be seeing the minx again very, very soon.

In the meantime, I needed a fix; something to take my mind off the sepia skinned goddess. Tonight, my quest diverged from the need to bury my troubles between the legs of a woman who'd be down for a one night stand. As tempting as it was, I wouldn't find release in the tight wetness of pussy tonight. *Not while trying to shake the scent of a very particular one from my memory.* No. Tonight, I needed another type of release.

Being attacked spurred the notion, I guess. I needed to lose myself in a back alley brawl. Not in the fight myself. Although punching a bloke square in the mouth was indeed a good way to let off some steam. But watching a good fight, would have to do the trick. I wanted to lose myself in the echo of fists against sweaty skin and raucous cheers of a crowd pumped up on adrenaline.

To find the kind of fight I was looking for, I walked down a dark alley with nondescript doors and awnings just off of Lucky Street. Once I reached the door I was looking for, I gave two slow knocks followed by three rapid ones with my knuckles on the hard steel. Ten seconds later, a small piece of metal slid back revealing an eye-level opening in the door. I uttered a single word. *Honduras.* The bolt of the locked door clicked and it was opened just wide enough for my body to slide through and enter.

There were several code words that could be used for entry into the establishment. But only three people on this earth knew the meaning of the one I'd used to gain entry to the eighteenth century, pub style speakeasy.

Most code words got you entry to the main lounge and bar of the old world style gentleman's club. Honduras got you access to the *King* of the establishment. And he was precisely who I'd come to see.

I followed the raven haired beauty in the direction of a set of doors beyond the horseshoe bar stocked with over 100 artisan and big name gins and spirits, real ales and excellent wines. The waitress opened the doors and stepped aside, letting me pass. She gave me a discreet nod and took her leave. But not before closing the doors tight behind her.

Upon entry into the darkened room, lit only by the light of several computer and security monitors, I was met with a back view of Evan McLeod, now known simply as King. He was intent on watching a panel of security monitors that each showed different locations around the world. A few were dedicated to various locations around Atlanta.

The back office of the speakeasy doubled as his surveillance command center. The establishment hid Evan's real dealings—underground private security for the very rich, very secret society of people whose very existence depended on them being in the know.

"Still playing superhero, ay' King?"

He was an MI6 operative with me years ago. Like many of us, once out of the game, he chose a role in society that allowed him to live in the light while still thriving on the outskirts of clandestine activities of the night. Hell, I wasn't even sure if Evan McLeod was his real name. It very well could be a chosen government name, giving him a clean exit from the agency.

My question was asked to King's back as he continued monitoring one of the screens, this time with a bit more scrutiny before he slowly turned around. Only the raised right corner of his mouth giving way to his joy in seeing an old friend.

"And I see you're still the toughest son of a bitch I know dressed in a laser cut suit, dripping fine wine and bathed in caviar but still able to rip out a man's jugular without getting a spot of blood on those fine *'I-talian'* loafers, agent O." He said in the lowest, slowest Texas drawl.

Women used to love the sound of that shit. To them, he was a good ol' handsome cowboy. His soft voice hid a razor sharp mind that would not think twice about dropping a bad guy in any part of the world. A Texas boy on loan to MI6 from the CIA back in the day.

Both of us laughed heartily as he threw out his arms and moved towards me, encasing me in a bear hug. His heavy limp and uneven gait was a reminder of our last mission together.

He'd sustained the injury from a raid we'd been on together down in Central America. The raid was on a small village that had been taken over by traffickers. We were sent in to rescue a group of kidnapped children from Honduras. We'd received intel that the children were about to be shipped via cargo container to a brothel in London known for soliciting kids.

We were lucky to get out of that camp alive. King almost lost that leg when he ran into oncoming bullets to grab one of the little girls who'd fallen behind and was about to be re-captured by one of the traffickers.

"Brother man," he said, snapping me back from a long ago memory. "What you doing on this side of the pond again?"

"You remember that nasty business you helped me with last time I was here? The ex-NFL Football player wreaking havoc on the daughter of the businessman that my firm provides security, yeah?"

"Yeah, I remember that. I was glad to see that *sombitch* being dragged off the Falcon's training field at Flowery Branch. It was all over the news." He responded; arms now folded giving me his full attention.

"Well, that same daughter along with her partner, just won a Michelin Star for that restaurant. The security at the restaurant will need to be beefed up. I'll be here for a little while doing just that. But Mr. Baijan wants that security overhaul to include the whole development and all other sites where future restaurants might go."

King whistled. "Damn, Daddy Warbucks ain't sparing a dime to keep his princess safe. That Parque Place development is a multi-million dollar location and he's footing the bill on revamped security for the whole damn thing?"

"Indeed he is. I have a meeting with the responsible firm in a few days to basically rework their security strategy. Leboo Baijan doesn't play about his," I stated matter-of-factly.

After filling King in on why I was back in Atlanta, it was time to get the information from him that I came for. Information I could get from one of the many monitors in the room. Because agents such as ourselves rarely made house calls to catch up, he wasn't surprised when I told him I needed to know where there may be an underground fight going on tonight.

"Ahhh. Still into that sordid shit, hunh? He asked rhetorically as he turned towards one of the monitors that played feeds around Atlanta. With a few clicks of a remote control, the feed changed to a parking lot of what looked like an abandoned warehouse in some seedy area of town.

"There's a fight out in McDonough tonight." He pointed at the screen, then stepped closer giving it a few taps directly on the flat surface. "Looks like some real movers and shakers are showing up tonight." He whistled. "Man, look at that parking lot. The main event hasn't even started yet, but the high rollers are rolling in," he stated in reference to the Range Rover, Bently and Maserati pulling in to be parked.

As he continued touching and swiping small pop ups around on the screen, I stared at the video of real time footage at the secret fight location. Just before he turned to give me the coordinates of the location, a black clad beauty in a body contouring strappy black dress stepped out of an SUV.

I stood transfixed. The dress had a slit so far up her thigh, the slightest move would reveal her nether lips. I could imagine that only the barest scrap of fabric would suffice as panties to protect her honey pot. *Or would she be so bold not to wear any?*

She wore a pair of black rubber-soled jackboots strung up to her knees. Even with her hair different from the upswept curls at the party the other night, I knew it was her.

Not even the fauxhawk of Bantu knots down the center of her head or the pair of shades could disguise *Red* on the ultra-HD quality video on King's monitors. Ms. Delia Aguillen-McGhee had just stepped out of a black-out SUV at the same fight I was about to attend.

I quickly took the address King provided.

"Here–"

He could barely get the proffered word out before I hurried to the door, leaving him with an utter look of shock on his face at my rapid departure. I didn't stop to explain. I needed to make it to that fight before it was over.

Chapter 4 – Delia

I SAT NEXT TO Rudy in the all-black Range Rover that I hired to take us to the event. I never drove my two door Mercedes coupe in case we had to make a quick getaway. You never knew what may pop off at one of these backstreet events.

Rudy had been quiet for the majority of the ride. We'd only just received the address for the site the night before. When we were about five minutes out from arrival, I felt his eyes on me.

As usual, I was prepared to ignore anything that came out of his mouth. He'd say something stupid to gauge my mood which would let him know how much effort I was going to put into my fight tonight.

If I said nothing in response to his antics, he knew I'd put up no fight and take the beating dished out. If I cursed him out, I'd put forth some effort. The outcome of my fight could be fifty-fifty in favor of me winning or losing. If I entertained his corniness and even smirked at his irritating jokes, I would fight to win... He was only guaranteed a good payout tonight from betting on me if I chose the latter.

"Endyra better be glad this isn't a weapons fight, Deels," He said.

Here we go.

"One stomp from those black-ass military boots and that chick will be out cold," Rudy chuckled, chancing a glance at my face to gauge my response after eyeing my knee-high jackboots.

I never knew what my response would be until the ritual between Rudy and I began and usually right before a fight. Tonight, I didn't reply. Simply adjusted my shades. Maintained a bored expressionless face under the blacked out square frames before preparing to exit the vehicle.

I reached for the handle to open the door before Rudy or the driver could come around to assist. But not before seeing the defeated look on Rudy's face. *Disappointment.* At that, I inwardly smiled. I didn't get why he always acted so upset when I didn't put up effort to fight an opponent. He'd just bet against me anyway and get his jackpot.

I liked to show up to the fight locations in advance of my fights so that I could get a feel for the crowd and who was in attendance. That meant my look pre-fight needed to be a bit more glam. *Edgy.* But glam all the same to match the vibe of the other onlookers.

This helped me maintain my anonymity as a fighter but allowed me to also observe the crowd. Most people were so drunk or high by the start of the fights that they didn't recognize me as one of the fighters. When I did enter the cage, my rich bitch persona would be long gone. Replaced by a stripped down, make-up free face, bare feet, black sports bra and boy shorts.

Even at these events, I navigated at least two worlds. Stepping out of the blacked out SUV with Rudy in toe, I was Delia Aguillen-McGhee, daughter of millionaire real estate moguls Emiliano and Shayla Aguillen. My dad had passed away around the same time I'd started my mixed martial arts training, but my mom was very well known around Atlanta. By the time I stepped into the ring, Black Viper, made her entrance. A scary name that I unfortunately was not interested in living up to. Rudy picked that dumb shit.

"Serious business, Deelz," Rudy said, catching up to me before we made our entrance into the warehouse. His expression earnest. "But are you ready for the big league after Endyra?"

I slowed. Confused about what he was asking. "Big leagues?" I questioned. I narrowed my eyes at Rudy, pressing him to get on with it. "What are you talking about?"

"I guess I should have mentioned it. The winner of this fight will advance to fight Storm for the "Raining Pain" title.

Oh hell no. What I didn't need was a title. Hell, I barely ever wanted to win a fight. I wouldn't have even shown up to this shit had I known any of this.

"God damn it, Rudy," I hissed before pressing through the crowd to enter the abandoned warehouse that had been transformed to look like a torch lit terror-dome, save for the scantily clad waitresses serving high-end bottle service to the swanky patrons who were quickly filling the space.

Rudy's and my relationship was a transactional one; he got paid, and I got the punishment I sought. He nor anyone would ever understand my motivations.

I was pissed because, the winner of this fight tonight would automatically move on to a title fight. Because this fight tonight was a lead up to a title, more people would be here. That meant more people who might recognize me. I definitely was going to lose big tonight. No way I could be entered into an actual title fight with Storm.

Inside my head, a torrent of emotions and thoughts raced. I never drank before a fight. But this time I was so pissed at Rudy for withholding information that I grabbed a glass of the free flowing bubbly and downed it before heading back to the locker rooms. No one would be back there yet and I needed to clear my head.

Changed and sitting on one of the benches in the locker room, I replayed my training sessions in my head. The hours spent in the gym honing my skills, pushing my body to its limits. Every punch, every kick, every drop of sweat was a testament to my exceptional skills. I could easily annihilate Endyra. As soon as the thought of winning entered, so too did the memory of my sister's little face, contorted in pain. I didn't deserve to win any fights. I didn't deserve anybody's titles.

"*...aaaaannnnndddd The Black Viperrrr!*" I faintly heard the announcement from the overhead speakers. Time to go get beat up.

Chapter 5 – Okiyo

"**H**WY 155 HEADED SOUTH," the GPS blared in the Uber Black I'd requested. Better to have a local drive me than one of Leboo's hired men. I was off tonight and something about using his resources for my personal exploits didn't sit well with me.

We drove through dimly lit roads where city lights were replaced by expansive manicured lawns and huge brick homes. Then eventually morphed to a more secluded industrial area lined with trucking docks and rows upon rows of long metal structured warehouses.

We finally stopped at a more isolated building. If not for the luxury car show in the lively makeshift parking lot, the structure could be mistaken as abandoned. Perfect place for a secret fight club to convene.

I used the information provided by King to access the event with little question. I was wanded through the open garage door. That meant no guns were likely inside the building. The parking lot outside was probably a different story.

Once my eyes adjusted to the low ambient torch lighting, I could see that the warehouse turned arena was packed. There was a sea of revelers all mingling around the huge ominous cage that took center in the room.

By the time I'd arrived, an undercard match was already underway. No one was paying attention. They were here for the main event who I'd surmised the fighters names were Endyra and Black Viper from the suspended posters hanging overhead.

Endyra was clearly favored to win. No one bothered to post any pictures of the other female fighter. Only her name was included on a life sized poster of Endyra. Endyra vs Black Viper, the caption read.

"Humph," I uttered even more interested in seeing this main event. These must be really good fighters I surmised because if it wasn't Ronda Rousy or Meisha Tate, women were usually relegated to the undercard fights. Sad, because women's MMA fights were often more brutal than the men's fights. Brutal was exactly what I was looking for until I'd seen Delia on that screen.

I ventured further into the crowd headed to the back of the room which had a slightly elevated observation area. I'd have a better view of the room from that vantage point and was hoping to spot a glimpse of her in the crowd.

In this part of the room, overhead neon lights flickered, casting eerie shadows that danced among the mingling crowd. The scent of sweat mixed with expensive colognes and adrenaline hung heavy in the air, creating a heady atmosphere that crackled with excitement.

Rich and powerful patrons mingled with their less affluent, yet equally dubious counterparts. Their stations in life, as diverse as metro Atlanta itself. But their reasons for being here tonight were the same. They were all here for adrenaline rushing mayhem.

My senses were on high alert. *Where was she?* The main event was about to start and I was hell bent on seeing Red. Needed to see her again. But once the fight started, that would be damned near impossible in this thick crowd still packing in through the open roller door.

I finally made it to the elevated area and took my place among the other spectators. The cage had been cleaned and reset for the showdown. I scanned the crowd again, this time in a systematic sweep, looking for the knots of hair atop her head. *Fuck.* The whole crowd swayed in unison towards the cage. The collective wave of movement along with the flickering lights made it impossible to focus on anything other than what was taking place in the cage.

I couldn't for the life of me understand why this woman was occupying so much space in my mind. Maybe it was the allure of the unknown, the mystery she carried that intrigued me. I'd been with some of the most beautiful women in the world. Yet, none of them lingered in my thoughts after the moment passed like she did.

There was something different about her—the way she moved, like a dancer with an edge, every step calculated, yet somehow instinctual. She had the elegance of a performer but the sharpness of someone trained to survive. I was skilled out of necessity—trained by the weight of my past. But her? What drove her to be like this? That was the burning question that kept me restless.

Maybe you're a sucker for mystery, Genius. I chided myself. I was usually the mystery, the one people couldn't quite figure out. But she reminded me—*of me*.

I was starting to think that the only way to get her out of my head was to somehow get her in my bed. But even as I thought it, it rang hollow. Something told me that one night with Delia would never be enough, and that realization should have had me running for the hills. Instead, a deep sense of deflation settled in my gut as I scanned the crowd once again. No sight of her.

The anticipation in the arena reached a fever pitch. The crowd's murmurs grew louder. The air crackled with electric excitement while drinks continued to flow freely, adding to the charged atmosphere.

"Fuck." I muttered under my breath. The lights dimmed in the entire room, save for the single spotlight on the announcer who was now in the center of the cage with a microphone. Operation find Delia in this crowd over.

"Ladies and gentlemen, it's time for the moment we've all been waiting for." The commentator's voice boomed over the loudspeakers. "Two fighters, locked inside the cage, ready to unleash the beast on each other—"

The crowd roared so loud it was hard to hear him even over the speaker.

"In the red corner, we have the reigning queen of the Pit! The undefeated champion, Endyra!"

His words trailed off again, giving way to the crescendo pitch of the crowd. The deafening roar reverberated through the arena as Endyra stepped into the spotlight. *Endyra.* The name sounded like something out of a Mortal Kombat game.

Her presence commanded attention. She stood about 5'10 inches, but was ripped with sinewy muscles. Not bulky, but defined and rippling from her neck down to her calves. Usually that kind of height on a woman fighter was a hindrance, but she knew how to use it to her advantage. She was undefeated. If not for all the tattoos, especially on her face, Endyra might have even been considered pretty.

"And in the blue corner, the challenger, the underdog with a heart of steel, the Black Viper!" The crowd's booing would have made any contender second guess going up against Endyra. I was afraid for the poor girl. It didn't bode well for her. The Black Viper emerged from the shadows, her face blank and eerily calm.

Recognition struck me like a bolt of lightning as I laid eyes on Delia and the memory of our encounter in the dark hallway flooded back like a fast replay. Her beauty and ferocity had stained my brain. She was a force to be reckoned with, a wild card in a game where the stakes were high and the rules were constantly shifting.

Oh this fight was about to be good and this crowd that heavily favored Endyra was in for a rude awakening. A lot of gamblers were going home lighter in the pocket tonight for sure. I couldn't stop the smile from spreading across my face.

I couldn't shake the feeling that Delia's and my path were destined to cross.

Moving to the edge of the crowd, I sought a better view of the impending showdown. The air crackled with anticipation as the two fighters squared off, their eyes locked in a silent battle of wills. Endyra exuded confidence, her movements fluid and calculated. But Delia was a dark horse and as the underdog she had nothing to lose and everything to gain.

The bell rang, and the match was on. My eyes were locked on the two women in the ring, every muscle in my body tensed as if I were in there with her. Outwardly, I kept my composure, but inside—*swear!*—I was electrified, riding the same rush as Delia. I wanted to see her knock the wind out of Endyra's sails. I didn't bloody care if I was the only one in this place cheering her on.

Delia's movements were fluid as she side stepped Endyra's brute force. This happened three times early on in the first round and I was baffled at why Delia didn't take at least two of those opportunities to exact a couple of body shots when Endyra's left side was left open. Then there were moments when she could and should have played offense and took the fight to Endyra, but she held back allowing Endyra to effectively corner her and issue some vicious body blows.

Delia didn't even attempt to block them. There was an almost euphoric look on her face as she absorbed each blow. *What in the bloody hell was going on here?* Why wasn't she fighting back? Hell, she put forth more effort fighting me in that hallway.

Each blow that Endyra connected reverberated through the air, sending shivers down my spine. I forced myself to release the breath I was holding. I wanted to, but was unable to tear my eyes away from the spectacle unfolding before me.

The fight wore on and on like this. Round one went by with Delia only throwing three swings. Each of them connected which meant her connect percentage was at a 100%, but they weren't effective at all in slowing Endyra down. Round two was much like the first. But now it seemed as if Delia was intentionally baiting Endyra to charge and pummel her, but put up no defenses when

Endyra took the bait. She'd taken some serious blows but miraculously dodged every one of them that was thrown at her face or head.

By the time the third and final round came, I'd given up any hope that Delia was going to win this fight. Even in the dark arena, I could see the skin of her rib cage and torso turning deep red where she was getting hit the most. I almost felt the pain that she was obviously going to feel even more tomorrow and the day after.

Twenty seconds remained in the fight. All but giving up, Delia stood straight up. Breaking the cardinal rule in the ring. Protect yourself at all times. Her arms hung long by her sides and then she cocked her head to the side and raised a single brow at her opponent. I couldn't see Endyra's face as she was facing away from me, but the slight tug of her head back beyond her shoulders clearly read, shock and confusion. Then she shrugged it off and gave Delia what she was asking for. A hard punch straight to the center of her abdomen.

It was a body-caving punch, and I watched as Delia grabbed her stomach, doubling over, wheezing for air. The referee moved in, ready to call the fight.

Honestly, he didn't need to; only about five seconds remained in the match. Then, just like that, the entire room went still as Delia lifted her head, her torso following. She froze midway, and our eyes locked. There was a long pause, and I saw her brow scrunch at me.

Even with the mouth guard in, I could almost read the expletive she mouthed when she saw me.

Realizing her opponent was still in the fight, Endyra charged forward, rearing back to throw a head shot that would have knocked Delia out cold. As if by reflex, Delia swung. Her eyes never left mine. But for the first and only time in this round, her fist connected square with Endyra's jaw.

The champ's knees buckled, and she fell backward, hitting the floor of the cage. A knockout. A collective gasp waved through the arena as the favored home team fighter lay stiff in the ring. Delia stood motionless, her expression frozen, until the referee snatched her hand up into the air, declaring her the victor.

I tried to make my way up to the cage to congratulate her. But before I could get through the crowd, Delia took off. She pulled her arm out of the referees grasp, bee-lining for the door of the cage. It crashed open and she was through it, pushing her way through the crowd to leave the arena. I was so confused at what had just happened. Not the how of her winning. A knockout was a knockout regardless of how the rest of the fight went. But the why she apparently didn't want to. I aimed to find out though.

Chapter 6 – Delia

"D ELIA—" I FLINCHED AT the hand that tapped the bruised muscle just below my left shoulder blade. Rhi's face scrunched in concern before smoothing, coming to her own conclusion about my wince. "You jumped like I punched you in your spine or something. Rough night?" My boss studied me quizzically with a conspiratorial smirk on her face, adjusting the strap of her Birken on her shoulder in preparation to make a mad dash out the door.

I shrugged, non-committal. Not wanting to feed into what she was thinking. I'd led her to believe on many occasions that my soreness and sometimes gap-legged walk was due to a rough night with a lover that had me walking funny. Similar story I'd shared with my sister on a few occasions when she bothered to ask about my wellbeing. No doubt, Iya has shared the same with my mother. They were as thick as thieves. Better that than, I got the shit kicked out of me, *for real,* last night.

"Nah, you startled me is all."

It was partially true. My mind was in a million places. But she really did poke me right in one of the bruises caused by Endyra's body shots. "I hadn't realized you'd walked in," I sputtered.

I wasn't in the mood for our typical end of day girl chats. I certainly didn't have the brain space to spin up some fantastical dating story— *lie*—to keep my boss out of my real business. Truth was, I'd given up casual dating quite some time ago. It was hard to explain away the bruises to my boss. Imagine having to explain them to a lover.

"Umm-kay," She emoted unphased, glancing down at her watch, distracted. "Thought you may have had another one of those Twister and baby oil nights." She chuckled, referring to the story I'd told some months back to explain away a gash on my forehead from another fight. She looked up from her watch, now looking distressed. "Nevermind. I need to get out of here and get to the airport. Can you look over this contract package for me? Our updates are due back to the client tomorrow night but Kendrick's flight just landed and I'm late."

I'd booked her husband's flight for her last week. Had I been focused on work rather than preoccupied with *how in the fuck* I'd won that fight last night— better yet, if I wasn't replaying the moment I locked eyes with *him*, I might have done my JOB and reminded my boss that she needed to leave twenty minutes ago.

Because what the hell was he doing at my fight last night? If I remembered correctly, he was introduced as head of security for the rich *Kenyan* dad of the restaurant owner that just won the Michelin Star. *How could he have possibly learned about a secret fight out in bumfuck McDonough?*

Rhi looked at her watch impatiently, shaking the papers in her hand. This time I was fully wrenched back to the present, safe from the pool of mahogany eyes I'd been swimming in. *Sheesh, Delia... get it together.*

I took the papers. "Yeah. Get out of here. I'll take care of this for you right away." I looked up at the wall clock before reassuring, "If you leave now, you'll likely beat the traffic and get to your hubby in no time."

It would be a stretch at a quarter to five. In all reality, she had less than a millisecond to be out the door before Atlanta's unruly ass traffic had her three hours late picking up that hunk of a husband.

"You're right! Let me get out of—" She stopped mid-sentence before cursing under her breath. I looked in the direction she was now looking in with a huge fake smile plastered on her face, waving.

"Damn it," she hissed through her teeth like a ventriloquist. "I forgot to put the meeting I set up with Mr. Bamdi, our new security consultant, on the calendar for today."

I froze, half listening to Rhi. It was him. A wave of pure unadulterated anxiety washed over me. This motherfucker was here to drop a dime on me for attacking his ass the other night. *Shit. Shit. Shit.* And the fact that he actually saw me in a cage fight last night—and win... just added fuel to the HR dumpster fire that he was surely here to start.

Wait what? I was so shaken at the sight of him that understanding of what my boss had just said was delayed. *New security consultant?* I managed Rhi's calendar. *What meeting?*

Rhi continued talking through her closed teeth as he spotted us and began making his way over.

"That's what I get for not getting you to book this damn meeting. I totally forgot about it, and you usually keep me straight," she whined, still through a clenched-tooth smile. I looked up at her from my still-seated position, curious. She sighed, continuing to fill me in. "Yeah. We set it up in the middle of that damn party, and I meant to ask you to book it," she rushed out in a hushed whisper just before he was in earshot.

"Mr. Bamdi. Welcome to 3W. And prompt, too," she stated, chancing a furtive look down at me, fake smile still plastered on her face. Looks like Kendrick's ass was about to be taking an Uber home from the airport.

"You remember my assistant Delia, right?" He nodded, eyes low as he slowly dragged his gaze up from my patent leather pumps to my face.

I felt a subtle prickle of heat climb up my neck, settling into my cheeks under sweep of his gaze.

"The vision in red from the party," he said, his deep voice rumbling as he extended his hand to mine. "The way you moved so effortlessly in it," he paused, narrowing his eyes as a corner of his mouth raised in a lopsided smirk, "How could I forget?" He reached out to shake my hand.

Standing by watching the exchange curiously, Rhi chimed in. "Delia, please show Mr. Bamdi to the conference room. I need to make a quick call to my husband." She grabbed her phone from her purse, but before walking off to make her call in private, she added, "I'll also go see if Stan, my boss, can join us. Be right back."

My small hand was still lightly gripped in his larger, stronger one by the time Rhi stepped away. Feeling scorched by his touch, I pulled my hand away clumsily, flushing from embarrassment all over. Standing, I turned towards the conference room, then threw the words over my shoulder. "Follow me, Mr. Bamdi."

"Please call me, Okiyo," he replied, following close behind. I simply nodded, not chancing a glance back so he wouldn't see that he was affecting me. I also didn't want to risk my eyes getting stuck on his chest and the way that damn suit jacket hugged it and his defined arms.

He wore a three-piece, grey Tom Ford today. Still laser cut to his body, only this time, instead of a fancy pocket square like the night at the party, the chain of a pocket watch peeked out. A classic man, *indeed*, I thought, sighing inwardly.

I forced myself to focus on the task at hand, walking a few steps ahead to keep my composure. It was just down the hall, but every step felt heavy with anticipation. I kept my shoulders tight and my breaths controlled, determined to stay professional.

But everything about him—his confidence, his accent, or just the way he seemed to fill the room—it had me all thrown off. I couldn't let it show. Not now.

By the time we made it to the conference room, my nerves were less frayed. Didn't matter that he had a valid reason for being here, I was still on guard. I reminded myself that this was the same motherfucker from the other night that I'd attacked and he very well still could drop a dime on my ass to HR. *Be cool Delia.*

Not letting my guard down, I pointed him to a seat near the head of the long conference table. I made my way down its length to sit near the center, aiming to put some distance between us and to keep my faculties in place. *Still too close, but it would have to do.*

"Would you like some water?" I pointed to the group of bottles across from him on the table rather than getting it for him.

I wanted to ask what he was really doing here but didn't want to make the situation any worse. If he didn't say anything about it, neither would I. And if he did, then I'd just have to say that the *motherfucker* followed me and I got scared. All true. And still not justifiable to the extent I took it. My shoulders sank.

The next few minutes we sat in silence. Him studying his phone, while I stole a few glances at his side profile. Rather than conceited, he had a confident air about him that spoke to him knowing his station. I didn't detect any sense of cockiness, just that he was a man about his business. Totally on point with everything he did. *'Miss me with that,'* vibes was the energy he gave off.

He proved to be all that and more. He was even a bit charming. Nevertheless, he still knew my dirt. I wasn't going to let my guard down in his regard.

Rhi and Stan made it to the conference room. As soon as Stan's introduction was made and all pleasantries concluded, Okiyo Bamdi stood and politely walked us through the reason he was here.

Without using a single accusatory or inflammatory word, he let us know just how lax the security was at several 3W developments. He focused specifically on the major developments in Atlanta, but was very clear that the problem was widespread at other locations around the country as well.

A quick glance around the table showed it was clear that he had both Rhi's and Stan's rapt attention. Mine too, but for very different reasons. The sound of his voice affected me. The way he carried himself was mesmerizing. Aside from Rhi, none of the leadership at 3W could hold a candle to this man in the *'I'm a boss'* department. And his knowledge of physical security and the surety with which he told us about ourselves, had all of us nodding in agreement at what he was saying.

"Out of extreme caution and care for the safety of his daughter, my boss Mr. Leboo Baijan wants to work with 3W to tighten the security posture of several of your sites. Specifically the site where Gastrafrique, his daughter's restaurant is currently located, and all other sites that have been marked as potential sites where new restaurants will open." Then Okiyo dropped the mind blowing statement that came next. "Mr. Baijan will cover all costs."

Stanton Jeffries literally sputtered. "Ah, well, Mr. Bamdi, you lay out a thorough case. I agree that we need to fix these security gaps," Stan drawled in his southern twang, waving his hands out across the marked up blueprints Okiyo had spread across the table. "And he's going to foot the entire bill to retrofit all these plans too?"

"That is correct." Mr. Bamdi pulled another stack of papers from his leather satchel. "Here is the full agreement. Take a look and let me know if you have questions. Otherwise, I'm ready to get started as soon as you agree and sign."

He leaned back but then quickly sat back up again.

"Oh, I almost forgot. If you agree, I'll need someone who is familiar enough with all the identified plans that can work with me to get this done quickly. It should take only about a month to get the new strategy in place, plans revised and the new security protocols ready to implement."

When he sat back again, I mentally relaxed. I'd been so focused on his every word that by the time he finished, I was spent like I'd been helping him put his whole spill together. When I looked back up and down the table, three sets of eyes were on me.

Rhiyan must have noticed the shocked look on my face because she seized the opportunity to repeat herself, as if to hammer it home. "Delia is the logical choice to assign to you," she said with a smile, a knowing glint in her eyes. "She's been involved in reviewing all our plans before they get stamped by the lead architect. Plus, I'll be away for a few weeks, working virtually from our home in Hawaii. This is perfect timing, as she won't have me breathing down her neck."

What the fuck just happened?

While I sat there dumbfounded, Mr. Bamdi gathered his belongings, then stated to the group, but eyes on me, "I'll be in town for the next six weeks. I look forward to four of them working with you, Ms. Aguillen-McGhee."

Stanton stood, reaching out a hand to Okiyo. "I'll take a look at the agreement, but for now, looks like you're the new security consultant for 3W."

They shook hands and both took their leave. Rhi tried to skate out but not before I cut my eyes at her, hissing at my boss, "You couldn't at least ask me if I'd want to be assigned to the new security consultant before your decision?"

"Oh don't worry. You got this, Delia. No one knows those plans better than you—"

"Umm, the architects who drafted them!?" I questioned rhetorically, cutting her off in my haste to get her to change her mind.

"Except, they are all busy being architects on other assignments, right?" She cut me right back off, framing her question in the same rhetorical way. "Something you could be doing too, if you'd only go take the license exam. So you're it," she said, shrugging her eyes up with a sweet, tight lipped smile to soften the blow of the finality of her words.

After a beat, she threw her Birkin over her shoulder and grabbed her other belongings. This time making a real dash out the door to go be with her husband.

Chapter 7 – Okiyo

I ENTERED THE BAIJAN residence and headed to the security wing off the main entry. The home was big enough to fit an entire command center conspicuously inside, with enough room to quarter at least six of my men. Billionaire that he was, Leboo Baijan bought a huge home in the posh West Paces Ferry neighborhood of North Atlanta. As his head of security, I had full access to the security gates at the entrance of the neighborhood and had personally overseen the setup of the surveillance system around the colossal home.

The security wing was fitted with creature comforts, a kitchenette and above average baths so that the security team could live on site. Except for me, that was. I'd been appointed a swanky, two bedroom loft downtown as my attentions would be focused external to the family estate.

I tried to convince Leboo to allow me to handle my own living arrangements but he wouldn't hear it. I'd be staying on for a while after the family and my men departed in the next few days back to Kenya. Because my stay was work related, he footed the bill.

The center of the wing housed the controls and surveillance monitoring systems where I found my once driver, now surveillance analyst, Deke. He gave me the daily update. While he did so, I reviewed the monitors and did my own perfunctory check of the grounds. Satisfied that my men were at their respective checkpoints and the outside of the residence was secure, I made my way to Leboo's office.

He was expecting me. I knocked once then let myself in without waiting for his reply. I hadn't made it two feet into the room before he handed me a heavy, crystal snifter of two fingers of whiskey, neat. He patted me on the back, welcoming me silently into the space as he rolled his eyes at the large screen on the wall behind his desk.

He was in the middle of a video call with Bishara, head of housekeeping back at his home in Nairobi. Leboo stood, arms crossed, one hand pinching the bridge of his nose in mild irritation whilst Bishara ranted, moving frantically to and fro around the kitchen. Her arms flailed as she recanted the latest antics of Mrs. Kwamboko Baijan, Leboo's not so lovely wife.

"And, ohhhh, Mr. Leboo, she be on the full war-*pawth,*" she said in her heavily accented English, "*Evah* since that article come out 'bout Ms. Andra and Mr. Kobe's Michelin star." She long sucked her teeth, a gesture that meant many things in East African culture, in this case, she did it to emphasize her next words.

She leaned closer to the camera of the video monitoring system, looking behind her to ensure the lady of the house wasn't in earshot. In a conspiratorial whisper, she continued. "Mister... when the young Ms. Mackena call here the other day saying that she and *ha' olda' sista* went *shoppun' togethah'*, this woman done went mad. Slam every door in this house."

Bishara didn't even pause to take a breath. It took everything in me not to bowl over in laughter.

"Ohhh she be big mad, Boss. Maybe you stay there a few more weeks!" She stepped back wringing her fingers and face squinched in mock concern.

This time I did laugh out loud at her antics. Leboo only quirked a corner of his mouth up in a lopsided smile as he shook his head at his housekeeper who was known to talk mess about, Kwam. Leboo and I both knew that ol' Bishara, though really trying to warn Leboo of what he was about to step into when he made it back home next week, really was poking a little fun at Leboo's mean ass wife.

When she heard my laugh, her face lit up like a shiny bright penny. "That be, Okiyo I hear there with you?"

Leboo finally spoke, "Yes, he's here and we have some business to tend to, Bishara. I'm going to go now. Ok?"

"Yes, yes. You two handle your business. But Okiyo *don'tcha fahget nah,* we be due for a call. Somebodies *gotta* make sure *ya' eatun* right and taken *care'a ya'self.* And Mrs. Bishara not talking about working out on that body all times of the day. I'm talking about settling down with a wife. *Gettun ya'mind* right *fa* when she start popping out them babies."

"Bye Bishara," both Leboo and I said in unison. He went to hang up the call, but not before Bishara, yelled, "*Mrs.* Bishara to you two rapscallions." Her raucous laughter reverberated around the room before the call went dead.

"That Bishara is a mess," I stated, moving towards Leboo's desk so we could get down to business."

"And that she is," he said taking a seat on the other side. "But she loves you like you were her own child so you better get to finding that wife like she said. Or you're going to have hell to pay!" He laughed heartily at his own words.

I smiled. "Don't know if that will be happening anytime soon, but Bishara certainly isn't going to stop trying to marry me off." Shaking my head at her antics.

"Ah, she's harmless. Just wants to see you happy is all."

I agree with Leboo on that. How welcoming she'd always been towards me was a sobering thought. I'd been head of security for Leboo Baijan and his family for six years now. And from the very moment I was introduced as such to the family and the staff,

Mrs. Bishara Okiofor welcomed me into the arms of a motherly embrace.

Over the years, I'd grown quite fond of her too. There were many occasions when I'd sit with her in her cottage off the main family estate and we'd sip tea as she regaled me with stories of the late Mr. Okiofor. They never had any children. She'd lovingly called me her honorary son because 'somebody need to care *'bout* you boy,' she'd often say.

At first it made me feel uncomfortable, but I never felt compelled to stop her from saying things like that. I grew up with no parents — a victim of genocide, separated from my family and ultimately adopted into a sterile London society where I felt isolated and invisible.

One day I shared this exact thing with her. I immediately regretted it. She cried at the realization that the words she often said in jest, that she was the closest thing I'd had to a mother, was very close to the truth. I'd lost my real mother and rest of my family when I was six. The wealthy British family that had adopted me back then was a far cry from family.

Returning from my trip down memory lane, I got to the business that I'd come to discuss.

"The meeting with 3W went well."

"No doubt it did," he nodded his head, raising a brow. "I need my daughter safe and how could they refuse an offer to get a state of the art security strategy implemented at their sites. *Free of charge.*"

"They wouldn't," I agreed.

We talked a bit more. Before leaving, I shared the final details about his and McKenna's return trip back to Kenya.

"Half of my team will accompany you and McKenna back to Kenya. High visibility and full coverage until you're home and secure."

Leboo nodded, his expression softening. "That sounds good. And Andra?"

"The other half will remain here," I continued, "focused on Andra and Kobe. They need round-the-clock security, especially with their upcoming trips. There won't be any gaps in security."

Leboo gave a small approving nod. "Good."

I paused for a moment, sensing the shift in his gaze as he looked at me with a bit of a smile. "And what about you, son? You'll be working solo. Wait. Did they assign someone from their team to assist?"

"Yes. They did." I'd be working alongside the beautifully confusing Ms. Delia Aguillen-McGhee. She was an enigmatic mystery even after we'd had the pleasure of meeting informally and formally. None of this I shared with Leboo but his question brought me back around to thinking about her.

He nodded his head in approval. "Good. Well what's the plan in your spare time? You'll have a bit more room in your schedule now. Think you might try appeasing Bishara's wishes to find a lady?" He chuckled.

I couldn't help the hint of a smirk. "Is that an official assignment, sir?"

Leboo chuckled more, shaking his head. "No. But it might need to be. You know she's never going to get off your back about it."

I sighed, a mix of emotions tightening in my chest. "I know, I know. Maybe one day I'll settle down—but for now. I've got work to do."

He smiled. A warm, fatherly look settled on his features. "Well, get on with it. Just know, there's more to life than work."

"I hear you."

"Alright then," he said, standing up and extending his hand. "Take care of things here, and stay sharp."

I stood, taking his hand in a firm shake. "Safe travels, Leboo."

"And you, Okiyo—get out and enjoy the city," he said, with a knowing twinkle in his eyes.

"No promises," I replied, giving him a slight smirk before turning to leave.

Delia Aguillen-McGhee. My thoughts were fully back on her as I left the Baijan estate.

I aimed to find out why she was such a walking contradiction. A great fighter who won't fight back in a competition. Also, lauded as the most capable to help me with the security revamp, but only has aspired to be the 'secretary.'

By the time I wrapped up my meeting with Leboo, I was already plotting an operation to get to know the Viper. *I wonder where she works out?* I needed to blow off some steam. She was a good fighter. No harm in sharing a gym, was it?

Chapter 8 – Delia

THE KITCHEN AT MY mom's house had always been the center of all the action. Especially before my dad had passed. And even though she could very well afford any top of the line personal chef and kitchen staff, my mom wouldn't allow another woman besides my sister and I to step foot in her kitchen.

'Let another woman cook in your kitchen, she has direct access to your man' was just one of her classic Shayla-*isms*.

Tonight was no different. Mom rushed around the kitchen preparing the food for the surprise celebration dinner she'd planned for tonight. She hadn't started tossing orders over her shoulder yet, so I stayed out of the way tucked neatly in the corner by the massive charcuterie board she'd put together. The thing was full of delectable finger foods. I stayed quiet and helped myself.

She stirred the pot of collards on the stove. Then dashed over to the in-wall oven to check on the pot roast and corn tamales. She always cooked her tamales in the oven, rather than on top of the stove. Something about them being more healthy that way. None of us cared about that. They were delicious and we just wanted to eat them... *all*.

To some, collards and tamales might be a strange pairing. But they used to be my dad's favorite meal. The two dishes were a staple in our blended Black and Mexican American household. It was almost as perfect a pairing as collard greens and cornbread to me. Similar flavor profiles. At any rate, the delicious aroma, a mingling of soul food and Mexican had my belly grumbling. I was starving.

She pulled out the fancy silverware that was gifted to her by her mother and sat them on the center island. No doubt getting ready to ask me to go set the table in the formal dining room. Mom only whipped those bad boys out for special occasions. Tonight was one such occasion. My baby sister was getting proposed to.

The proposal was supposed to be a surprise. Mom passed this dinner off as a work event to celebrate the recent success of the real estate firm, where both Iya, my sister and her boyfriend, Justin worked.

Surprise my ass. I smirked at the thought. I didn't buy it. Something about the way my mom wasn't all stressed out cooking this dinner was a major clue. She couldn't hold water where Iya was concerned. They really were as thick as thieves. If mom really was keeping a secret from her favorite child, she'd be stress yelling orders at *me* by now. *Oh... She was way too calm.*

"Delia stop standing there eating all the damn cheese and crackers and go and start setting the table. The guest are starting to arrive."

Spoke too soon.

I still wasn't convinced Iya wasn't in on the planning of her own engagement party. That order wasn't barked strong enough. The curse word combos not intricate enough. *If anyone ever wondered where I learned to curse? ... Just check my matriarchical pedigree.* Stressed Shayla would be cursing out the stove burners and kitchen knives at this point. Company in the house, be damned. Stressed Shayla wouldn't give a rats ass about them hearing her losing her shit in this kitchen either. They could get it too.

I popped a few grapes into my mouth. Then reached into the cabinet behind me to grab the fine China that matched the silverware. I grabbed a big stack of the heavy dishes, carrying them to the formal dining room on slippered feet. I'd kicked off my heels in the mudroom off the garage when I'd first arrived, planning to change back into heels when the party officially started.

"Don't you break my good dishes, now," I heard my mother yelling at my back. I ignored her. Thankful to be out of the kitchen before she tried to put me to work for real.

I was extremely happy for my younger sister. She was living the dream. She worked in my parents real estate firm and was doing extremely well as an agent. Her contribution to the firm started immediately after she'd joined the team. A lot of the firm's extraordinary growth over the last three consecutive years could be attributed to Iya.

Iya opted not to go to college. A total *three-sixty* from the plans we'd discussed so much in our youth. Then, she'd been excited about following in my footsteps to go to school to become a famous architect. Things had definitely changed. After spending a couple of gap years traveling overseas, she came home and got her real estate license instead.

Iya and I were much closer back then, even though I was five years older. We'd grown apart. Mom couldn't be more proud of Iya. She'd been running the firm alone since dad died of cancer just before my Sophomore year of college and now she had her favorite child to come work for the family business.

Me on the other hand, I'd finished school and gotten my architectural degree, but had lost my passion for it. Hell I wasn't even sure mom even cared what I was doing half the time. I wasn't Iya. I'd stopped being jealous and hurt by it a long time ago. At least I tried to convince myself of that.

I quickly shrugged off my dark thoughts. It wasn't my baby sisters fault that mom gave her all of her attention. They'd basically pushed me to the side the moment Jordy Hefflin's court case concluded. Guilty as charged... for Sexual Battery. A felony but perhaps the mildest sentence that a perpetrator could get for exposing himself to and trying to force himself on Iya. She'd done her best to fight him off. He got less than 3 years. The motherfucker was out before I'd even graduated from Tech.

I didn't blame my parents for wrapping Iya in all of their protective energy. This happened on my watch. They'd trusted me to look out for her. But I was too busy chatting it up with my architectural idol and I failed my little sister and their baby girl.

I'd kick my ass to curb too... I felt like I'd lost my entire family back then. My mom because she'd wrapped Iya up in a protective shell and never took her eyes off of her for a minute. My little sister was untouchable by everyone and everything—including me. Then we all lost my dad.

Iya had mom and I learned to emotionally fend for myself. We'd both been through therapy. Iya's seemed to work. Mine, not so much.

The house was decorated beautifully with several vases of white, lavender and purple floral arrangements. A thoughtful touch. Lavendar was Iya's favorite color. *Wait a minute. Are these Dahlias?* Yep. Another clue that Iya's hands were all over the planning for this event. My mom hated Dahlias.

She always said they were a waste of money. Because why did such pretty flowers have no smell. I think the real reason was because they reminded her too much of dad. Dahlias were the national flower of Mexico, his home and he used to love them too.

Of course, I knew that Justin was going to propose tonight. My mom had shared that much with me when she'd call to make sure I'd be here. She'd let slip that she'd stayed in her room for days crying when in honor of my dad, Justin performed the traditional *perdido de mano* by formally asking her for permission to marry her youngest daughter.

Seemed she'd worked through it because, she couldn't be more ecstatic about Iya getting married than she was tonight, hosting her surprise party. And I still wasn't a hundred percent convinced that it was the secret she'd claimed it to be.

I set the table secretly wishing some of the fanfare she gave to Iya could be for me for a change. It had been quite a long time sense my family got excited about anything I did. *And why would they?* Education, elite but doing nothing with it. Job, nothing to write home to mom about. And God knows I was nowhere near getting proposed to.

Several of the invited guests, to include the full staff of my parents firm, and Iya's and Justin's coworkers had arrived. Justin and Iya had met at work and had been dating for the last three years. We were all mingling in the formal living room when Mom excitedly entered the doorway tapping her fork on her crystal champagne flute. "Everyone Iya just pulled up." The chatter in the room faded as she proudly looked at all of us, eyes lingering on Justin. "We all know what we are gathered here for but please, I implore you do not let the cat out of the bag. Just act normal!"

This woman was really putting on like Iya really didn't know she was about to be proposed to tonight. I chuckled inwardly. Everybody else might have been fooled. I stopped by my condo right after work to change into a strapless black bodycon dress, a pair of black red bottoms and touched up my makeup to ensure none of the bruises from Endyra's punches were visible.

I did all this because if Iya had any inkling of this party being in honor of her, she'd come dressed to the nines. And I could never let my little sister out dress me. I might have been invisible; the black sheep of the family even. But an ugly duckling I was not.

And my suspicion that Iya knew about her own engagement party was confirmed when she walked in looking like a total baddie. This was supposed to be a straight after work event. I definitely know she knows now because who went to work in an iridescent silver body skimming dress that looked like it was tailored just for her modelesque figure?

She was stunning. Compared to my average 5'-6" height, Iya stood almost a full 6' tall with the slim physique of a swimwear model, with just enough curves to give her mass sex appeal.

Iya knew she looked good. She strutted in late. Planned, I'm sure. Grand entrance made. I almost burst out laughing when she had the nerve to come in looking surprised, "Oh wow! I didn't realize all these people were going to be here. Thought it was going to be just a few of us from work over for dinner." *And the award for best actress goes too...*

I may have been the only one who noticed the conspiratorial wink my mom gave Iya before tapping her champagne glass again. "Come on everybody, let's make our way to the dining room."

Midway through dinner, I was ready for it to hurry up and be over. I was tired from the lack of sleep I'd gotten the last couple of nights stressed about this new work assignment with a certain proper gentleman that had my full attention. I almost jumped with joy when mom finally stood up and cleared her throat. *Thank God.* She was about to set it up so Justin could finally propose.

"I'm so glad all of you could make it tonight. I know you've all worked hard today, but we wanted to just show a little appreciation for all the hard work you all have been putting in." She paused briefly looking around the table, eyes finally landing on Justin as if silently getting his assurance that he was ready to pop his question. He confidently gave her a single nod to confirm before she continued on. "And now I want to give Justin the floor to say a few words."

After a deep clearing of his throat, Justin stood, nervously bringing his refilled champagne glass to his lips to take a quick sip of courage.

He swept his eyes to my mom. "Ms. Aguillen, first let me thank you for accepting me into your firm and family as Iya's boyfriend. Also for putting this fine dinner together."

Everyone was sitting up straighter in their seats while mom was grinning from ear to ear looking like she was about to swoon and fall out of her seat from sheer happiness. I just sat back and watched totally tickled.

Iya was on the edge of her seat, looking very much like the Morgan character played by Paula Patton in the rom-com "Just Wright" after she'd finessed an engagement from the main male character played by the rapper Common.

Justin now moved from his seat to stand near Iya. He looked down at her lovingly. You could almost hear a pin drop when Justin cleared his throat again, his gaze softening as he knelt before her, opening the iconic Tiffany blue box he'd pulled from his pocket. The sight of the ring—a sparkling cushion-cut diamond—had a few gasps rippling through the room, and Iya's hands flew up to her cheeks, her eyes wide in perfect surprise.

"Iya, from the moment I met you, my life would never be the same," Justin began, his voice carrying just the right amount of emotion. "You're strong, beautiful, and you make me a better man every day. I can't imagine my life without you."

He paused, taking a deep breath before asking, "Iya Aguillen, will you marry me?"

Tears welled up in Iya's eyes as she nodded furiously. "Oh my God, yes, Justin! Yes!"

Justin slipped the ring onto her finger, and they sealed the moment with a kiss as everyone clapped and cheered. My mom looked like she might burst from happiness.

I smiled, genuinely happy for Iya. She deserved this—her fairy-tale engagement. But as I watched them, I couldn't help but feel a pang of longing. Not jealousy, just... curiosity. What would it be like to have someone look at me the way Justin looked at Iya?

My thoughts wandered briefly to someone else, someone whose face had a way of appearing in my mind lately. I pushed the thought aside, clapping louder as my sister beamed at all of us. This was her moment, and she deserved every bit of joy.

Chapter 9 – Okiyo

I SAT BACK IN my seat, fingers steepled under my chin, totally satisfied with the facts I'd found in my research of Delia. Almost any bit of information that you wanted to find on any given person was available to you in just a few keystrokes. My art of digging through a person's past, present, and making informed decisions about their future activities came from the many years as an agent. And one who fights must train.

I decided to do a triangulation between where Delia worked and her home to find all the MMA gyms in a ten mile radius of both. I was able to find her home address through a Google search and all MMA fighting gyms in between. I further narrowed my search by looking for those that provided capoeira training. That brought my options down to two gyms that she must train at.

I was well versed in capoeira, jujitsu, Taekwondo, and other fighting styles and recognized at least three that she was also aware of through her blows at me. The most rare of her fighting styles was capoeira which is why I narrowed the search there. Not many gyms taught this ancient Afro-Brazilian fighting style. I have to admit a part of the reason why I was so keenly interested in this enigmatic woman was because I was impressed.

Armed with the information of Delia's potential whereabouts for training, I closed the lid of my laptop and grabbed my keys and hit the door. The first gym was in walking distance about six blocks away from my rented condo. I tried that one first. And if it just happened to be the right gym, either of the two for that matter, I was dressed to enjoy a workout myself.

I entered the first gym and quickly surmised that Delia was not a member. The gym was too sterile. Perfectly white walls and rows upon rows of neatly aligned weight benches and racks was not it. The staff members that lazed around the check in all resembled Flo from the Progressive commercials. I backed out quickly. Not even wasting time to inquire about a membership.

Delia's fighting style was grimy. *When she actually tried.* I'd expect the gym she trained at to be a bit on the grimy side too. How else would any of it fighters have the street creds needed to gain entry to a secret fight society.

I called an Uber to take me to the next location. It was in walking distance of the first gym. However, it was late afternoon and her workday would be ending soon. If my hunch was correct I could accidentally run into her there. Before I exited the Uber, I knew this was the right gym.

It wasn't a bad location per se, just not as exclusive as the first gym. The building had no sign above the stainless steel door that faced a side street rather than busy Courtland Street. The name of the gym was Blaze. When I opened the door and entered the huge Blaze logo that graced much of the back wall of the gym confirmed I was in the right place.

I did the necessary and enrolled in a temporary membership at the front desk. I surveilled the room while the receptionist clicked away at her tiny screen to complete the setup. There she was. I spotted Delia in the back corner of the gym. She appeared to be in a heated conversation with a sleezy low life looking fellow.

I kept my distance as I began warming up near the body bag area. It gave me the perfect vantage point to work out and keep my eye on her in case I had to put the man she was talking too down if he got too aggressive with her.

It did indeed look like they knew each other. I was able to relax a bit because of this but stayed vigilant. Where I came from, small clashes could easily become big brawls in an instant. Even though Delia was quite a capable fighter, I'd break him or any other man in half if he came at a woman, in this case her, improperly.

By the time I'd started throwing a few body shots at the bag, Delia ended her conversation with the little guy and made her way to the ring. I watched her companion go to lean against a wall intent on watching Delia spar. A tall wiry guy in full protective gear, to include a kick guard, must have been her sparring partner. He stood at least a foot taller than Delia and looked to be in peak shape. I stayed mostly hidden, but moved to get a better view. I wanted to see how she was going to hold up to her sparring partner.

She immediately attacked. Her initial assault strong. She aimed a crushing blow with her shin to his midsection. But she pulled back. I held the body bag still. Moving even further around it to make sure I'd seen what I thought I had.

Then she did it again; went in for a deadly strike to the man's head, but quickly pulled her punch. *Why the fuck was she pulling her punches?* The *blimey* was fully decked out in protective gear and she was smaller than him. Nothing she could do would seriously injure him.

After witnessing about four more of these instances, I moved even closer to the ring. I was now openly observing her in disbelief. I checked my surroundings in the wall size mirror across the back length of the gym and noticed several people starting to take notice of me. I was new and obviously they were a small family of fighters here who all mostly new each other. Of course I stood out to them, but not a single one of them paid a bit of attention to the travesty going on in the ring. It was like they were used to seeing this mediocre performance from her.

With me, she had actually put up a real fight. I could understand that night she may have felt threatened in a way. I did follow her down a dark hallway after all. Maybe she only put up a real fight if she felt threatened by something? Someone?

I needed to make my presence known. Maybe then she'd at least try in that ring. She clearly had skill. I'd done my research on her. Only a sprinkling of wins under her belt and more than a dozen losses. I only had to see one fight paired with what she was doing in this ring right now and I bloody well wanted to pull my hair out. She had all of the skills of a champion fighter but there was something in her head keeping her from her greatness. *What was it?*

"Swear!" I yelled out loud, rushing up to the ring. I bloody couldn't take any more of this. "You could have easily swiped left with that right foot sweetheart. Take his legs out why don't you!"

Delia and her sparring partner stopped mid squabble. He had to look over his shoulder to see where the yells were coming from. She had to look around him to see where the demands on what she should do in the ring were coming from. Recognizing me, her face scrunched. irritation was etched across her brow. I could care less about her irritation. The whole bloody gym should be irritated by this farce.

She shrugged off my words and got back in her stance to continue her sparring round. Her partner took her lead and did the same. They started at it again.

This time, she intentionally misses her opponents left ear with the right hook that she threw.

"He has on headgear, sweetheart," I stated facetiously, intentionally taunting her now. Apparently her sparring partner was used to her play it small performance. "Your partner has skill. He very well could have ducked when you came at his head just now. What are you doing, Love?" My taunts were coming faster now and Delia was becoming unhinged. Again, I could care less. I wanted her to do something. *Hell*, attack like she did the other night.

"Are you even trying to hit your opponent?" I asked, still calm on the exterior, but doing angry somersaults on the inside. "No amount of force from you could hurt the big guy. So use your small size and out maneuver him." This time my goading worked.

"How about you bring your punk ass in this ring and see." To no one in particular, she yells in frustration, "Can someone get this motherfucker out of here?"

I looked around at the few onlookers who were starting to move closer to the ring to see what all the commotion was. I looked back at Delia, shrugged off her tantrum and shook my head. Silently questioning, who was going to get me out of here? Little Tubby who she was arguing with earlier? That was a laugh.

"Nah sweetheart. You'd provide no competition," I stated matter-of-factly moving even closer to the ring. Just a little bit more of me fucking with her head and she'd invite me into the ring again, this time for real unlike the bluff she'd made earlier, and I'd get to show her how to fight. "The way you were throwing your punches, I wouldn't even have to duck. Wouldn't even break a sweat sparring with you."

"As I said," she rolled her eyes and neck, hands on her hips. "Bring your punk ass in this ring and find the fuck out." She turned her back on me this time, moving back to the center of the ring. She didn't look back but tossed over her shoulder, "I remember almost kicking your ass in four inch stilettos and a ball gown the other night."

She was seething at this point. Getting madder when she turned around, her eyes narrowed menacingly when she realized she was facing me instead of her usual sparring partner. I'd climbed over the ring rope quietly during her rant and tapped ol' boy out promising everything would be cool.

Standing face to face with Delia now, I stared straight into her eyes before stating, "Almost doesn't count, sweetheart." As if struck by a thought, I cocked my head to the side and reached up to stroke my beard. Then I leaned in close to state, "And as I recall, you rather liked my hand around your throat the other night too."

My words were barely audible. Only she knew what I was referring to. I spoke close enough to her cheek that she couldn't escape the seductive tinge of my words or the innuendo behind them.

That was straw that broke the camel's back. I thought being faced with a threat was her trigger. I was wrong. Delia Aguillen-McGhee didn't like to be seen. She certainly didn't like that I saw through her bullshit; her contradictory nature. And I saw it all and could now use that as a tool to extract some effort out of her. The sexual connotation of my words were yet another tool to amplify the effect.

Before I could get the words out of my mouth good she was lunging at me. I side-stepped her attempt sending her crashing into the ropes. Little man had the nerve to slither under the ropes and jump between Delia and I before she rushed me again. My look alone withered him and he backed all the way up into the corner before slithering back out of the ring.

I looked to Delia, threw up a hand and beckoned her to me. Any fighter knew that such a gesture in the ring was akin to a duel. *Fair fight only.* I could see her contemplating my request. Moments went by before she rolled her eyes in submission and stepped to the center of the ring. Hands up. And when I yelled *hite*, she knew exactly what to do and attacked.

She came in with a quick kick to my abdomen. From what I'd seen, it was her go to move. I let her connect. The force of her strike was good. Her aim precise causing me to stumble back a bit.

"Good. You actually do have some skill."

At my goading she attacked again. A three punch combo. I blocked but was impressed that she didn't pull her punches this time. The sound of her gloves smacking against my palms reverberated around the gym.

She tried another combo, but this time I countered, dropping down into a low roundhouse. She quickly jumped over it. She stepped back then popped right back into her fighting stance. This time southpaw. Behind me I heard someone say in surprise, "That's Delia in the ring with ol' boy? Oh shit!"

She counterattacked quickly running at me then leaping and coming down with a straight right fist. I sighed, feigning boredom before side-stepping her attempt. I then grabbed her arm and flipped her over my shoulder in a none vicious body slam. She was on her back but there was still fight in her.

She grabbed two fists full of my shirt around the sides of my neck and pulled me into her while bringing her knee up to catch me in a body shot to my side. I tightened my core, blocking the shot. As we grappled on the ground, I couldn't stop myself from getting really close to her ear, "How does it feel to be pinned beneath me to the floor, Delia? As good as it did when you were pinned between me and the wall at Gastrafrique?"

Her breath caught in her throat. I'd intentionally used those words to goad and disarm her. What happened next, totally disarmed me.

Her grip on my neck loosened, arms falling limp by her sides in submission. Just as I was about to push myself off of her, she snaked one hand between our bodies and grabbed a fist full of my dick. She then pushed the forearm of her other arm under my neck as she rolled her body over mine. We ended up with me pinned to the mat, while she hovered over me in a low straddle never letting go of my balls.

"How does it feel for the family jewels to be cupped and jiggled by a girl?" She smiled sweetly as I slapped the mat three quick times, tapping out.

Of course, Delia didn't actually cause me to tap out. We'd barely even scratched the surface of a full blown fight. She did however catch me completely off guard with the dick move. Not that it hurt. No. It wasn't pain, but excruciating pleasure that shot through my body like a million tiny electric shocks. What actually happened was this beautiful, soft yet steely hard vixen had me mesmerized.

Realizing that everybody in the gym now had their eyes on us, she tensed then sat straight up and rolled off me. I quickly followed suit. Then made sure to say loud enough for all to hear. "Good fight. I knew there was a fighter in there some-where." I jumped out of the ring then went to grab my few belongings preparing to walk out of the gym.

Everyone else was still standing around with looks of shock on their faces. Delia had actually put on a show. I'd refused to let her play soft. Perhaps she'd gained the respect of her fellow gym mates.

Chapter 10 – Delia

RUDY ENTERED THE GYM as I was doing a few rounds on the punching bag. I'd just finished working on some speed work and noticed him take the long way around the gym to avoid Okiyo. He'd been in the gym every day since our impromptu sparring match—three days ago. So far, both Rudy and I had been able to avoid him. I wasn't sure what I was going to do in the next few days when I actually had to start working with him.

Even now we were on opposite sides of the gym. Over the last couple of days we moved around each other as if our interactions were choreographed. Every so often, I'd feel his eyes on me and would have to fight the urge to look up or over in his direction. Other times, I'd sneak glances his way and would curse myself for doing so.

His body was cut, muscles defined with a razor sharp edge. I mean the man didn't have an ounce of fat on his body. He took to working out without his shirt on and it never failed that if I chanced a glance at him, my eyes would zero in on the sweat sliding down his chest in rivulets. *Damn he's fine.*

I could tell Okiyo was older than me by a few years from the tinge of gray that peppered his beard. Maybe 10 years or so, but of course it could have been more... His Motherland-melanin drip was on point and his skin was silky smooth. *Girl, get it together.*

I forcibly retrained my eyes on the punching bag that was eye level before me. The next few weeks were going to be *long.*

He'd already infiltrated my job. And no amount of begging Rhiyan to take me off this project had worked. His larger than life presence had permeated my gym, too. And now my fucking thoughts. *Ugh!*

Now clear of Okiyo, Rudy quickly sauntered over to me. I could tell by the way he moved and the shit eating grin on his face that he was excited about something. This typically meant he had found a fighter who was willing to fight me with my deplorable record. Well, a little less deplorable now that I'd won an actual bout that mattered.

"I see you getting even better with that roundhouse Delia," he said starting to stutter when I sneered at him.

"And how would *you* know I'm getting better, Rudy?" I hadn't done the move he referred to since before I'd gotten in the ring with Okiyo. He was just trying to open up the door for conversation, so

I chuckled as I continued doing combo punches on the punching bag.

"Yeah, well, you know the other day you held your own in the ring with old boy over there," he said tossing his head in Okiyo's direction. "It got me to thinking."

"So you're thinking now, huh?" I couldn't help the jab at Rudy as I continued. "It's amazing how you don't fight anymore. Yet, you're always in the mix. So what exactly are you thinking in this regard?"

"Yeah well I've been mixing it up on *your* behalf outside of here too. And since me and the whole fucking gym know you can actually *friggin'* fight now, it's time for your punk ass to step up. And since you won your last fight—" he paused, face screwed up like he wanted to say something else but was hesitating.

"Go on," I encouraged, "you've already disturbed my work out. Spit it out."

"Naw, I'm just saying. I lost a lotta fucking' money on that last fight of yours by the way. I could have sworn you let me know you wasn't going to even try."

"That's what the fuck you get for betting against me," I couldn't help but chuckle out loud. He was absolutely right. I had no intentions of fighting during that last bout. Me winning was just as much a surprise to me as everyone else. Rudy included.

" Yeah, well, no more of those weak ass low effort, low payout fights either. You've been called out. Storm has you on her radar."

I stopped hitting the bag after he mentioned that name. Storm was one of the best female MMA fighters in the Southeast and the entire Eastern seaboard. Her notoriety reached all the way down to Miami and back up to New York and Philly. As a matter of fact she had her face on a small billboard going into midtown and a few more in some of the seedier parts of town. I'd heard about how dirty she did her last opponent. The bitch was crazy.

She still fought underground and in some of those seedier areas. Same circuit that I fought in, it's just that I'd never been in the winner circle from a fight that actually mattered before now. *Fuck. How the hell would my fights remain anonymous, being called out by a fighter who actually was showcased on ESPN?*

There was no way I could fight Storm. Number one, she was known to knock her opponents out. If not in the first round, early in the second. Number two, she was too powerful a puncher for me to just take her punches. I'd quite literally have to defend myself or exit the cage on a stretcher. And third, as if a third reason was needed, I could fight Storm, could possibly even avoid getting knocked out, but that defeated the whole fucking purpose of using these fights as my atonement.

"No fucking way." I stated and continue hitting the punching bag.

"Why the fuck not, Deelz? You can beat her if you just tried." He was getting animated, arms flailing as he continued trying to convince me why I couldn't turn this fight down.

I didn't readily answer his question.

"Come the fuck on, Delia. You've been taking these petty ass fights, knowing damn well you can fight! And after seeing what you did in the ring with black Jason Statham over there, you can easily take Storm down. Or at least get in the ring with her ass! Just let me know what's up so I know how to bet my money and potentially recoup some of the loss from your last fucking fight!" He was all but screaming at this point, drawing attention from others. "We need this payout, Delia," he said, calming down, voice almost pleading.

I finally stopped hitting the bag and rounded on him. "No, Rudy. *You* need this payout. I'm just supposed to get in the ring with her and risk life and limb so you can win a stack to blow on God knows what? Nope. Plus I'm not *even* ready to fight a fighter like her!"

"Well we got a week and a half to get you ready," he countered. "And if you don't take this fight, no one is going to waste their time on you again. Not me anyway!"

That had a sobering effect. He was right. If I turned this fight down, my fighting days would be over. I'd be stuck to deal with the shame and guilt of not protecting my sister. I'd tried the therapy route before and it led me here. No amount of talking it out made the feelings of abandonment or rejection of my family go away. Only the pain seemed to numb the thoughts.

"With what trainer Rudy? You?" I said in a last ditch effort to get out of this. It was becoming clear, I had no choice but to get in that cage with Storm.

A little small greasy grin started spreading across his lips as he paused and just stared at me. And then he turned his head and looked across the ring at you know who.

I followed Rudy's direction with my eyes. "Oh fuck no. Hell no."

"Here me out, Deelz," Rudy said, hands up to pause me long enough to not walk away from whatever nonsense was about to spew out of his mouth. He continued talking in a hushed tone through his teeth. "Dude over there, asshole that he is, he could get you ready. And I don't know how he knows your moves like he knows them, but the way he was coaching you and fighting you at the same time the other day lets me know that you respond to him. He'd make you a perfect coach and it's only for a week and a half."

I was busy thinking about Rudy's words and my spirit was aggravated by how much sense he'd actually made. And also, why had I responded to Okiyo in such a way. My pause gave Rudy several moments head start in Okiyo's direction.

"Rudy, I said no. What's the point anyway? The winner would have to go—" *...Fight in Mexico.* I called behind him in futility. My words trailed off. *Dammit Rudy.* I began speed walking to catch up to him, but was too late.

Okiyo had just finished kicking the bag when he paused, pinning Rudy with an impassive stare. His eyes narrowed further and further into slits as Rudy got tentatively closer.

Okiyo looked over Rudy's shoulder and saw me walking up as well. I could see the tension literally release as his face smoothed into a more open gaze at me. Never taking his eyes off mine, he asked Rudy, "What can I do for you?" His voice and posture were that of a perfect gentleman rather than a panther ready to strike when Rudy first pulled up on him.

All that base Rudy had in his voice for me was reduced to a babbling stutter in Okiyo's presence.

"So um, yeah," Rudy started quickly turning towards me as if he was second guessing himself. He cleared his throat as I too stared at him waiting for him to continue. Hoping he wouldn't. Finding the courage from deep down in his ball sacks I guess, he did just that—*continued*— and I rolled my eyes. "Delia and I, *umm,* we was thinking you know, after you and her sparred the other day... *Man,* "he paused, wiping the bead of sweat that had formed on his brow before speeding on to say, "You really got some nice moves and we wanted to ask if you'd be her trainer for an upcoming fight?"

"Never mind, Rudy here is overstepping." I glared at him in disbelief.

Okiyo stood, arms crossed, legs wide glaring at Rudy in annoyance.

Not giving in, Rudy continued yet again, "She has a big fight coming up in a week and you know," he swallowed hard, "She's a little bit outmatched but I think after what you guys did together in the ring the other day, Delia can take Storm down."

There. He'd said it. And when I should have been putting up a huge fuss to shut this shit down, I, just like Rudy, was intent on hearing what Okiyo had to say.

"She's not ready." The rude motherfucker then turned away to continue hitting that stupid body bag!

"Yeah, but you saw what she can do in the ring, didn't you? I mean, she beat Endyra *man*, and then went toe to toe with you just the other day."

Okiyo chuckled at Rudy's weak argument. "By accident," he chuckled again, shaking his head, leaving both Rudy and I confused.

So he repeated himself, eyes back on me, but talking to Rudy. "She beat Endyra by accident. And her going toe to toe with me is just comical."

"Accident? What's he talking about, Deelz?"

I totally ignored Rudy's question. This asshole was right about me beating Endyra by accident. But something about the way Okiyo said that shit and laughed, pricked my ego. I was fuming. My anger was not missed by Mr. *All Seeing* Okiyo and he doubled down continuing his assassination of my fighting ability.

"Storm, you say?" Okiyo asked, holding his chin in thought.

Rudy nodded his head up and down vehemently.

Again, Okiyo chuckles as if to himself this time. "Well Storm has a really quick strike, and Delia here pulls her punches." His eyes were back on me as if he were reading my soul through my eyes. "Even when she knows she has an advantage, she doesn't take it."

He prepared to turn back to his bag and begin his work out again. Then tosses over his shoulder in finality. "As I stated, she ain't ready."

I don't know why I did it, when I could have just as easily taken his answer and moved on. *But noooo...* Silly me had to open my big mouth.

"You don't know me enough to tell me I'm not ready for anything. Just because you waltz in here and give a few pointers does not make you some sort of fucking MMA master. Trust me, *sweetheart*," I said, mocking his accent and condescending reference to me previously. "You're not that fucking desirable. I'm good and

I'm ready when I say I'm ready. Not when you say I am. *Who the fuck do you think you are, Okiyo Bamdi?"*

"That's exactly who the fuck I am, *sweetheart*." he tossed the word right back at me like an insult. "And you're just a young lady who talks big talk and plays small. As I stated, you ain't ready." He paused , rubbing his chin again. This time in deep contemplation, but still scrutinizing me heavily. After a few beats, his eyes softened from the steely stare just a bit before he continued. "But I can get you ready if you change that loser's attitude."

Fuck, fuck, figgety, fucking fuck. Fuck my life and fuck Rudy for getting me into this shit.

Chapter 11 – Okiyo

SWEAR. I'D NEVER BEEN so bent on being in anyone's company, let alone that of an insipid woman with the petulance of a toddler. Yet, I'd gone and done the most to be in the company of one Delia Aguillen-McGhee.

I'd had to settle—*thus far*— on our 'companionship' merely being two people sharing space in the same gym. Even that consisted mainly of my inconspicuous observations of how she trained.

I cursed myself for it. The need to see her. Be in her presence. Yet, it all became worth it when I'd catch her studying me with curiosity when she thought no one was looking. Once, I'd even caught her and she graced me with a venomous eyeroll.

Today, however, marked a turn in our nonexistent relationship. I came off the fifth floor elevator at 3W and walked right into the bullpen of architects working diligently on whatever task they were assigned. The 5th floor belonged to Rhiyan Carson's team and was exactly where I would find her assistant.

I'd not made it five steps into the space when I saw her standing by the same architect she'd worked to evade so diligently at the Gastrafrique party.

The sight of them standing close, heads bent together over some document, ignited a heat low in my belly. It wasn't just proximity that had me on edge. I felt this way because Delia commanded attention effortlessly, even when she tried to stay in the background. And seeing him so close to her, the way he looked at her profile while her attention was on the plans spread out on the table below, only made me realize that he saw it too.

I didn't like how close he was to her.

In conversation with her boss, Rhiyan Kekoa, at the Gastrafrique party, she went on and on about how great her assistant was and if only she'd take her license exam, she'd promote her to architect at the drop of a dime. It's when she'd basically offered Delia up for the first time when I inquired about the security plans that were put together for Gastrafrique. According to Mrs. Kekoa, Delia was the glue that held the team together.

I'd just made it within earshot and from what I could hear, Rhiyan was right about Delia. Fittingly, her work persona was totally opposite of hers in the ring. *Walking contradiction indeed.* She didn't hold back on this guy like she did in the ring.

I watched the exchange from a distance, my eyes narrowing as this *Devon dude* was busy running his mouth at Delia. He talked a good game, but I could tell he was one of those pricks who thought he was the smartest person in the room.

"It's a commercial space, so the hallways need to be five feet wide. The one you changed can be six, but it'll cut into the conference room that the client specifically asked to be bigger." Delia's voice was steady, professional, but I could hear the subtle edge in her tone. She wasn't here for his nonsense.

Devon, not even phased, pushed back with an arrogant grin. "Yeah, but I'm thinking we could use the extra foot for some decorative features. Maybe a seating area, you know? Somewhere for folks to wait before meetings. It'll look good, trust me."

This guy. I could feel the heat rising on the back of my neck. He didn't get it— *at all*. He was trying to play designer when he didn't have the range, and even worse, I could see he was flexing to impress Delia. She wasn't having any of it. She handled him like a pro.

"No," she said firmly, cutting off his fantasy about a seating area. "The client didn't ask for any of that, and it's not in the scope of work. Rhiyan already approved the initial layout, and asked me to take them to the lead architect for his signature. If you push the hallway to six feet, it's going to throw off the balance of the entire floor plan."

Devon didn't give up, because of course he wouldn't. "Look, the client won't even notice. Once they see how open it feels, they'll love it."

Delia didn't blink, standing tall against him. "No. I'm not taking these to anyone for approval until the plans reflect what the client actually wants. You need to fix it first. If you want to pitch something else, you'll need to do that before you ask me to get these signed off."

Devon thought he'd gotten the best of her, but Delia wasn't backing down. Watching her assert her authority like that—quiet, controlled, and absolutely unshakeable—was something to admire.

When she saw me standing there, her spine stiffened at the look I gave her over this clown's shoulder. A silent *why the hell are you entertaining this nonsense?*

She left Devon and the plans at the table and headed to the breakroom without another word to him.

I followed her, catching up just as she was refilling her coffee cup. This was definitely a different side of Delia. In the cage, lots of talent with no grit, but here... here she was precise, calculating, and assertive. There was hope for her after all.

"And here I thought you'd play it small at work too. Bloody impressive what you did back there." I couldn't help but throw the jab at her while she fixed her coffee.

"Get off my back, please," she groaned, continuing about her business of making coffee.

"You clearly know what the client wants, though. I'm beginning to understand the praise your boss gives."

I moved into her personal space, reaching around her to grab a cup for coffee as well.

I stepped back quickly, as she rounded on me. Coffee sloshing all over the place as she did so. The conviction she showed in telling Devon to go fuck himself was fully turned on me.

"Here you go with this bullshit." She huffed, breezing past me on the way to her desk. Without breaking her stride, she tossed over her shoulder, "Will you please stop acting as if you know anything about me."

I put the coffee cup back, not really caring for the bitter substance and followed her to her desk. I relished taunting her. Relished it even more after seeing her boss up. "Well, what I fail to understand, Ms. McGhee—"

"Aguillen-McGhee," she corrected.

"A million pardons," I offered a feigned over apology before continuing, "what I fail to understand, Ms. Aguillen-McGhee, is how one with enough talent to get hired by one of the most prestigious architectural firms, not only in Atlanta but globally, agreed to be a glorified secretary?"

I'd already been informed that she was only the license shy of being and architect, but I had no expectation that she would answer my question. Thought she might even respond by attacking me.

Surprisingly she didn't. She cooly pulled out a pair of air pods and plugged them firmly in her ears and ignored me.

Knowing full well she could still hear me, I continued on to get my desired effect. Raise her ire. I laughed on the inside at the fact that the same goading in the gym would have her inviting me to a battle. Here, she was unflappable.

I tapped her on the shoulder. "Nevermind that question, but I do need you to look over the blueprints for the new security protocols at the Parque Place at the Hamlet site."

"I don't work for you!" She snapped, ripping one of the buds out of her ear and turned in her seat to glare at me in wild amazement at the notion that I'd given her a task.

"According to the memo I received with both your boss's and her boss's signatures, indeed you do for the next three to four weeks," I stated unbothered by her incredulity. "First thing in the morning, I need you to meet me over there. No. Change that. I will pick you up at 8:30 AM and we will ride together to talk with the security contractors," I paused, fighting to hold in a satisfied grin at rendering her totally speechless. "We'll need to have the old plans swapped out with the new ones I've created. With your suggested edits of course." I pulled out my phone and continued. "You should have the new plans in your inbox right now."

I moved to take my leave but couldn't help but notice Delia's wide mouthed stare in my direction.

"But wait," she sputtered, clicking a few buttons on her keyboard to open her email to take a quick peek at the floor plans of the new security layout. "You redid these plans in less than 24 hours?" She continued staring at her computer screen in amazement. She turned around in her swiveling chair, eyes raised, lips parted as she looked at me incredulously. "I just sent those over to you yesterday. It took the lead architect almost four weeks to lay out the security protocol for that site."

"Well Ms. Delia, Rhiyan sent me the amazing notes that you took during the planning of the security protocols. Made it super easy for me to see the flaws, weak points and I was quickly able to make the right adjustments. I must say, it is you who exceeds *my* expectations. And as unimpressive as that fight of yours I had the displeasure of watching, I'm moved by your ability here, *Secretary*."

I couldn't help the dig, relishing the stank look of scorn she gave at my newest nickname for her. Our 'situationship' was getting to be most interesting and my decision to train her in the ring was solidly made. This of course, would cause a slight delay in our schedule to visit the first site tomorrow.

"Oh and Delia, one final thing before I take my leave. I'll be picking you up from your flat." I stated it so matter-of-factly, she didn't know how to respond. "Please do share your building number with me at this number." I reached into my breast pocket to hand her my card, which she hesitantly took. "Oh, and please, don't bother wearing this get up."

"Get up?" She gasped, finally breaking her silence. Even gave herself a surprised once over as her eyes followed the wave of my hand up and down her body, referring to her office attire.

It wasn't a dig. I rather liked the feminine flair of her pants suit, silky blouse and pointy toed heels. She actually dressed like the skilled architect that she should be. *Walking contradiction, indeed.* "Bring a bag with your office attire in it. Be dressed for battle when I get there. Our training starts tomorrow.

Chapter 12 – Delia

I AM CONFLICTED.

He'd infiltrated my work. Had come into my gym, challenging me. He'd totally gotten under my skin. Both from the sexiness that oozed off of him and the unasked for challenges that he kept throwing my way.

To make matters worse, I'd been up all night like a nervous twit. Mind teetering back and forth between calling him up to curse him out and let him know I wouldn't be bullied into fighting or stepping up at anytime, anywhere, by anyone. My private bravado applied to the ring and at work.

Then my sentiments totally swung in the other direction and I'd start fretting over what workout outfit I was going to wear in the morning. This went on for the better part of my evening, until I took the bait, settling on a pair of hot pink tights and a matching sports bra. I begrudgingly tossed a pair of slacks, a blouse, undergarments and all my other morning necessities into a hanging garment bag for work before finally climbing into my bed to go to sleep.

I'd somehow given in and accepted Okiyo as my work mate and training partner overnight. Curiosity about how all of this—training plus us working together over the upcoming weeks— would play out, had won.

Regarding him being my trainer, it would go one of two ways. Him making me into a champion or me making him into a fool for thinking he could.

At work, however, the outcome wouldn't be so black and white. I had no doubt that the security project would go smoothly. I'd already seen his expertise in action. What freaked me out was how unpredictable my body's reaction was to him in those damned suits. *Sheesh*. I both wanted to jump his bone and eagerly just watch him do his thing.

Funny how in the gym, I just wanted to claw his eyes out. Maybe that's what would make it all work—his tendency to motivate my aggression.

I was up and outside waiting at the front door of my building for him to pull up after I'd texted him my address upon waking this morning. Just like he'd asked, no—told—me too.

Even while I waited for him to show, I couldn't stop thinking about him. He was persistent and pushy. It pissed me off to no end that he saw straight through my every attempt to stay in my own little mediocre world. I was repelled and drawn to his surety *about me* at the same time.

No one had paid this much attention to me or cared enough to push me in a very long time. The fact that he barely even knew me, but did, both scared and intrigued me.

Okiyo Bamdi had officially gotten in the way of my atonement.

Thus far, it had worked for me. Eating the punches and feeling the pain helped numb my feelings. In one fail swoop, Okiyo Bamdi had put a mirror up right in front of me and had me questioning who the fuck I was and what she really wanted.

He had me in my head playing the what if game. *What if I allowed myself to fight to win? What if I got my license to practice architecture? What if? What if someone actually cares?* Hot tears of confusion welled up and stung my eyes and I quickly swiped them away just as a black Range Rover pulled up promptly at 8:30 AM.

Hoping my eyes weren't red, I swung my gym bag over my shoulder and clung tightly to the garment bag with my work clothes in it as he came around to open my door for me.

Once I was settled into the backseat beside him, it didn't take Okiyo a hot five seconds for him to start being a jerk.

"Ah, so you do take direction well." He looked over at me as if approving my hot pink workout gear.

I closed my eyes for a brief moment. Taking a deep breath, I met his gaze head on and in as much of a British tone that I could muster, I sarcastically said, "Why yes, my jolly good man. I do follow orders well. And just so ya' know ol' chap, I have me' sparring shoes and gloves tucked away neatly in this here gym bag too." I patted my bag for good measure and hit him with the sweetest grin I could pull out of my ass.

To my total and utter surprise, Okiyo burst out laughing. Head tilted back and eyes crinkled at the corners. It gave me a moment to study his features openly. Amazed at the thought that he was even more handsome when he laughed.

His open laugh was contagious. I rolled my eyes while stifling my own giggles. I threw my hand up to my mouth in mock shock. "My God, he actually has a sense of humor. Pray tell!"

The moment helped lighten my mood. Made me see him in a different light. He presented as detached and no nonsense. But I actually got the sense that he was just extremely loyal and about his business.

I mean, he was staying back here in the States overseeing a security project to ultimately ensure his boss's daughter was safe. He was also going out of his way to train me.

Sobering, I asked, "Why did you decide to train me?"

His brows raised at the question. "Honestly, I wasn't going to. You are deplorable in the ring. But then I saw your passion at work and realized it was the same passion you have for fighting but just don't show it. I guess—" Just when I thought he would leave it there, he gave me a bemused shrug and continued, "I guess I want to understand why."

Fair enough. I looked down at my hands. I knew my reasons, but wouldn't be trying to explain them today. Likely not ever.

"Well, you're stuck with me now." I looked at him expectantly. "What kind of workout do you have in store for me today?"

He returned my direct look with a lop-sided smile. "I guarantee, when you find out, you won't be giggling or mocking my accent again," he taunted with a raised brow.

I groaned inwardly, knowing he wasn't joking at all.

Moments later, we pulled up to the gym. Okiyo jumped out to my door. He placed a hand on my elbow to assist me out of the SUV.

"You balance being a gentleman and jerk out rather well."

I moved past him, stealing a glance over my shoulder just in time to catch the subtle smirk curving his lips.

I didn't know whether to groan or moan. That look—dangerous, sexy and unreadable—it sent a ripple through me. So much for him only bringing out my aggression to fight in the gym. Another 'F' word definitely came to mind right now. *Get it together, Delia.*

After checking in, Okiyo called over his shoulder, "Finish putting on your gear and meet me in the ring." His tone was clipped and back to the no-nonsense tone I'd grown accustomed to. "Today I want to learn the styles you can fight in." In a warning tone, he continued. "And Delia, don't come at me with that punk shit that I saw you do in the ring the other day. Either go hard or go all the way the fuck back home. Cut the bullshit if you want to win."

Win. There was that word again. Deep down, I absolutely wanted to, but the truth was after making myself believe I didn't want to for so long, the concept just felt foreign to me. That and I still had real concerns about my family finding out. They were too much apart of my why.

Then the pendulum of my emotions swung. I was pissed all over again about how I got tossed into this predicament about having to choose to win or lose all over again. Because truth be told, had Rudy just shared the small detail that the fight with Endyra was a lead up to a title fight, there would be no need for Okiyo to be training me. Now I was going to have to fight for my damn life or get fucked up in the process.

Let the training begin.

I stood in the center of the ring while Okiyo stood in one of the corners with his arms crossed. The gym smelled like yesterday's sweat. I tried to mask my nerves but I felt like he saw right through them. I stopped trying to hide them. Just stood in the center of the ring looking stupid, twiddling my uncovered thumbs and waited as he scrutinized me.

He came over, ever the calm and imposing figure, and circled me.

"All right. Let's see what you've got. You pick. Show me one of your fighting styles."

Simple enough.

I nodded and took a deep breath to steady myself. Then dropped into a classic Muay Thai stance, fist up and elbows ready. Okiyo's eyes flickered waiting for me to make my first move. As soon as I shifted my weight on my back foot to do just that, he stopped me. He then moved in close to correct my stance.

I felt heat radiating from his body. I bit my lip as his hand lightly touched my waist while his other reached down to slide his fingers under my foot so he could adjust it. The contact sent an electric current from the very sensitive arch of my foot straight up my leg and inner thigh. I bit harder on my lip and did an involuntary Kegel to steady myself. *Focus Delia.* Seemed that had become my mantra in regards to him. When he straightened, our eyes locked for the briefest of seconds before he pulled away.

I tamped down the butterflies that were threatening to rip my stomach open then took a deep breath to slow down my pulse. I threw a few swift punches followed by a powerful knee stroke.

Okiyo blocked and dodged them both effortlessly, barely having to even move. I shifted to a different stance, transitioning smoothly into Brazilian jujitsu. I attempted a takedown, aiming for Okiyo's legs but he countered.

"Good job," he said. "You're versatile but you're still holding back and if you do this in the cage with Storm she will eat you for lunch."

The burst of nerves quickly went away as I narrowed my eyes at the slick comment. He was right, but I didn't want to admit it. I'd always played it safe and never pushed myself to the limit. But something about him made me take a step back and reassess my approach.

"Capoeira," he said. It wasn't a question it was a demand and I acquiesced.

I hesitated only for a moment before launching into the fluid, dance like movements of capoeira. My kicks were graceful, yet powerful. As usual. Okiyo intercepted them all with ease. He stared deep into my eyes as we sparred. It felt like a silent challenge lingering in the air. Every time our bodies came into close contact, I felt an undeniable pull. His firm grip on my waist, the brush of his chest against my shoulder it was all too much and yet, not enough.

"Come the fuck on Delia. Stop hesitating. You need to fully commit to your strikes." I shoved hard at his chest, pushing him off of me. This time I switched to a more aggressive stance as he continued, "You got the skills." I attacked blending Krav Maga elements into my capoeira movements. "What the hell are you afraid of," he hissed.

Our faces were mere inches apart. I felt his warm breath on my neck. My heart pounded wildly. *I feared he could hear it.* That's how close we were.

I stepped back to get space enough to drop low, spinning on the ball of one foot to swipe his legs at the ankle. He jumped then aimed a kick at my temple. I did a back roll to get out of the way.

We were moving so fast. He was coming at me hard but I held my own and then in the middle of an intense sequence I slipped on the mat.

Okiyo grabbed me. With quick reflexes, his arms wrapped around my waist to steady me from falling. This was now the second time he'd saved me from a fall since we met.

For a brief moment we stood there my back pressed to his chest. His strong body against mine. And though his breathing was steady and slow, I felt his heartbeat as strong and wild as mine had been earlier.

I took the opportunity and I moved with renewed vigor, my strikes faster and more forceful. He continued to counter each move, never allowing me to land a clean hit.

We continue for a while in this manner, me attacking. Him countering.

He began coaching me. His voice low, deep coming from his chest between each counterattack.

"Your biggest fight isn't with anyone in the ring. It's with yourself. You've got the skills, the strength, everything—but you're holding back. And if you don't figure out why, if you don't face whatever's got you pulling your punches, you're gonna lose. Or worse, get hurt. Stop playing it safe right fucking now, or don't bother stepping into this ring with me again."

His words struck a chord. *Go harder, Delia.* My worthiness was at stake. I needed to show how hard I was willing to go in that cage. In life. It occurred to me that he may be right. *But was I able to get out of my own way?* I did not know and I felt a surge of frustration.

I've trained for years. But for what? I'd never truly given myself the chance to win. I was defeated before I even tried. Not this time.

"Ahh," I let out a guttural cry, countering again. "I'm not afraid."

"Then fucking prove it."

He lunged at me quickly. His attack was relentless, pushing me to react without thinking. My instincts took over. It was either that or get kicked in the chin. He gave me no choice but to stop holding back, I let my training take over.

I drove a sharp kick into his midsection, feeling the solid impact beneath my foot. Without losing momentum, I followed it up with a quick right hook, grazing his jaw. His head tilted just slightly in acknowledgment, and for the briefest second, I caught a flicker of something in his eyes— approval, maybe.

But he didn't back down. No surprise there. Okiyo absorbed the hit like it was nothing, his expression cool and unreadable, as if he had expected this all along. His words came out low, calm, almost like a command, "That's more like it."

He dodged my next punch with effortless precision, but there was something different in the air. It wasn't just a test anymore. He was pushing me—really pushing me now, and I could feel it in every muscle.

I went for another strike, faster this time—two quick jabs aimed at his side, followed by an elbow. He blocked, his strength solid, but I didn't miss the slight shift in his stance. He was feeling me out, but he respected the heat I was bringing.

"Keep going," he muttered, eyes locked on mine, his voice steady, calm. The praise was there, but so was the challenge. He wanted more. He expected more.

And I wasn't about to disappoint.

I was spent after that volley. He took a step back, signaling the session was over. I was breathing hard. Sweat dripped down my face. But I felt a spark of confidence I hadn't before.

"Good session. We can build on this. You have the potential to beat Storm, but you need to unleash everything you've got. No more of that low effort shit, Delia."

I nodded, determination burning in my chest. With Okiyo's guidance, I was about to win my first title match. On purpose this time.

"Go get showered," he said, climbing out of the ring and heading in the direction of the men's locker rooms. "Meet me out front and we'll head to our first site visit."

I followed close behind, deviating to the women's locker rooms deep in thought.

What if I won?

For the briefest of seconds, hope blossomed that I could. The idea was taking shape in my head. It wasn't farfetched. Yet, there was still something very real to hesitate about. That's how winning went. Always another challenge.

If I won, then I'd be the logical contender in the "Terror Dome" fight in Tulum Mexico. I didn't often think of Mexico. Even though I was half Mexican. I was born and raised in Atlanta, Georgia. My mother was black and most of the family that Aya and I grew up around were also black.

This could be an opportunity. Aside from the beautiful stories my dad had told us about his home growing up, I knew nothing about the place. What he did share was how beautiful it was growing up near the beach. He'd tell us about how he'd often sit with his friends atop some of the Mayan ruins overlooking the Caribbean Sea. And how he missed the salty ocean breezes or the scent of street food when he and abuela Auggie, his mother, who'd past away when I was about ten years old or so, would go to the bustling street markets to sell some of her pottery. He made it sound so beautiful.

But when we'd ask him why he never went back to visit and take us too, he'd usually have a far off look of sadness in his eyes and blow it off by simply saying. "Those were the old days. Mexico has changed so much. Not for the tourists so much but for the locals, life had become hard. Plus, our life is here now. We live the American Dream, Nina. Where else could the poor son of an immigrant single mother who cleaned houses, such as myself get a great education, then go on to marry the most beautiful, successful woman he's ever seen, and provide you and your little sister with the finest that life has to offer. Mexico. *Psss!* I don't need to go back."

I'd long since put the thought of my father taking us to his home country out of my mind. But now, with the possibility of winning this fight. I very well might get to see it in the beauty that he used to describe it so long ago.

First, I had to decide if I wanted to win the fight. Then, I had to win the fight. And then I needed to take off from work. Ugh... I hadn't even thought about what this would mean for work. That meant I'd need to tell my boss some fantastic lie about why I needed to take a week or two off... My family probably wouldn't even notice I was gone. This was a bit too much. But damn. Winning this fight was getting a bit more enticing.

Chapter 13 – Okiyo

To my surprise, Delia had done very well for our very first session. Something had changed in her almost overnight. She knew more fighting styles than I'd guessed and actually took the instructions I gave her for improvement in stride without putting up much of a fight. I was glad that she was now pushing past her inner blockages.

We still had some work to do on her going all in on her opponent rather than playing it safe. But at the very least she was attempting to get out of her own way.

This both delighted and concerned me.

Admittedly, I agreed to train Delia because I wanted to get closer to her. Shake this silly growing desire to know more about her. I thought that once in her presence for an extended amount of time, I'd quickly tire of her tantrums. I'd hoped they would trigger my natural desire to detach and she'd give up her weak efforts of training for this fight. But no. It all backfired.

I only wanted to be closer to her and she was putting up true effort to prepare to win this fight. I honestly didn't think she'd go through with it so I hadn't even weighed the consequences of her actually getting in that ring. Let alone winning. After the session today, those two things, definitely the first, possibly the second, were happening.

This changed things dramatically. I felt unsure for the first time in a very long time. I needed to make a choice. Either talk her out of this bout or double down on getting her fully trained and ready to fight Storm. And if she beat Storm, a big IF, then there was no way I could detach and leave her to fend for herself.

And then there would be Mexico. The location of the battle brought me crushing fear for Delia. Unbeknownst to the average person, the beautiful tourist destinations of Cancun and Tulum were underscored with some of the nastiest Cartel activity. It hadn't yet boiled over to affect tourism so it was not widely discussed.

But where underground fights and black market gambling were concerned, the Cartel's; Sinaloa, Los Zetas and El Chapo's old gang were certainly involved. *Brutal* couldn't sufficiently describe the fight scene there. For now, I would keep all of this close to the vest. No need to unceremoniously introduce fear in Delia when she'd just crossed a seemingly major internal block of her own.

My cell rang, effectively cutting into my thoughts as I finished dressing. It was Andra, confirming our appointment during the lunch hour today. I ended the call after giving her the ETA for our arrival at Gastrafrique to discuss the security upgrades there and for the entire Parque Place site.

Parque Place would be the first full site to get the new security protocols. It was the site of the flagship location of Gastrafrique and Leboo's top priority. The security at this site would become the model for each site where one of Andra and Kobe's Gastrafrique restaurants would be located.

Delia and I were going over the plans in the back of my Range Rover on the way to the restaurant to meet with its owners.

"I see why we are putting the cameras in over here. Seems like a perfect amount of coverage where the retail stores are and the restaurants, but is it necessary to have this amount of cameras in the residential area?" She asked looking down closely at the small print denoting the cameras on the half opened blueprints.

I leaned in close to see where on the plan she was referring, causing a collision of our heads as she suddenly popped up to look and see if I was following where she was going with this.

"Oh," she exclaimed, reaching up to soothe the side of my head where the corner of her glasses scratched me. "That's going to sting. I'm so sorry." She just as quickly pulled her hand away to reach into her bag to grab a tissue. The smell of her Bond no 5 perfume pervaded my senses from the closeness of her wrist before she pulled it away.

"No need for all that," I said, pulling out my pocket square.

"Wait. It will get infected." She said, quickly pulling the scrap of fabric out of my hand to douse it with a small bottle of hand sanitizer then pressed it to the small welt that was beginning to form.

"Ouc—"

"It may sting—"

We both said in unison.

Apologetically she tried to pull the antiseptic laced silk square away. I caught her hand and held it in place, not ready to lose the feel of her touch. For a moment, neither of us moved. Just sat there with her hand pressed to the side of my head, while mine pressed against hers.

She cleared her throat and gently pulled away. She readjusted in her seat, settling the blueprint back on her lap.

"Besides so many cameras in the residential area, I didn't have any other comments from my review last night. These plans are really good." She smiled, offering a tentative glance in my direction."

I asked her to review the plans knowing they were sound, but I wanted to know if Delia was as good as her boss claimed her to be. Strangely, her approval meant a lot too.

Aside from new CCTV cameras, the new security protocol would also include state of the art, but very unobtrusive access control points for both patrons of the retail spaces and to the more private residential areas. I totally received her point. Too many cameras in the residential area along with the increased access control would seem intrusive. *Great eye for detail.*

"I'll make the changes to the plan. We can easily move the extra CCTV cameras to the outdoor greenspaces."

"Even better. Lots of kids use the skate park and the small lake for paddle boating. I'm sure parents will appreciate the extra security there," she said continuing to study the plans while biting her lip. She did that a lot.

I was beginning to love watching her think. She tilted her head to the side appearing to ponder her own words. "The more I think about it though, there's a lot of break-ins and car-jackings in that area. Insurance premiums are through the roof. With more cameras, the residents could get some price breaks. Maybe leave them." Her eyes jerked up. She almost caught me studying her profile. "Wait, the electrical plans showed a computer room and data center in the security control room. Will there be enough storage for all the feeds from these new cameras?"

Damn. She is smart. Not even an architect, but knew about electrical schematics and computer storage systems?

"Impressive. And to think, you tried to get out of this detail. I see why you were offered up to take part." I nodded my head in appreciation. "Yes, it will be a massive cost, but no expense has been spared by the Baijan family. We can add cameras to both areas. The onsite servers, cloud storage and redundancy will all be upgraded. The new plans include more footed patrol men and women around the site and will be equipped with connected communication devices for faster emergency response in case all this new technology fails."

She nodded her head approvingly at me this time. I liked the feeling it gave me.

We pulled up to the restaurant's valet parking area. Looking past me out the window to see where we were, Delia's face lit up.

"I didn't realize we were actually going to meet them at the restaurant. I've been dreaming of the food at Gastrafrique since the Michelin Star party."

I chuckled, jumping out, swiftly opening her door before either the driver or valet could. Offering her a hand, I responded, "Well it is the main reason for the Parque Place upgrade. May as well get the perks, right? I hope you're hungry."

"Famished after that workout you put me through." Another smile from her. I was indeed winning today.

We were seated at a private table in the back of the restaurant in no time. I'd laid the plans that we'd be going over to the side and picked up my menu. I nodded at Ms. McGhee—*McGhee-Aguillen*— to do the same. I took a moment to study her unobstructed as she perused the menu. I admitted, I was both curious about and intrigued by Delia.

She was different from most women I'd encountered. I found most women were infatuated with the idea of marriage. Yet, had no clue what it meant to be in partnership with someone. I didn't get this impression from Delia. *I wonder if she wants to be married?*

I squirmed uncomfortably in my seat. What a strange thought for me to have about someone when I didn't even know if she were single. *Wait. Was she dating someone?* I should just ask her. And who the hell was I to question most women, when I had no *bloody* idea of what it meant to be in partnership with anyone either.

The crazy part about all of this, I was feeling things that I had no business feeling. Firstly, I have to be at least 10 years her senior and here I was supposedly focusing on the security plans. Yet, I sat here staring, lost in the flawlessness of her beautiful skin tone.

I admired the delicate fingers that held the menu that she studied so thoughtfully and deliberately. They had the capability to be lethal but their elegance on the mat paper mirrored the grace she exuded with her every move. It was almost impossible to ignore.

I was lost in my thoughts, and from the way Delia's eyes were scanning the menu, it seemed she was just as focused on deciding between the dishes. We were both caught off guard—a furtive glance at her showed surprise on her face— when Andra cleared her throat, standing at the table looking back and forth between Delia and I.

"Well now. I was beginning to wonder if I was going to have to go take another table's order. You're so caught up in that menu," she turned sweetly to Delia. "Hard to decide, isn't it, Girl? And you," she swung her attention and signature braids in my direction. "The menu wasn't quite the focus of your attention, now was it?"

Delia looked back and forth between the two of us. A curious smile on her face, as she tried to decipher Andra's meaning. Before I could give her question any consideration, my eyes were drawn to her abdomen which was directly at my seated eye-level. I hadn't noticed the slightly pronounced protrusion of it two weeks ago at the party. Now, however, it was unmistakable.

Seeing where my gaze had gone, she bracketed the top and bottom of it proudly and struck a pose in true Andra fashion.

"Congratulations are in order I see," I smiled as I rose to give her a hug.

"They sure are in order." She splayed her hands graciously, then looked back towards the kitchen. "You can give them to the man who knocked me up. He'll be joining us out here in a little bit. And do I owe you a congratulations, Sir?" Her eyes volleyed sweetly back and forth between Delia and I.

Messy ass Andra.

Her eyelashes fluttered as she waited on a response that she knew she wouldn't get from me.

Delia, however, sputtered, "Oh, no. I've been assigned to help Mr. Bamdi with plan reviews for the security upgrades. I work for the firm who designed and developed your restaurant and the rest of the Parque Place site."

"I know who you are dear. We didn't get a chance to meet at the party but I remember seeing you. That red dress you wore was fierce." Andra smiled, dipping her head around to me, conspicuously whispering, "It definitely caught the attention of black James Bond over here," she laughed, preparing to slide into the booth beside Delia. "Scoot over girl, my hips need more room."

"I see you've not lost your knack for sneaking up on people," I said to Andra as she sat.

Laughing openly she retorted, "Look who's talking! I must say, I didn't think it was possible to catch the *CIA ninja* slipping. But here it is, twice in two weeks I've caught you— mesmerized." Not giving me a chance to refute her claim, Andra turned abruptly in her seat, "See anything interesting on the menu that catches your eye."

"Umm, yes. Too much perhaps. It all looks so good but I was hoping to find those little meat pastries that I had at the party." Delia's face twisted in bliss as if she could taste whatever the dish was.

"Oh yes." Andra chuckled, "You're talking about the *bobotie*. It's a South African dish and you're in luck, Kobe just added it to the sampler platter. How about I get us a couple of those out here? It has *bobotie, ugali, fufu*, and a little *jollof rice*. Some of everything. How does that sound?"

Delia nodded her head profusely, lips shrugging, index finger raised and quickly dipping to Andra's suggestion, "Yes to all of that." The giggle that escaped her lips made me smile and Andra laugh out loud as she flagged down one of her waiters.

"Dedrick can you bring us out two of the sampler platters and tell Chef Abara to make sure it has extra *bobotie* on it, please. I'll be having a sweet tea to drink but bring Okiyo here and Old Fashioned. I'm going to need him to loosen up if he wants me to listen to these boring ass security plans," she smiled over at me knowingly. She looked over at Delia, eyes raised to inquire what she'd like to drink.

Delia quickly responded, "I'll just have a water with lemon."

"Suit yourself. Bring out a rum and coke for Chef Abara. He'll be joining us in a second."

The waiter took the order and headed to the kitchen. A warm smile crossed Andra's lips. She tilted her head to the side, looking at me.

"Even though you literally called to remind me of this meeting, I forgot that fast about it. I guess this baby brain phenomenon I keep hearing people talk about is a real thing. When I saw you two over here, for a moment I'd hoped you were on a date with this beautiful woman." She smiled sweetly at Delia who was shaking her head back and forth to ward off Andra's misperception.

"You don't have to tell me, girl," she laughed at Delia. "It was just wishful thinking on my part. Okiyo, here is all work and no play. Even though any single woman in his presence usually is a swooning fool over him," she said, rolling her eyes and chuckling. "But you seem to be holding up pretty well around him, Delia."

I was getting ready to ask her to cut it out but as if on cue, the kitchen doors opened and Kobe came out followed by a waiter carrying a large tray laden with the sampler platters and the drinks we all ordered.

Wiping his hands on a towel, the chef joined us at the table on my side after leaning in to give Andra a kiss on the lips. "Hey everybody, what's all this talk about Okiyo daydreaming?"

"Shut up," Andra playfully reached across the table, popping a laughing Kobe on his shoulder. "I texted you that in private."

They both chuckled while I sat there taking them in. They really were good together. The joy and mirth on their faces, even if at my expense, was a testament to what a true partnership was. I'd never had that before. A furtive look at Delia revealed her eyes softening as a wistful smile played on her lips at the sight of these two love birds too.

"Bon appetite, everyone," Kobe raised his rum and coke and we all clanked our glasses together. "We can talk about the new security plans while we eat."

"I'll cheers to that," I jumped in, glad to change the subject to anything other than my dating habits. "We've finalized the security strategy for Gastrafrique and the rest of Parque Place. We only need you two to review and approve the changes to the restaurant though." I pulled out a smaller PDF version of the plans specific to the restaurant, passing them across the table.

Andra took the papers and began looking them over as she handed them one by one to Kobe to do the same. She was indeed a jokester, they both were. But after Andra's ex-lover wreaked havoc on the place, putting Mrs. Abara, Kobe's mother in the hospital, security was priority number one for them. With all the success and a baby on the way, I'm sure it had to be even more important.

I wondered if Leboo knew already that he was about to be a grandpa. Would certainly explain further why he'd be willing to foot the entire bill for these upgrades.

Between bites of food, Delia and I walked them through the plan and strategy to upgrade the security systems on the doors and cameras in the restaurant. Delia even explained how the plan tied into the overall site plan. Andra raised her eyes at me, acknowledging what I'd already began to see in Delia. She was quite a woman.

I slid the signature page for the plans over to Kobe once he'd finished going over the documents. I needed their signature for any of the work to begin. We'd also finished eating. Delia sat back in her seat, clearly full and satisfied from the massive portions she'd eaten. I laughed inwardly. She certainly could put away some food. My kind of girl. *Swear. Another unbidden thought about her.*

Once the business concluded, we shared a few more pleasantries with Andra and Kobe. I nodded my head at Delia, signaling the time for our departure.

She nodded, taking the hand I offered to help her rise from her seat. Kobe did the same for Andra.

Before we took our leave, Delia attempted to shake both Andra's and Kobe's hands. Andra wasn't having it. She pulled her into a full on hug. "Nice to meet you, Delia. You'll have to come back and dine with us again. Bring your family. It's on the house."

Perhaps I was reading into it too much, but Delia winced at Andra's suggestion to bring her family.

"I will take you up on that offer," she said more reserved. "Congratulations on the Michelin star and the baby."

Chapter 14 – Delia

WE PULLED UP TO the last site of the day. We'd changed the plans like many of the others to retrofit the new cameras and sensors for the alarm systems. I had to admit, this was all bringing back the joy I used to get just at looking at the beautiful artistry of skyscrapers in magazines. To bring something so technical and complex as blueprints and schematics of building systems, electrical and lighting plans to life was almost a God-like ability. I used to dream of having that ability.

It was late and the sun was starting to set. This week had flown by. Early morning training sessions with Okiyo and all the site visits and security checks made the days a blur—in a good way. I'd begun looking forward to what each day had in store. We were definitely ahead of schedule though. That was a good thing in theory, but meant that this too would come to an end faster. I looked at Okiyo and felt a pang of sorrow at the thought. At this pace, we'd be done in less than three weeks. I'm sure he'd be leaving to go back to Kenya soon after. The thought was sobering. I liked him. *I liked him a lot.*

We were on the rooftop of the building with the foreman and a few of his men. They along with Okiyo were huddled around a worktable, going over the new layout. Okiyo had pointed out a major flaw—a missed entry point to the rooftop that nobody else had caught.

That was typical Okiyo—on point. *Solid.* Always finding the things our own architects and engineers had missed. I had to give it to him. He knew his shit. For the newer plans, he didn't just fix the problems; he made sure they never became problems in the first place. The more time I spent with him, the more I realized it wasn't just his skills I was starting to respect. It was everything else that came with it.

I stepped away from the group while they finished up, drawn to the edge of the rooftop. From here, the noise of the city was just a distant hum, and for a moment, everything felt peaceful— calm, almost too calm given how hard we'd been pushing lately.

Training with Okiyo each morning had me running on fumes, yet somehow, I wasn't exhausted. The opposite actually. I felt more alive than I had in a long time. We'd fallen into a rhythm—early morning sessions that had me throwing punches and kicks I didn't even know I was capable of, followed by full workdays reviewing security plans with contractors and teams.

Okiyo was hands-on, always there, making sure every detail was accounted for. I couldn't help but admire that about him. Being out here, seeing the construction sites in person instead of just looking at the blueprints, gave me a new appreciation for how all of this came together. It was something I usually didn't get to experience firsthand as Rhiyan's assistant. But with Okiyo... I was right in the thick of it, seeing it through his eyes. And the more I saw, the more I realized how much I respected his process. But even more, I realized how much I missed the girl I used to be. The passion he had for security plans was the passion I used to have for blueprints and amazing architecture.

Okiyo was an amazing fighter and trainer as well. It had only been a week since he'd started training me, but already my confidence and my ability in the ring had doubled—tripled even. Yet, I was still extremely nervous about this fight.

For starters, the fight date was still a mystery. When Rudy had rushed in to tell me it was official, he'd said we had a week and a half to get ready. That may be true, but we all knew that to keep the locations secret, it could be that amount of time or a few days earlier or later. I prayed it wouldn't be earlier. I needed all the time I could get to train. I was fully committed to winning this fight.

Just a week prior, I wanted to blame Rudy so bad for throwing me into this mess. That wasn't fair. He didn't make me swing and knock Endyra out. I was so shocked at seeing Okiyo at my match that it was all reflex and timing. It was almost comical now that I thought about it. At any rate, I was still nervous. Not that I wasn't physically ready, but I wasn't sure my mentals were.

I never fought a main event before. Besides Rudy, I'd never had anyone in my corner rooting for me either.

He was my trainer. Technically, kind of my boss... more like a mentor. *Damn. May as well say he's your everything, Delia.* I looked back at him then. The thought was certainly laughable, but watching him do his thing left me wondering, *what if?*

It certainly had me wanting... Sometimes it seemed like he was my friend, though the word "friend" felt off the moment I thought it. Especially now that we were spending so much time together. *What if we could be more than friends?* He certainly stayed on my mind. His voice. His focus. Hell, his brain. It was annoying how brilliant he was, probably one of the smartest men I'd ever met.

And when he let that guard down enough for me to catch him smiling, my heart didn't just skip a beat—it tripped. Don't even get me started on the rare times he actually laughed. That sound could melt panties.

Who was I kidding though? This was strictly business. He was all work, all gentleman. He wasn't thinking about me like that, and I was starting to feel ridiculous for hoping otherwise. I'd fight, I'd win or lose, and when all this was over, he'd be gone. Back to Kenya.

And I'd be nothing more than a blip of a memory of someone he'd met on a work assignment.

I shifted my thoughts to more relevant concerns. The fight. Winning would make me a standout, and that alone could become a whole different problem for me. The underground fight scene in Atlanta was seedy. Drug dealers, dirty cops, politicians—all of them were a part of these events.

My family wasn't exactly under the radar. My mom's firm was one of the top real estate firms in the Southeast. Hell, my mom and sister probably brokered deals for half the high rollers at these fights. My anonymity wasn't just for me—it was to protect them, too. Their reputations at least.

I sighed, leaning over the rooftop edge, the breeze cooling my skin as I stared out at the city.

I turned slightly, glancing over my shoulder at Okiyo again. He stood from the table, taking a long stretch after leaning over the plans. He flexed his neck to one side, then the other, and I caught a glimpse of those muscles rippling under his shirt. His movements were efficient, controlled, the same way he did everything. Even in this setting, away from the gym, he was still a picture of strength and precision. I couldn't help but notice the way his suit, custom-fitted, moved with him like a second skin.

I watched as he folded his arms across his chest, surveying the rooftop with that ever-present coolness. Our eyes locked briefly before his jaw clenched as he tore his eyes away from mine again, attention back on the foreman who'd asked him something.

I sighed, turning back to the view of the city. Just like that, my mind back on him.

He knew so much about me—my training, my weaknesses, my damn limits. And yet, I knew so little about him. I knew just enough to be intrigued.

Here I was, pining after a man I barely understood. A man who, as Andra and Kobe had so subtly put it, they'd never seen with a woman before. He was secretive, stealthy, like he was hiding something. Maybe there was a woman back home—someone he kept quiet about. Or maybe he wasn't even into women at all. That thought quickly left my mind.

I couldn't figure him out. And yet, I couldn't stop trying either.

And then there were those moments. The other day, I'd caught him staring at me after we trained, and I could've sworn there was a question in his eyes. It was almost as if he was wondering why I was even doing this. He said he believed I could win, but was that just part of the job? Was he only saying what he thought I needed to hear?

I shook off the thought, but I couldn't fully dismiss it. Maybe he was just being professional. Then again, sometimes the way his eyes lingered, the way his voice softened, made me wonder if there was more to it. If there was more to how he viewed me.

I felt rather than saw him join me at the edge of the roof. His presence was always steady, like the city skyline we both stared at. I glanced sideways at him, taking in that calm, focused look I'd come to respect—more than respected. His closeness stirred something deep inside me, but unless he gave some kind of sign that I affected him too, I wasn't about to embarrass myself.

"You ever played Twenty One Questions?" I asked, not taking my eyes off the skyline ahead of us.

"Can't say I have. How does it work?"

"I ask you a question, you answer with the first response that comes to mind."

"Ok. I'll bite. Shoot."

"What do you do when your not working or in the gym?"

"I read a lot."

I could definitely see that.

"How many pairs of jeans do you own?" I chuckled, already knowing what his answer would be.

"None. However, I do own several pairs of joggers," he chuckled.

"What's your favorite book? Had to ask that since your favorite pastime is reading."

"I have three favorite books. In no special order: 'The Spook Who Sat By the Door,' 'The Alchemist,' and 'Mastery' by Robert Green.' And I never said my favorite pastime was reading."

I chanced a glance at him at that response. "What is your favorite pastime, then?"

"Wouldn't you like to know," he smirked, raising a single eye-lid as he stared unflinchingly at me.

Heat spread up my neck into my hairline. I had a million questions, but that answer paused me.

I turned to fully face him now. "Andra called you 'CIA ninja' the other day. What does that mean?" I asked quietly.

Okiyo chuckled softly, but there was a shadow behind his eyes. "Just a nickname from a dear friend," he said, brushing it off with ease.

"Nah." I wasn't going to let him brush me off that easily. "It's got to be more than that. You seem to know so much about me. Yet I know next to nothing about you—aside from the fact that you fight like no one I've ever seen before and you've got the mannerisms of a proper British gentleman. It's all rather, secret squirl-*ish* if you ask me."

I tilted my head up to catch his eye, wanting to see if there was a crack in his polished exterior. But he was already looking away, closing himself off again, just like that.

"How about we focus on your upcoming fight," he said, his tone flat. The conversation about him—or lack thereof—over.

I sighed, frustrated, and leaned back against the low railing. Crossing my arms, I looked down at my heels, trying to swallow the impatience bubbling up inside me. "It's hard to focus when I don't even know when the fight is. How am I supposed to prepare for that?"

I felt him shift beside me, stepping closer. There was a warmth to his presence that was almost reassuring. "That's why we train as if the fight is tomorrow. That way, even if it is, you'll be ready."

He was always so composed, so controlled. It made me want to break through those walls even more. I wanted to *fuc*— I stopped the thought before it started.

I nodded, tamping the heat spreading over my body down, focusing on his words, wanting to believe his words. I did agree with him about training like there was no tomorrow. He was a good teacher. And I was giving it my all to get ready. *But did he actually believe I could win?*

"This fight puts me in an awkward position," I shared.

"How so?"

"For starters, I've kept the fact that I fight in these back-alley matches a secret; from my family and work."

"And that scares you?" He asked, his voice calm but probing, trying to understand what the problem was, I guess.

"No," I shot back, a little too quickly. My shoulders slumped as I sighed, softening my tone. "Well, yeah. I guess it scares me. I'm not sure I want my family to know. Fighting has been how I cope with failing to—" I pulled back. Not wanting to share details about my strained relationship with my mom and sister. "I just don't want to let anyone down."

It wasn't just about keeping the fight secret anymore. It was about losing my coping mechanism. But also about my changing desire to win. It felt selfish to want to win at anything when I'd let someone rape my baby sister. I didn't deserve to win, but God, I was starting to want to so bad. I was so torn.

I felt him watching me, waiting for me to go on, and it tugged at something inside. Not since therapy had I shared how guilty and ashamed I felt at what happened to my sister. I saw where that got me.

Quack ass doctor had the nerve to say, "You weren't raped. Why don't you just get over it if your sister seems fine." I wanted to punch him that day. Wanted to fight something. It's the day I found Blaze. I walked in off the street, signed up for a membership and jeans and t-shirt, went to the back and wailed on a body bag. Rudy was the one who'd stopped me and asked if I wanted to train.

After that day, I never went back to therapy. Mom was so busy making sure Iya was ok, it was almost a year later that she'd realized I wasn't going. Fighting became my guilty pleasure and the keeper of my secret shame and guilt.

But the way he asked about my fears—his keen interest in *me*, unlike my mother's ability to make me feel invisible, made me want to rip open my chest and let all the hurt and pain pour out of me. But I didn't.

I shifted uncomfortably, glancing at him from the corner of my eye. "It's just... this fight—I mean" I hesitated, searching for the best words to code my true feelings. "Let's just say, winning this fight will put me in a new class. I've just not been sure I wanted to move up like that."

He didn't say anything, just listened, letting me talk.

"Now, I am sure. You've kind of made it impossible for me not to be. Hell, I'm starting to feel like I matter," I chuckled, wrapping my arms around myself. "Like I'm not just going through the motions of training for the sake of training any-more, you know?"

I could hear the slight waver in my own voice. He remained quiet still and I kept right on talking.

"When I'm training with you, I feel like I'm finally being seen. And that... it scares me."

He finally spoke. "Why does that scare you?"

I shrugged my shoulders, shifting my eyes to the ground and answered truthfully. "Because I'm starting to rely on it."

The words hung between us, heavy and vulnerable. It wasn't just about being seen as a fighter, but about being seen as some-thing more—something I hadn't even let myself feel before.

With Okiyo, I felt like I was more than the assistant, more than a fake ass fighter, more... And now, the reality of this all being temporary, terrified me.

I turned away slightly, feeling exposed but glad I'd let that part out at least. "I guess I'm scared of losing that. Of going back to feeling... invisible again."

I could feel his presence beside me, steady and grounding, but I didn't dare look at him. The silence stretched for a while.

When I did finally look at him, Okiyo's gaze was intense, unwavering. Then his usual steady demeanor faltered. He exhaled sharply, as if shaking off whatever had crossed his mind.

"I don't know what's going on in that pretty little head of yours," he finally said, his voice a little softer than before, "But you do matter, Delia. More than you actually know. I see greatness in you. Especially in your work. I want you to see it in yourself. Perhaps this fight, winning it, is precisely what you need for you to see what I and everyone else sees. You're ready to win."

Seeing the mixture of fear and frustration welling up inside of me, he pulled me in for a hug.

I was so shocked, I only stood there. It was several moments later that I finally released the breath I didn't realize I was holding. With each passing moment, I relaxed into him. Until he finally grabbed my chin, tilting my face up to his. "You are ready, Delia. Maybe you've always been. Just needed someone to show you."

"You seem to always say the right things in my regard. You're always so composed, so mysterious. What is your story, Okiyo?"

His gaze faltered again, I saw a wave of sadness before he quickly masked it. He then smiled—a rare, almost gentle expression that threw me off balance. "Maybe one day," he murmured, resting his chin atop my head.

I waited, hoping for more, but instead, his voice shifted back into that familiar, controlled tone. "But for now, we need to make you the best fighter you can be."

And just like that, the wall was back up.

He released me from the hug and turned on his heel to walk towards the entry door back into the building from the roof. I watched him for a second, his broad shoulders disappearing inside. The pang of disappointment that hit me was acute, but was quickly replaced by another feeling.

Determination.

I was going to win this fight. Not just in the ring, the fight to get to know him in this limited time we had together. He couldn't hide behind that cool, stoic mask forever. He saw through my bullshit. Well I wanted to peel back his layers.

"Fine," I muttered under my breath, as I pushed off the wall and quickly followed after him, my footsteps echoing against the concrete. I was already planning my next move.

Chapter 15 – Okiyo

THE GYM WAS ALIVE with the usual sounds of clashing gloves and rhythmic grunts. Delia and I were in the middle of a sparring session. Her movements were now extremely precise and fluid. Sweat dripped down her face as she gave her all to each move and combination I'd given her for the day.

She's ready. Yet I struggled. My personal desire to protect her conflicted with the need to push her to be her best in the ring against such a vicious opponent.

Storm was a different beast. I'd done my research on one Astoria "Storm" Strummond. This girl was a real pill. Multiple stints in juvy between the ages of 10 and 18. Daughter of a big time drug dealer from back in the day in New York. A setup for a true villain origin story.

This was weighing heavy on my mind. And just as I was about to call for a break, the gym door swung open. Rudy strode in with an air of urgency. He walked right up to the edge of the ring.

"Listen up! This is not a goddam' drill. The fight has been set. Less than 24 hours away."

The whole room fell silent. I looked over at Delia. Her eyes locked on mine. I fought to keep my expression unreadable. No matter how much trepidation I felt about this fight, I'd keep my calm for her sake. I merely nodded at Rudy. Then addressed Delia directly. "You got this. Just remember everything that we've trained for. Let's break for the day so you can rest up."

I walked out of the ring and went towards the locker room to shower. My mind raced. The trepidation wouldn't leave. Delia was physically ready, but Storm's ruthless reputation added a layer of psychological warfare.

If I hold back information about Storm, Delia might not be prepared for the intensity of the fight. This could put her at a disadvantage. But if I tell her, it might push Delia to go too hard and push her own limits. Yeah. It might increase her chances of winning, but it also increases her exposure to getting hurt. I thought through the strategy of getting her to lay in wait and set a trap for Storm.

After our sparring session, both Delia and I were back in the car getting ready to go to the first site visit of the day. I turned to Delia, having made up my mind to bring up the conversation about Storm.

I grabbed her hand, taking her by surprise as I began. "I need you to know what you're going to be up against in this fight." She stared down at our intertwined fingers. I'd even caught myself off guard when I did that, much like when I pulled her in that hug on the rooftop last evening, but she didn't pull away. So neither did I.

I continued on, "Storm has a violent history. And it's going to get extremely aggressive in that cage. She's not gonna be phased by textbook moves. You are going to have to fight as dirty as she does. The girl has a rap sheet—"

"A rap sheet a mile long," she paused, lips pressed into a thin line as if contemplating how much to tell me. "Yeah. I know. I've done my research on Storm." Confidence now fully bloomed on Delia's face, while pride bloomed in my chest at this astonishing woman. "Appears that Storm was left to fend for herself as a kid when her Dad was sent up state for a life sentence and her mom was strung out on drugs."

"All true," I added. "By age 23, she was also hemmed up on a murder rap that she beat. But what's not in her public record is that it was by a plea of insanity. She spent a few years in a psych ward before nearly disappearing off the map until she reemerged on the scene in Atlanta."

Delia stilled, while processing what I'd just laid on her. I needed her to know this so that she could decide if she truly wanted to go through with this fight. Admittedly, I didn't want her too. Storm was a wildcard and rules would not apply in the cage with her.

As I was preparing to let Delia know that there was no shame in backing out, she squeezed my hand and dipped her head to catch my eyes, ensuring I paid full attention to the words that came next.

"She will be ruthless in the ring. I know. She has nothing to lose. But I have everything to gain from this fight." Her face slowly split into a confident smile. "Your belief in me is a major part of me figuring that out. I want to know what it feels like to win a real fight."

She laughed softly, almost to herself, pulling her hand gently from underneath mine and placing it on top as she leaned in closer. "Thank you for caring about my well-being, Okiyo Bamdi."

My brows shot up, "Oh?" I questioned, wondering where she was going with this.

"Don't 'oh' me. It's written all over your face. Right now, even. At first, I thought that look of concern meant you didn't believe I could win this fight. But all this time, you've been worried about my safety because I'll be fighting a straight-up lunatic." She patted my hand as if trying to reassure me, her touch stoking the fire that was already starting rage inside me.

This woman was going to be the *bloody* death of me.

I chuckled, releasing some of the pent-up tension that had coiled in my chest. Her confidence, that fierce fire I'd always admired in her, was shining brighter now. She was more than ready for this.

"Let me make you proud, O."

Her words sank in, and as if on command, the pride I already felt for her swelled. My pulse quickened as I leaned in, drawn to her like gravity itself was pulling us together. The confident Delia, the woman in red who had audaciously attacked me the night we met, was right here, close enough to touch. I wanted to grab her, to dig my fingers into her hair and kiss her until neither of us could breathe. I wanted her in every sense—her body, her mind, her soul.

But just as my lips hovered inches from hers, the truck lurched to a stop. The world snapped back into focus.

We were at the site.

Her thigh brushed against mine, and she hadn't moved her hand yet. Our eyes locked again, the air between us so thick with unspoken desire that I could feel it pressing against my chest. The moment stretched, and it was as though the whole world held its breath with us. She looked at me with a silent promise, a shared understanding that something had shifted between us, something inevitable.

I was the first to break the contact, pulling back before I crossed a line that would blur everything we'd built. To act on this now would be reckless, a disservice to the fight she had ahead.

Twenty-four hours seemed like an eternity, but I could wait. I *would* wait.

For now, she needed me to be her mentor, not her lover.

As I watched her throughout the day, her focus was unshakable. She was locked in, ready to take on whatever came next. And maybe, when this fight was over, she'd finally understand the man standing beside her wasn't just here to train her—I was here for her.

But then there was the part of me, the one that never stayed in one place for too long, that knew this couldn't last. I didn't do attachments, didn't do staying put. It was safer that way, for both of us. And yet... for the first time, I wasn't so sure.

During a quick lunch break, the tension between us was still there. Over the sandwich she'd just taken a bite of, her eyes searched my face. She was beautiful. I wanted to look away but was too captivated to do so.

"CIA ninja?" She raised a brow, catching me off guard. "You said you would share something about you." She blinked sweetly, waiting on my response.

"I did, didn't I." I hesitated, then decided I would share a glimpse of my past with her.

"I used to work in intelligence."

"No," she said in mock surprise.

"That obvious?" I asked.

"Well, you've been reading me since day one. I'd imagine that's one of the secret squirrel tactics you learn at *The Farm*."

I laughed at the term she'd used.

"You watch too much television. Also the *Farm* is where your FBI trains in Quantico, Virginia. I was a British foreign intelligence officer; MI6."

"Ahh," she responded, impressed.

"I retired from that life about six years ago and opened my own security firm. I rarely share that information with anyone, so consider yourself lucky."

"Duly noted. Explains your secretiveness and all-knowing aura." She mused out loud. "So did you tell Andra this or did she just guess?"

I raised my brow, smirking at the memory of the first time Andra had called me CIA Ninja.

"Not quite either. Around the time that Andra first came to Nairobi and before she discovered who her father was, I was assigned directly to her security detail. It had to be inconspicuous. Rather than outright tell her that she had security, it was under the guise that I was assigned by the studio that filmed her tv show as her transportation liaison.

When she asked me what a transportation liaison does, I explained simply that I liaised. Nonplussed, Andra fumed at my lack of answers.

Then there was the time I called her out about being in love with her then best friend Kobe. I politely let her know that he wouldn't be too happy with her attending Giraffe Manor without him. It had been something they'd planned to do together.

They'd talked about it on social media. And before you ask, of course I stalked both of their IG feeds. She denied being in love with him, but was way too concerned with how I knew they'd planned to do that excursion together. When I explained simply that I'd done my research on her—" I paused, recalling the look of irritation on Andra's face that day.

Delia was fully engrossed in the memory I was sharing.

"Well, you've met Andra," I chuckled. "That day she took to calling me CIA Ninja. At least that's the tame version of the nickname she'd given me. When she'd first said it, the 'nja.' on the end of Ninja was really a 'gga'."

And with that, Delia bowled over in laughter. Literal tears streamed down her face. When she finally sat up straight, and between gulps of air, she nodded her head, "Yep. I get it. The CIA nigga. It fits." She screamed and folded over laughing again.

Chapter 16 – Delia

F IGHT NIGHT.

Again, I was deep in thought in the backseat of an SUV. This time, not a hired car. Not beside Rudy. I watched the city blur by through the window of the chauffeured Range Rover I'd become used to. Okiyo sat quietly beside me. His presence alone was a steady anchor. I could only imagine how off kilter I'd be if he wasn't here beside me.

We were headed to East Point, to an equally abandoned warehouse that sat on the side of the tracks that no one wanted to visit. Not even during daylight hours.

This was it. The moment of truth. No more hiding. No more playing it safe. There was no way I would survive this fight without that mindset. I was going to have to annihilate Storm or get fucked up trying. And I was too cute to be fucked up. The thought made me laugh on the inside.

"I can feel the jitter of your nerves, you know?" Okiyo said breaking the silence and the cycle of what ifs running through my head.

"That bad, hunh?"

"Something about the way you've been gnawing at the corner of your lip, and bouncing that leg of yours, gave it away."

I immediately stopped the bouncing. Hadn't even been aware I was doing it until he pointed it out.

"I've told you this a thousand times already. You've got this. We've trained hard and I know you're ready. But I have yet to ask you before I let you get in this cage. Do you believe you're ready?"

He turned his body towards me. I struggled to make eye contact because I was already in a vulnerable state and his presence sometimes overwhelmed me. No way I could hide the fact that he made me just as nervous as this fight. His demeanor was calm, unflappable as usual. He saw my erratic energy as just nerves for the fight and not me being on the edge of my seat wanting him too.

I hadn't tried to hide my interest in him the other day, but he pulled back. Andra's insinuations about him being into me were not missed. I largely ignored them to not make the lunch awkward. His *for duty's sake* regard of me showed that he cared, but it was a bit too chaste for me. Especially when all I thought about was how it had felt to be pressed between that wall and that wonderfully made chest of his on the night we first met.

It both irritated me and made me want to press him for more. Him opening up and sharing a more personal side of himself equally motivated me to show him that I could win this fight. This night would not end in defeat. When this was all over and I had Storm's title, I was shooting my shot with him too.

When I finally looked at him, I was resolute. "I'm ready." I stated simply. "I'm about to turn that 'Storm' into a light drizzle."

Having no clue of my double meaning, Okiyo chuckled and patted my hand. "Alright, then. Let's go dry up her little downpour."

I turned my palm up to intertwine my fingers with his. I squeezed it with confidence as we pulled up to the arena. He'd unknowingly just shaken on a deal that would be sealed tonight if things went my way.

Met by Rudy, we all entered through the back of the makeshift arena. Rudy went to secure his bets and find their seats and just as any good trainer would do, Okiyo led me to the locker rooms to get ready for this fight.

I could already hear the announcers amping the audience into a frenzy as we got closer to the title bout of the night. Okiyo wrapped my hands with tape. His motions precise and deliberate. I could feel his energy too. Where it zinged with anxiety before, now it was calming. It felt like a mix of pride with just a hint of concern now.

Continuing to bend over my taped knuckles, he spoke.

"Storm is going to come at you hard and fast. She's aggressive and unpredictable. You've got to stay in control, understand?"

I already had my mouth gear in so I simply nodded my head at his question.

"Use her wildness against her and you got this fight, champ."

I allowed his words and final instructions to wash over me. It was game time. That was all the encouragement I needed. I stood and walked to the door. Ready.

'I'm on a New Level' by ASAP Ferg blasted over the speakers as we made our way to the cage. The heavy base mimicking my heartbeat as I entered my zone. The words radiated the energy of the crowd through my veins. I'd chosen it as my entrance music for this exact reason.

The arena lights dropped and the crowd parted like a sea. The spotlight blinded me but it didn't matter. I moved through the crowd as if divinely guided to the center of that cage where I'd come out victorious tonight. Rudy had been waiting outside the locker room but now flanked my left side while Okiyo trailed behind. My silent enforcer.

My adrenaline was on ten as we slowly inched closer to the ring. I was so deep in the zone that I didn't care if the crowd cheered or if they booed. I was mentally preparing to whoop Storm's ass.

I didn't expect much fanfare and knew that she would be coming out to many more roars and applause than I would. Yet, she would be no match. I had too much to prove. And yet, was still turned on by the sense of punishment that I would receive in the ring. I had an advantage. I didn't run from pain. I ran to it, bringing a level of intensity to the fight Storm had never seen before.

I was in the cage. Okiyo and Rudy made their way to their seats. There were no corner nor cut men or women in street fighting. If there was blood, I'd just have to relish the taste until I walked out of this cage as a champion.

And then there was Storm.

My music ended and hers began. 'Wake Up in the Sky,' by Gucci Mane, Bruno Mars and Kodak Black filled the Arena and East Atlanta's own, Gucci Mane actually led her procession, spitting his own bars to the instrumental as Storm and her entourage made it to the ring. She entered and the arena went dark as her music faded to silence.

For a moment, everything was silent and still, the only sound being the faint rustle of movement and the distant hum of the audiences energy. Slowly, the lights were raised to a dim glow, casting a soft, eerie light over the ring. The illumination high-lighted Storm first, then increased to include me in the glow. The atmosphere became electric, and the tension palpable as the audience held its collective breath, waiting for the fight to begin.

I heard none of the announcers pre-fight commentary, nor the rules he was required to say. I only heard one word. *Fight!* And we got to it.

Just as Okiyo predicted, Storm surged forward like a predator. I felt the rush of air on my cheek as her fist whizzed past my face. *You missed me.* My mind raced to stay ahead of her relentless assault. She came at me with a flurry of Muay Thai strikes, her elbows and knees flying with deadly precision.

I blocked a knee aimed at my ribs and countered with a quick jab to her midsection, she barely flinched. *Okay. No problem.* I stayed in control.

Use her aggression. Okiyo's words played in my psyche. I shook off the punch that she'd landed to my left shoulder. I shifted my stance, transitioning into capoeira. My movements became more fluid, unpredictable, as I dodged her next attack. I spun on my heel, aiming a roundhouse kick at her head. She blocked it with a raised arm.

The impact of her block sent a jolt through my leg, but I didn't let it slow me down. I followed up with a low sweep, aiming to destabilize her.

Storm stumbled but recovered quickly, her eyes flashing with anger. She lunged at me, her fists a blur. One punch connected with my jaw, sending a shockwave of pain through my head. I staggered back, but ate that shit. I tasted blood.

Focus, Delia... It had become my mantra. Don't let her aggression throw you off your game.

I dropped into a defensive stance, channeling my training in Brazilian jiu jitsu. Storm tried to grapple with me, but I twisted out of her grasp, using her momentum against her. I caught her in a wrist lock, but she powered through it, breaking free with a vicious elbow strike to my side.

She was a great fighter. I staggered, not sure if I was gonna be able to keep up with her. Pain flared, but I gritted my teeth and held on.

The crowd's cheers blurred into a distant roar as I reengaged my concentration on the fight.

Focus, Delia. Storm's wildness was definitely her strength. It was hard to tell what skill she was going to present and even harder to tell which direction her onslaught was going to come from. There was no rhyme or reason to it. Making it hard to anticipate. But I would trust the process no matter what. Hell, all this time I'd been worried if Okiyo believed in me. Did I believe in him? Yes. I. Did.

She came at me again. Her movements erratic. But they would be. I had her number now. There was predictability in her unpredictability. Control was my counter weapon. Her wildness was now her weakness. I could exploit this and it created an opening for me.

I fainted to the left, then launched a series of quick strikes. Muay Thai knees, capoeira spins, jujitsu grappling moves. Each blow landed. Each move carefully calculated. I could see the frustration growing in her eyes.

It gave me a moment to look over and I caught Okiyo's eyes in the sea of people. He nodded his head and mouthed one word. *Win.*

I squared my shoulders and blew out two shaky breaths. Storms next punch was wild. That was all I needed. She was left wide open and I seized the opportunity to slip inside her guard. I landed a solid uppercut to her jaw, followed by a swift elbow to her temple. She staggered and I pressed my advantage home.

With a surge of effort, I executed a flawless kick, catching storm square in the chest. She fell back, hitting the mat hard. The referee began the count but I barely heard it. My breathing was ragged. My body ached and sweat stung my eyes as I leaned over palms on top of my thighs as I waited for Storm to get up.

But she didn't. I stood tall when the referee reached the ten count. The crowd erupted. I raised my fists slowly until the reality of my victory sank in. Then I looked over at Rudy. He was already on his feet, jumping for pure joy. The payday he was about to receive was bigger than it had ever been before. I had done it. I had won.

Then I turned my eyes to Okiyo. I was midway through a second, maybe even a third jump for joy. But he wasn't celebrating.

There it was again—that look of concern, anxiety, etched across his face.

As if in slow motion, he stood from his seat and sprinted toward the cage. His mouth was moving, but I couldn't make out what he was saying. It looked like he was yelling. The crowd's cheers and chants were deafening, but all I could focus on was Okiyo. He was pointing urgently, his eyes wide with alarm.

That's when I turned to see what had him so worked up. The thought alone—Okiyo, worked up—was baffling.

My eyes swung back to the center of the cage. She was on her hands and knees the last time I'd looked, the referee hovering over her. But now she was a blur of motion.

All I saw was her fist coming straight at me.

Chapter 17 – Delia

Darkness. Then light. It cycled as if someone was turning a light switch on and off in my head. Pain. Flashes of light that turned out to be the penlight of the fight physician checking my eyes disrupted the images of the fight replaying in my mind. Then blackness, again.

I didn't know if I was in a dream. The last thing I remember was literally jumping for joy and my eyes locking on Okiyo's. His face didn't show joy though. I thought he was proud of me. *Why the concern?*

Then it all came flooding back. The referee's count fading into a distant echo. I had won. I'd done it. A glimpse of the roaring crowd cheering. Storm's fist. An explosion of pain.

I opened my eyes to see Okiyo's filled with fear. My vision blurred momentarily. Then crystal clarity. It wasn't a dream. I remembered seeing Storm's wild eyes before she released her cocked fist and hit me. I also remembered the mat rushing to meet my face before I was out cold.

I recalled the physician saying, "That's a nasty blow she took to her temple. She's ok. But she's gonna need rest. A few days of rest."

Ironically, I'd lost a lot of fights in the past but still managed to avoid getting hit in the head or my face. I won tonight. Kicked Storm's ass pretty bad as I recalled and got knocked the fuck out. Go figure.

I'd been in and out but remembered Okiyo carrying me out of the cage. I'd kept my eyes closed because the lights made my eyes hurt and my head pound. It was easier to succumb to the blackness. I didn't need to see him to know it was his arms that cradled me to his chest.

The scent of his woodsy cologne encapsulated me. I was safe. Protected. He pressed me to his chest as he carried me out of the arena. I felt his beating heart. I remembered smiling—I'd won and I had his chest. Blackness.

This time when I came to, I was in a huge comfortable bed. I was alone in it, but his scent surrounded me. I turned my face into the pillow and drew in the distinct smell of him. I was in Okiyo's bed.

My eyes shot open. I was now fully awake in the darkness of his bedroom. *Where was he?*

I was awake but disoriented. I'd been dreaming about him while I was out. I recalled snatches of images from the fight morphing into vivid images of Okiyo's face. His Obsidian eyes, soft with worry as he gazed at me. In my dream, we lay side by side. I saw unchecked lust in his eyes. Felt his desire like warm honey pouring over me. In my dream, it was uninhibited desire kaleidoscoping with clashing fists, and stinging blows all merging with visions of our intertwined bodies. His dark smooth skin melded into mine.

The dream had been so vivid as my subconscious seemed to look down upon us together in his bed. Our nakedness was beautiful as our bodies snaked around each other. My head was thrown back into the pillows, anticipated pleasure on my face. My hands gripped his ass as he pulled his hips up, preparing to plunge into me. Just as his back and flanks tensed to enter me, a sound wrenched me awake.

I heard the sound again—words being murmured coming from the side of the bed. I rolled to peer over the edge and that's where I found him. He was curled up on a pallet on the floor. The room was dark accept for a sliver of light creeping through the curtains. I blinked, piecing together what was happening.

He slept fitfully. At first I thought he was shivering, but as I watched, he began tossing and turning. I could just barely make out the lines of his face in the dark room. His jaw was clenched as if in the fit of a nightmare. He groaned in so much agony that I tore from the bed to kneel beside him. I wanted to shake him awake but didn't want to startle him.

Even in my groggy condition, I felt guilty that this man, who had obviously taken care of me over the last hours, days? Whatever the timing I'd been out of it, he was sleeping on the floor beside his own bed.

"Okiyo," I whispered.

My heart ached at the sight of him in such turmoil. He was deep in REM sleep and didn't hear me. So I said his name again, louder. This time I did place a hand on his shoulder to gently shake him. *Oh God. Tell me this man is not reliving my ass getting knocked out in a fight I'd won.*

He stilled but continued to mumble incoherently. His body twitched again as if *he* was fighting something or someone. I wasn't sure what to do. My instincts finally took over and I pulled the comforter from the bed. I pulled it over his body in hopes of bringing him some comfort.

I was in the process of tucking the blanket around his shivering body when suddenly his eyes snapped open. With lightning speed, he grabbed my wrist and pulled me down on top of him. His eyes glazed over briefly before the smoke like veil lifted.

Fully awake now, he stared up at me, our eyes locking in the dim light. Realization dawned and he quickly released my wrist, his hands trembling slightly.

"Delia, I'm sorry. I didn't mean to—"

I cut him off, my legs instinctively locking around his hips, holding him in place. "I'm fine. You were shaking in your dream. Are you okay?" I whispered, searching his eyes. Getting lost in them. Our faces were mere inches apart. I could feel his heaving breath.

He didn't answer. Just stared up at me, his body gradually relaxing, his breathing slowing. The intensity of his gaze intensified, piercing through me. The raw emotion in his eyes tugged at me.

I'd planned to shoot my shot tonight. Not like this though. This was unbidden. Unplanned. I leaned in powerless to his allure, capturing his bottom lip gently between mine. Sucking. Tasting him. A shiver ran through his body, and I felt his hesitation in the way his hands gripped my waist—tight but uncertain.

It was like he couldn't decide between pushing me away or pulling me closer. His breath hitched as I deepened the kiss. His palms rose to cup my cheeks. They lingered there for a moment as his tongue swiped against mine before he gently pulled my face away. Our eyes met, and I could see it—his crumbling resolve, the unfiltered desire simmering just below the surface.

In my excitement at seeing his passion, a wave a dizziness washed over me. He pulled back slightly, still cradling my face close to his. "You're hurt."

I managed a weak smile before sinking down onto his chest. "I'll live," I said. In pain, but it was worth it to be this close to him.

"You took a pretty nasty blow to your temple. You shouldn't be down here." He moved to sit up but even in my dizzy state, I pressed deeper into him. He could have easily continued his motion, but didn't. He settled and allowed me to stay where I was. Cradled in his arms on his chest.

He tilted my head up to his again, eyes scanning my face. My head was indeed throbbing. But still I quipped, "But I won, though." It was a weak brag that made his eyes crinkle up in an almost smile as he nodded his head.

"You absolutely did win, Viper. You were incredible tonight." His face, serious again now. "But you definitely need to get some rest."

We lay together in silence.

I could have stayed in his arms like this forever. That was the last thought I had before I drifted back off into the darkness.

Chapter 18 – Okiyo

I STOOD IN THE kitchen. I was relieved that Delia had awakened from her concussed state in the wee hours before. She slept in my arms peacefully.

The feel of her body pressed against mine while she slept the rest of the night felt good. Too good. The dream that had come before it, not so much. I couldn't shake the melancholic feeling that remained even as I stood in the kitchen bathed in the fresh morning light. I mechanically stirred my cup of coffee. The aroma filled the air but my mind was far from the present.

I hadn't had a dream like that in years. Since before being recruited to become an officer in her Royal Service, perhaps.

My thoughts drifted back to the vivid dream— nightmare— that haunted my sleep. It was a dream of my childhood. A time I tried so hard to forget, but came rushing back with a force last night.

It started out the same way it always did. Chaos. The sound of deafening gunfire. The screams of the villagers was a haunting backdrop as bodies fell around me. My small hand was clutched tightly to my big brothers. Our father's voice echoed in my ears. "Run down river," he screamed. "Hide in the thicket beyond the village."

I remembered all too vividly how fear gripped my heart, but my big brother's firm grip gave me the strength to keep moving. We ran, our bare feet pounding against the ground. I remember my lungs burned with the exertion. The world blurred around me, reduced to a tunnel of survival.

My hand slipped out of my brother's. I turned and a warm spray hit my face. The world stopped. My little legs faltered and I felt myself being pulled backwards.

"*Brother!*" I screamed.

His hand was still reaching for mine. But now he was on his knees, blood blooming in the center of his chest.

"Come on big brother!" I panted, panic rising. His last words were a desperate plea. "Run, Okiyo. Remember where father told us to go."

My scream echoed as he fell face first at the river's edge. The sight was burned into my memory.

I snapped back to the present, the coffee in my mug swirling slowly. The pain of my past mingled with the fresh wound of seeing Delia hurt. Like my brother falling face-first into the dirt, another person that I just began to realize the depth of my care for, fell face first into that mat after Storm's illegal punch.

The dream was symbolic of the way Delia crumbled to the mat. It brought back all those memories of helplessness that I felt as a little kid. Both of my parents had been slain and I watched my big brother fall face first into the mud.

I shook my head, clearing the remains of the memory away. I took a sip of the coffee. The bitterness grounding me in the present. The memories of my brother's death had shaped me, driving me into the shadows, leading me to become Agent "O."

I admitted, cutting off my feelings in a very whitewashed proper British society left me, a little black Kenyan boy, to feel helpless and invisible. But in a way the invisibility forged me into the steel that I needed to be. It was necessary to do the cold callous work of an intelligence operative whose job was to quail the heinous crimes against humanity by boogeyman across the world.

But who knew a pretty little lady with a fluid capoeira style could awaken something so new in me. Something I hadn't felt in a very long time; care, passion and an intense need to protect her.

The sound of soft footsteps broke my reverie. I peered over my shoulder to see Delia standing in the doorway of the kitchen. Her eyes still slightly glazed from sleep but filled with a simmering fire.

I'd flirted with her. Pushed her buttons while simultaneously pushing my own because I was intrinsically connected to her. I pushed and she pushed back. There'd become a point where we'd both tumble over the edge. I was only here temporarily. Couldn't give her that thing she'd never stated, but I could clearly see that she needed. Someone permanently in her corner. I would break her heart. I needed to protect her even from me.

"Morning," she said, her voice raspy from sleep.

Before turning to her, I steadied my emotions. Masked my face, resolved to not be affected by the sweet sultriness of her voice. I set my cup down, turning towards her before leaning against the counter. Crossing my arms as a barrier between us. "How are you feeling?"

Doubt flickered across her face, or at least that's what it seemed like to me. She hesitated for a second, as if gathering herself. But then, she managed to pull up a smile. "Better. Still sore. Still a bit groggy."

She moved towards me, continuing, "I feel... safe being here with you. But I have to ask, why did you bring me here?"

"Because—" I faltered. She'd caught me off guard with the question. *Why had I brought her here?* "You were pretty out of it. In and out of consciousness for a while. You couldn't share your apartment number with me in that state," I paused. I already knew her address, but didn't want her to think I was stalking her. Even though I quite literally had been. "Also, the fight physician said you needed rest and I wanted to make sure you got it."

I told her the logical reason for bringing her to my flat. The simple truth was that I wanted her here with me. I needed to be the one to take care of her. Not Rudy, not anyone else.

"Rest for how long?" Her eyes caught mine. I read a deeper question in the uncertainty of her gaze.

"A few days should do it. Don't worry about the site visits. I can finish up at those on the schedule this week."

"Okay," she raised her hand absently to the tousled coils on top of her head, touching the reddish purple bruise that spread from the outer corner of her right eye, across her temple and into her hairline. I'm sure it felt worse than it looked. She appeared to search for her next words as if scared to ask them. "Well I guess I better call Rhiyan and let her know I'll need a few days—"

"No need to bother her. I've got the sites covered and you can just rest here."

What was I bloody doing? I could have had my driver take her home and I'm sure she could have called a family member to let them know her state. I'd just have to keep my hands off and truly let her heal up. *Easier said than done.* And she'd apparently made her way into my closet to change out of the outfit she'd fought in last night because though she was disheveled still from sleep, she was oh so sexy in one of my oversized dress shirts.

I side-stepped her touch. Moving beyond the reach she attempted for my hand as I moved slowly by. I tossed over my shoulder. "I need to go out for a bit. Will you be ok, alone for a little while?"

"I'll be fine," she smiled, reaching for my hand again.

I moved past her, allowing my hand to only lightly brush against hers. Even that small touch sent a wave of electricity through my groin. I needed to steer clear of her. "There's coffee in the pot and a number for food delivery on the counter. Feel free to order what you need. They have my card on file."

I didn't look back as I continued on to my bedroom to get dressed but I could feel Delia's eyes on me as I walked away. I imagined there might be confusion or hurt there. Last night, we had a moment, but I needed to put the wall back up to sort through my own feelings. My only thought was to protect her. My time here was limited.

After last night's fight, she would be pulled into many more as a headliner. As a champion, she would not be able to say no to these fights. Viper, the beast, had been awakened. Three weeks of the planned six I was scheduled to be here had already expired. I wasn't sure how I could protect her from thousands of miles away.

Chapter 19 – Delia

A COUPLE OF DAYS had passed by in warp speed since I'd been at Okiyo's. Per the doctor's orders, I was to rest up for a few days. I had free reign of his space, but Okiyo basically avoided me since we kissed. He'd switched effortlessly back into his detached nature.

I lay back on the couch, staring at the ceiling. Trying not to think about him, simultaneously ignoring the incessant ringing of my cell phone. It was my mother, again. Not asking, but demanding my help with planning the next event for Iya's pending nuptials. I couldn't right now. *Not while nursing my bruised ego from Okiyo basically going cold on me.* No. We had definitely shared a moment the other night. I could still feel the warmth and longing of his kiss. Now his ass was blowing me dust.

Admittedly, I was hurt by it. He'd done so much for me. *But who was I kidding?* To believe he wanted me beyond seeing me win in the ring. I mean, what an ego booster for him. Taking an all-out dud fighter and turning her into a champion.

"Ugh! This damn phone!" The shrill ringtone cut through my ruminations about Okiyo. Why did I answer it yesterday? Ever since I had taken her call and half-heartedly agreed to help her with the anniversary party for my sister, my mom wouldn't shut up about it and Iya's upcoming wedding.

Of course I wanted Iya's wedding to be spectacular. I wanted her to be happy and living it up in wedded bliss. But I couldn't help but feel a sense of jealousy at how easily everything just came to her.

She got it all. Even got on with her life while I was stuck wanting everything that she was getting. And it killed me to feel this way. But I couldn't seem to fake the funk anymore. Not since a proper gentleman, CIA ninja placed a mirror in my face and made me stare into it. The very things I'd convinced myself into believing I didn't deserve— to be seen, to be desired, to love— were the very things I longed for now.

All of this had me in a serious funk. My body was healing just fine, my mental state was anything but. It wasn't just the wedding planning or my mother's continued badgering. It was not being able to get closer to Okiyo. My plans to do so had failed miserably.

Even before my fight, I thought we were at the very least becoming friends. The sexual tension between us was unmistakable. Here I was in his home and sleeping in his bed— alone.

I just wanted to go home. This man was basically forced to take care of me in his space. That was it. I'd worn out my welcome. He didn't strike me as the kind of guy to want someone up in his space 24/7. Even if we were to have crossed the line the other night, I could quite literally see him hitting me with the 'so what you about to get into line,' the very next morning, i.e., don't forget your earrings, love, as he booted me up out of here. I needed to figure out a way to get back home and let the man breathe.

I folded over, gut punched at my next thought. It had never occurred to me that he could have had a woman friend or something that he probably had to put off because of me.

Those were my exact thoughts when I heard the door open and close, signaling Okiyo's return from another day of covering for me at the different sites.

He entered the living room, his eyes immediately finding mine before looking away quickly to place his keys and other things on the table just in the interior of the room.

Over his shoulder, Okiyo casually asked, "How are you feeling today?"

He barely made eye contact, like he was deliberately avoiding me. It made me feel like even more of an intruder, lingering in a space that wasn't mine.

"Better," I lied, forcing a smile that I hoped didn't look as awkward as it felt. "Almost as good as new. Ready to be out of your hair. I'm sure you'd like your privacy back."

He paused, his eyes flicking up to meet mine, holding there a second longer than usual. "I never said that."

Maybe not in words, but everything else screamed it. His distance, his cool composure—it all felt like he was waiting for me to leave. I couldn't shake the thought that maybe someone else was waiting to take my place.

"I know," I said quickly, trying to keep things light. "But you've been great. Letting me crash here and covering for me at the sites... I don't want to overstay my welcome."

His brow furrowed slightly, and I could see him weighing my words. "Delia, I know you've been healing well, but I can tell something's eating at you. What's going on?"

I let out a short laugh, more out of nervous energy than humor. "What? No. I'm fine. Totally fine."

He didn't buy it, his gaze lingering, pressing.

"I'm serious," I added, softer this time. "Really, I'm good. Besides, it's not like you don't have other things going on." I couldn't help the slight dig, though I kept my tone playful, trying to mask how much I wanted to know what those "other things" were. The way he'd been distant lately had me wondering if there was someone else—maybe multiple someones—waiting for me to be out of his space.

His mouth curved into a small smile, but there was something guarded in his eyes, like he knew exactly where this conversation was headed but had no intention of going there. "If I wanted my space, I'd have made sure you knew by now."

I raised an eyebrow, surprised by his answer. "Really? No hot dates lined up now that I'm almost out of your hair?"

"Not exactly," he said, chuckling low, his accent wrapping around the words in that maddening way. "But I didn't know you were so eager to be out of my... *hair*."

My heart did a weird flip at that, and for a second, I felt bold enough to push further. "It's not that I'm eager. Just... feels like I've been taking up too much of your time."

His smile faltered for a moment, as if he was debating whether to say more. But instead, he reached for his keys, toying with them on the table. "You haven't been. If I wanted you gone, I'd have told you by now."

I wanted to ask what that meant—if it meant anything at all—but just as I was about to, his phone buzzed on the table, breaking the moment. His eyes dropped to the screen, then back to me with a look of apology.

"I need to take this," he said, already moving towards the hallway. "We'll finish this later."

I nodded, trying not to let the disappointment show on my face as he walked out of the room. Before he disappeared down the hallway, I blurted out, "I have another fight."

He stopped, eyes narrowing at me and his jaw tensed.

"When?"

"Few days."

An emotion that I couldn't read was there in his eyes. The phone rang again and without a word, he walked away.

As soon as he was gone, I sighed, sinking back into the couch. Maybe I was reading too much into things. Maybe I wasn't. But the longer I stayed here, the more it felt like I was in some kind of holding pattern with him. At the very least, I wasn't confused about wanting to continue to take fights. He could continue to coach me or not but something had to give. I was more confused than before.

On the one hand I was relieved that his phone had rang because he couldn't press me further on how I was really feeling. How do you tell a man that you feel guilty about being in a space while at the same time frustrated that you want it to be more in his *personal* space.

The next day, much like the day before it and the day before it, Okiyo left early to go to one of the planned sites. I got out of bed immediately after he'd left and returned all the unanswered calls from my mother. We talked briefly so she could basically give me a laundry list of things she needed me to do. I acquiesced.

I tucked away my slight feelings of jealousy, guilt and hurt , replacing it with as much joy as I could muster to help with the wedding. But first, this stupid anniversary party.

The day went on and I tried to focus on the tasks at hand. Calling caterers, calling the venue that the wedding was to be held at to make sure they'd be able to accommodate Iya's and Justin's wedding date roughly three months from now. But after the third call, I was done. I couldn't focus on this. The more I tried the more I just wanted to cry. By the evening, I was exhausted, both physically and emotionally. This time I barely noticed Okiyo return from work.

Chapter 20 – Okiyo

INSTEAD OF ONE CALL the night before, two had come in back to back and I needed to make one to Leboo as well. It wasn't intentional but I gave up on continuing my conversation with Delia.

The first call was from King, hence the reason I was sitting at a table in the back of his bar preparing to sift through the details I asked him to pull on Delia.

The second call was from Bishara to let me know that Leboo and Mackena had made it back safely to Kenya. I'd made a mental note to reach out to one of my men to take her some of the tea that she loved.

On our call, she had a nasty cough that I wanted to make sure she was nursing. It was rare that Bishara ever got sick. As a matter of fact, in the six years of my employment with the Baijan family, I'd never known Bishara to take any time off, save for a few appointments here and there.

The conversation with Leboo to let him know that the work with 3W was running ahead of schedule went as planned. I was almost compelled to tell him I'd be taking some additional time here in the states before returning to Kenya but thought better of it.

At any rate, the call to Leboo was a reminder that my time in Atlanta was quickly coming to an end. A lot of that was largely due to Delia's reviews and input on how we should go about the upgrades with minimal disruption to developments already in the building phase and minimal changes to those that were already built.

Even with that going well, and Delia healing from the mild head injury, I was still very much on edge. So much that I'd taken to leaving out of the flat early in the morning and coming back later in the evening. Not because I didn't want to be around her. I absolutely did.

I wanted nothing more than to laze the day away with her, finishing the kisses she'd started the other night. Making love to her and worshiping her body like the Goddess that she was. My groin tightened at the sheer thought of her. And that was precisely why I put distance between us.

I wanted to give in to this yearning for her. My time here was temporary. Yet, my feelings for Delia were becoming finite, tangible, and undeniable. And this was the bane of my conflicted emotions. Because I cared so much for Delia, finishing my work and leaving didn't sit well with me. It would be heartless.

The woman was already being summoned for another fight. An intermediary one that would come before the title fight in Mexico, but she was just recovering from a head injury for Christ's sake.

The fact that Delia was entertaining taking this intermediate fight, could only mean that she had her sights on Mexico. The intermediate fight would serve to keep her sharp, but also help build hype around her if she continued to win. She wanted that title.

How could I leave knowing the war zone she'd be stepping into in Mexico. And with who in her corner? Rudy? No. I needed to understand what made Delia tick. What was driving her on this suicide mission in the cage.

She was still fighting something deep and dark within. One win was not going to cure that. One win, even a title, didn't mean much in the grand scheme. It was a dangerous illusion, something that could give her a swollen ego going into the fight in Mexico, thinking it'd play out the same way. It wouldn't.

So now, I was sitting in the back of King's bar nurturing a snifter of whiskey and preparing to sift through the information he'd gathered for me since our call last night.

The soft murmur of conversation floated around me, punctuated by the occasional clink of crystal glasses against polished wood.

King's was the kind of place where men came to let their thoughts unravel over whiskey and cigars, secrets disappearing into the low hum of jazz and dim lighting.

The scent of aged scotch mixed with leather upholstery filled the air, and the rustle of cards being dealt at a corner table added to the quiet rhythm of the room. But the world around me barely registered.

The file on Delia sat open on the table in front of me, its stark, clinical words in sharp contrast to the warm atmosphere of the bar. What I discovered there was gut-wrenching. It was all written out in the court transcripts—the details of her sister's assault, laid bare for anyone to read. The words hit me like a punch to the gut: how Delia had found her sister that night, the aftermath. It was all there.

I sat back in my chair, letting out a breath I hadn't realized I'd been holding. The bartender was moving behind the counter, glasses clinking softly, but his movements were lost in the background of my thoughts.

The truth behind Delia's fights—why she took those beatings without fighting back—was spelled out right here in black and white. Her guilt was written between the lines of those transcripts. She'd taken her sister's pain, her violation, and shouldered it like it was her own.

Fighting was never about winning for Delia. It was about penance. In her own words she blamed herself for not protecting her sister.

A group of men chuckled from the far side of the room, but their laughter felt distant. The weight of what I'd just read pressed down on me. She'd been fighting for a redemption that was never hers to seek. I closed the file slowly, my fingers resting on the worn edges of the paper.

In the dim glow of King's, I realized I was no longer just her trainer or her protector. I was involved now, inextricably tied to this woman. The bartender set down a glass with a soft thud, but I couldn't tear my eyes away from the closed file. Delia's burden had become mine too.

After reading the file on her, doing nothing about this thing between us wasn't an option. I could try to convince her to just spar in the gym. It's a controlled environment with less opportunity for her to get hurt. But who was I kidding? This trauma of hers preceded me. Body blows hadn't convinced her, how could I?

I could use these last few weeks here to truly get her to open up to me. Perhaps I'd not even have to reveal that I knew what was going on with her. Just be there to convince her to seek the help she needs outside of the ring. Perhaps it was a slightly better option than trying to convince her not to fight. However, it could take months, years even for her to peel back the layers of trauma. There was simply no time for that. And after I was gone, who's to say she would stick to therapy?

There was really only one option that would help Delia in the near-term. I could continue to help her with her physical training, preparing her for the fight in Mexico without addressing her mentals but making sure that she was in peak condition. That way, I could ensure she would be safe and also buy myself some time to convince her to seek a longer term solution for help.

Of course, this created another problem. One of bigger magnitude. One that would leave a big part of the both of us battered and bruised. It was the challenge of irresponsibly placing two hearts in close proximity, allowing time to inextricably tie them together, then ripping them apart because of duty.

As I mulled over these options, I couldn't leave her alone to heal the wounds that plagued her. I would train her intensely, ensuring she was physically ready, but I would also confront her gently about her past and see if I could also get her to seek therapy. Even after I was gone, I'd know that she was okay.

I finished my drink and stood to leave. My decision was resolute. It was time to face the angel and help her confront the demons haunting her.

Chapter 21 – Delia

HOW DID I READ him so wrong? We kissed, shared a moment and then he pulled away. I felt like a burden. I left Okiyo's place around lunchtime, feeling more rejected than ever.

Back in my own apartment, I tried to focus on something else. Like the anniversary party my mom had put together to celebrate Iya and Justin's three year dating anniversary. It was tomorrow night and I'd committed to going. I really wasn't in the right headspace to go but didn't want to let her down even though I didn't seem to exist to them.

So here I stood in the middle of my closet trying to put together an outfit. And who the fuck throws an anniversary party for an engaged couple in the midst of planning a wedding that's less than three months away? My mother. That's who.

This was all too much. I had my own stuff to worry about. Like how I was going to explain to Okiyo why I up and left his apartment without making things more awkward than they'd already gotten. For me at least.

This swirled in my head while I also felt like a fraud; faking happiness over all this hoopla around Iya's wedding. It wasn't that I didn't want her to be happy. Deep down, I just wanted a little slice of that good thing— being cared for and loved on by another— for me too. I sighed, feeling dejected and lonely.

The pile of discarded clothes grew as I tossed each option one after the other. Nothing felt right. I had a billion options in my closet. I stood there, looking at all of the bright colorful sequins, pen stripes, cutouts, body cons, minis and maxis, business casual, business formal, formal wear, high end and low end pieces that normally made me happy. Now each of the once coveted pieces just felt like a cold substitute for the embrace of family and loved ones that I didn't have.

Fuck. I didn't want to go. I stood there staring at the mess around me. This couldn't be all to my story... I needed more. I wanted more and I, I just... God help me! The sob escaped before I could do anything to suck it back in. Then the dam I'd been holding back my emotions with for so long broke. I cried.

I looked around at the abundance of things in my closet. Every stitch of discarded clothing on the floor highlighted my insecurities and my failures. I cried harder. First, crumbling down to sit on the ottoman that sat in the center of the closet. Then slid further down, landing in a heap at its base, now surrounded by the pile of clothes. No amount of effort could stop the torrent of tears falling down my face as I curled into a ball and just let them go.

The pressure from my mother to help with this wedding while my life was literally suffocating me was too much. I felt like an impostor. I didn't have the capacity to be happy for my sister when I wasn't happy with me.

Why couldn't I just move on from this as easily as Iya did?

I was so lost in my misery that I didn't hear the door to my apartment open. It wasn't until I heard the faint creek of the closet door that I realized someone was there. I looked up, startled, to see Okiyo standing in the doorway.

"Hey, hey, hey. Why these tears?"

Before I could wipe the blinding tears from my eyes, he was kneeling on the floor beside me.

And as bad as I wanted to fight myself out of his arms and pretend that everything was ok, I couldn't. I went absolutely weak in this man's arms and buried my face in his shoulder. The best I could muster was a weak, "How did you get in here?" Between my sobs.

"I have my ways." He muttered rubbing the back of my scalp. "Shh now."

"Fucking CIA nigga," I choked back my tears, wanting to curse him out for breaking into my home. But the slow massaging motion mixed with the sifting of his fingers through my dense coils soothed my soul in a way it had never been soothed before.

Of course I'd had many lovers over the years, none were more than a one night stand to a two week affair at best. This moment was more intimate than all of those hookups combined.

I should have been annoyed, concerned by his intrusion even. But instead, I felt a strange sense of relief. Here I was lamenting about feeling like a stranger within my own family and here he comes, holding me as if I was the only thing he ever cherished in life. And the world... my world was at peace.

His presence was grounding. The more he soothed, the safer I felt. My sobs eventually calmed to tears and shuddering shoulders as he rocked me in his arms.

I hadn't cried like this in a very long time. This maybe was the first time ever in front of someone else since I was a kid. And strangely I felt no regret or shame. I clung to him for dear life and cried some more while he remained silent and held me cradled to his chest.

This man didn't even ask me what I was crying for. It was almost like he already knew how to heal my broken heart. And I had no fight left in me to act like everything was ok. I let him absorb my pain, the shame and the guilt. I laid it down right at his feet and he accepted it and me as one on the floor of my closet surrounded by a sea of clothes.

After what seemed like hours of us sitting like this, Okiyo finally asked in a hushed tone. "You want to tell me why I found you crying on the floor of your closet?"

"Not really." I croaked faintly, "But something tells me that you're not gonna let me slide this time."

"I think it's time you opened up about it. I'm a pretty great listener," he said, tilting my face up to his with a gentle nudging of my chin with his finger.

"It's, umm," I cleared my throat. "It's so much. I don't know where to start."

"Take your time. I'm all ears."

"My sister's anniversary party. Well, it's not just that it's— I always feel like my mom pressures me to be there for my sister all the time, but only when it's convenient for her. I mean, I love my sister and I miss when we just were close you know. Umm... *shit*. I'm sorry. I know none of this is making sense."

"Keep going, love. For days something has been eating at you and I haven't really wanted to press. But finding you here crying in a heap of clothes," he said with a little chuckle as he held up a paper napkin sized skirt with fringe that slipped through his fingers. "I'm sure I'll be able to piece it together."

I took a deep breath, pulling my skirt from his hand and continued.

"My baby sister and I used to be really close, but as we grew up, there's just been a rift between us you know. My mom and her are very close now and it just... well I just feel left out. Then there's this anniversary party for my sister and her fiancé that my mom wants me to attend. It just seems that they only want me around when it's convenient for them or they need help. I just feel so alone."

I rambled through so many of the things that truly did hurt, making sure to leave out the part where his pulling away was a part of the hurt too.

"You're not alone Delia. I'm sure your family cares. And," his words trailed off leaving a space of silence between us.

I needed to close that silence.

"It's not all that's wrong but a big part of it." I continued. "I didn't want to be a burden to you. I'm sure you could have a thousand other things to do than nurse me up. I know you were just being polite and all. I'm sorry for wearing out my wel—"

"I care about you." He cut me off, but said those words so quietly, I almost thought I imagined them.

My heart started beating erratically as I mulled over his words trying to glean the meaning behind them before looking up at his face in confusion.

He gazed down at me, eyes trained on my lips. He wasn't smiling and though his face was kind, his words had a seriousness to them.

"I care about you, Delia. And I owe you an apology."

"An apology for what?" I asked as my eyes pierced his with the question.

"I'm very sorry for pulling away from you so abruptly. I need you to know that it wasn't you. I needed to gain control of my faculties else, I would have taken everything you offered me in that kiss the other night."

I squeezed my eyes shut in embarrassment that he brought up the kiss. I'd just been trying to make sense of it myself before he'd swooped in like a superhero to save me from my tears. Slowly opening them, my rushed words tumbled out, "I should be the one to apologize for that. I'd just. Well. I thought we were," I paused again to blow out a shaky breath. "I thought you felt what I was feeling."

This man had me stuttering like a fool.

"I felt it. Feel it. I wanted that kiss, Delia. Wanted you, but bad timing, bad everything." He wiped a hand over his face. "It wouldn't have been right taking advantage of you being hurt. I wouldn't have been able to live with myself."

"Trust me, there was no head injury involved in that kiss. I kissed you because I felt our chemistry and connection in the darkness of your room. When I came to and remembered you taking care of me while I was out. You'd even given up your bed and slept on the floor beside me so I wouldn't be in a strange place alone. All of that mattered to me."

I lifted up further in his arms, making sure he saw the conviction of my words in my eyes. "I wanted to kiss you the first time we met. Well, when you had me pressed between your body and the wall at Gastrafrique. Please don't apologize to me, Okiyo, for giving me what I've wanted for a while now."

We both sat in silence drinking each other in. I looked up at him boldly and continued. "I want you to kiss me now." My words trailed as I lowered my head. There. I'd said it.

He grabbed my chin and lifted it up so that our eyes met. I saw a kindness there that morphed quickly into passion, desire, and lust I'd not seen in his eyes before. By no means was this man smiling but a softness had replaced the steel that usually resided there.

Before I knew it our lips met. It was a nice kiss with his lips pressed softly against mine. Then he slowly began to pull away. *Oh no the hell he wasn't.* I wanted this and I wanted it now.

I pressed my palms to each side of his face, loving the electricity that his beard caused from the friction of me pulling him back to me. I pulled his lips back to mine. Moaning when ours touched again. This time I held tightly , pushing my tongue deeper into his mouth, savoring the rough yet gentle stroke of his against mine.

His arms wrapped tighter around me as he pulled me in close. The kiss deepened into something more animalistic. I wanted to hold this man so close. He was gripping me just as tight. The intensity of the moment carried us.

I desperately needed to feel this connection. I was seeking solace in him and he found an open willing partner in me. He picked me up and the robe that I had around my body began to fall open exposing my full nakedness. I felt and heard the audible hiss as his breath caught in his chest. The weight of our unspoken emotions driving us further.

Tears began to stream down my face again as he kissed each and every one of them away. Heat exploded through me as he moved his lips down to nuzzle the nape of my neck. I held on to his shoulders. My eyes closed as I savored the sensation of his tongue on that sensitive spot just above my collar bone.

He moved further down still. Capturing the solid bud of one of my breasts between his lips. I cried out. "Ahh," not able to hold it in as a bolt of lightning spasmed through the pit of my uterus as if there was a direct electric current between my nipple and my pussy. I spasmed and pulsated and the man had not even touched me there. My whole body clenched in longing for him to touch me everywhere.

Oh but then he did.

As if sensing what my body craved, his right hand slid over my taught abs and hovered just above the heated flesh of my vagina. The mere heat of his hand caused a pool of wetness to puddle between my hot thighs.

It was tantric. My lubricated walls were calling for his fingers to stroke me and he did just that. I whimpered in his arms like a soft kitten. Then with a lick and a flick of his tongue on my pebbled left nipple, he crossed his head over my body to toy with the right. More lightning bolts zigzagged and coursed through my body.

My toes clenched and curled as he slid two digits inside of me while his thumb wrestled with my swollen clit. I panted, releasing the covers that were clenched in both fists on the bed, to reach up and pull his face from my breasts back up to my lips. He rose easily to the occasion balancing on one elbow above me as he continued to finger fuck me with his right hand.

I kissed him hungrily, biting his bottom lip then suckling it back into my mouth. He kissed me back as fervently. No words were stated. None had to be. I wanted this man. I wanted him badly.

He pumped his hand and he twisted his thumb as I raised my hips to meet his palm. The room was so silent that our every breath and moan was like sexy R&B music of our own making. My wetness against the palm of his hand made a suctioning smacking sound that seemed to draw shock waves from my body like magic. The sound was hypnotizing and stimulating at the same time, causing a mystic eruption. I cried out as I exploded in the most fulfilling orgasm I'd ever had. This was just from his hand.

And again he was so in tune with my body he knew I wanted more. I wanted to give him more of me. As if in a vision, I imagined freeing all of him that was pressing a dent into my inner thigh and sliding down its length while I rode him with abandon. Then it dawned on me that I didn't have any condoms. I groaned audibly at that thought.

He had to be a mind reader because as he slid his fingers from my engorged wetness, he brought them to his lips and after tasting them, he whispered, "May I kiss you there too, sweetheart."

"My God. Yes. You can kiss me wherever and whenever you want to." I finally caught a breath and mumbled before he slid down my body. "I want you inside me but I don't have any condoms."

Saying nothing, he continued to press light kisses on my breasts and abdomen as he traversed my body until his beard was aligned with the apex of my thighs. I held my breath in anticipation. He kneeled at the edge of my bed. Pausing for a second, he opened me wide with the thumbs of both hands. I heard him take a deep breath, savoring my essence.

"Open your eyes, luv. I want you to watch me kiss you here, so there's never a doubt again in your pretty head that I don't want this as bad as you do."

"Lord have mercy," I moaned as he swiped my pussy from top to bottom with the tip of his tongue. He dipped his fingers back inside me then pulled the same two out that he'd used before. I watched my juices glistening on them as we both inspected my wetness before he slipped them between his lips, closing his eyes in bliss as he savored the flavor. Okiyo was now ingrained in my memory as a certified freak. And I was here for every bit of it.

My head fell back into the mattress as he nuzzled his nose into my wetness and then snaked his tongue out of his mouth and deep into the recesses of my pussy. I lost it. Back arching and hips raised to meet the assault he waged on my swollen labia. The sounds his mouth made were driving me crazy. I gripped the sheets again, holding on, "Ohhh," I quivered, allowing him to do all of what he wanted to do to me with that tongue and his hands.

Less than five minutes went by. Maybe it was only three before my abs tightened and my toes curled in an inhuman way as I involuntarily exploded for the second time by my mentor's, trainer's, and now lover's tongue.

He'd wound my body up like a taut string and even after an eruptive release, I wasn't sure how to release myself from the knot he had by body in. I had no power to remove myself from the grip he had me in until he released my thighs and climbed up to join me by my side on the bed. Before long, I was nestled in Okiyo's arms and he'd angled my body so that my cheek rested on his chest.

We lay this way deep into the evening, both falling asleep and waking well after the dinner hour. I woke up still lying next to him but I could feel that he wasn't asleep. He lay there patiently waiting for me to stir. I felt a strange mix of vulnerability and safety laying like this with him. Before long I felt his head angle down towards the top of my crown. I timidly angled my face up and locked on his eyes. What I saw there unlocked a part of me that held the secret guilt and shame I'd been carrying locked away for far too long.

I started speaking slowly at first—Resolved to share what was really eating at me. And he listened intently.

"It's hard for me to say this, especially at almost thirty years old, how much I'm affected by my mom and her pressure for me to be like my sister. She never misses the opportunity to remind me of my failures. Iya's my younger sister and she's getting married. And though I'm extremely happy for her, it's so hard you know. I feel like I'm drowning sometimes and it makes me doubt myself."

At a certain point, I started hemming and hawing again trying to find the right words to explain to him about why mine and Iya's relationship had changed so much and why it always felt that my mother never really trusted me around Iya any more after she'd been assaulted while on my watch.

After fumbling through the words, Okiyo gently placed a finger over my lips allowing me to go silent.

"I know about your sister's assault and how you've blamed yourself all these years," he said quietly.

I froze, my heart pounding. "What—, I stuttered. "What do you mean?" I questioned tentatively.

His words cut through my defenses, exposing the raw wound I had been carrying for so long. Okiyo pulled me into his arms, holding me tightly as the tears began to flow again.

"I should have protected her. She was just a kid and looked up to me and I failed her by taking her to an event that I was barely even old enough to be at."

"Delia you were just a kid, too. You could never have predicted that someone would do something harmful to your sister. And whoever has allowed you to believe that you were at fault; that you have to shoulder the blame for this is just bloody fucking wrong. It wasn't your fault. It was the sick son of a bitch who assaulted her. It was his fault."

"... But I should have protected her."

"No Delia. You were put in an impossible situation. Blaming yourself won't change the past. Playing it small and getting pummeled in a ring or cage will not give you retribution. You have to live for yourself and learn to fight for your own happiness. You are capable and one hell of a fucking fighter and an architect for that matter. And you damn well better start acting like it. The healing starts now."

His words, his embrace, and the sheer force of his presence broke something inside of me. It broke something that needed to be broken. For the first time, I felt a glimmer of hope that maybe, just maybe, I could drop this cloak of guilt and shame and just be. *Me.*

"Delia, we are going to get up from here and I'm going to leave you for a little bit so you can get cleaned up and dressed for work. I'm going to head back to my flat so that I can do the same."

It was 6 A.M. according to the clock on my bedside table.

In one fluid motion, he'd angled his fully clad body from beside me and was standing up pulling me towards him. My cheeks burned as I realized the robe that I had on still was now wide open and my full body was exposed to his gaze. And that this man just licked his lips and squinted his eyes at me in the most tasty way.

Pulling me past him he patted me on my ass as he directed me towards my closet to do as he said. I couldn't help but look over my shoulder at him. There was something about the way he watched me made me that made me feel strong. An emotion that was quickly backed up by his words as he slowly moved towards the door. "You're stronger than you think, little one. I'll be back in an hour to pick you up."

Okiyo did exactly as he said. He knocked on my door right on time, ready for our next site visit. We were almost done with the security assessments, and I was relieved that no one at the office questioned my absence since they all knew I was working with him. Today, though, I'd have to make an appearance. I'd do some desk work in the office while he did the site visits—Okiyo's idea, not mine.

The day passed quickly as I submitted security change requests and reviewed documents with the architects. Before long, 5:00 PM had arrived, and a wave of panic set in—tonight was Iya's anniversary party, and I still hadn't settled on an outfit.

Just as I started thinking about what I was going to wear, Okiyo texted to say he was ready to drive me home. A few minutes later, I was in the car with him, and without a word, he reached over and handed me a large white box tied with a gold ribbon.

It wasn't until I fingered the pretty ribbon that I fully took in the sight of him. Calm and collected as always. Also not in the same laser cut suit that he wore to work this morning. He was now in a three-piece charcoal grey one and I swear it fit him so well that my pussy involuntarily clinched. My mouth must have been hanging wide open because he quickly chuckled at my bemused face before ordering, "Open it."

Still in total confusion I did exactly what he said and before long was pulling open beautiful tissue paper to expose the most exquisite gold dress. Also in the box was a bottle of Baccarat 540 Rouge. I was speechless. In absolute stunned shock.

Without the words I could only raise my eyes to his questioning.

With a broad smile now on his face he stated, "I think you mentioned needing a date to a party." His eyes twinkled and one brow lifted as if anticipating my response to the statement he just made.

"I believe my words were, I didn't want to go to the party. But since I promised my mom, having a date makes it better." I grinned like a silly fool as he chuckled even more.

"Well it's settled then. We'll swing by your apartment and you can get freshened up and dressed and you won't even have to sift through the mess that you made in your closet yesterday."

Chapter 22 – Delia

I STOOD IN MY full length mirror, adjusting the dress that Okiyo had skillfully picked out. *For me.* When did he have a chance to go buy me a dress? And how did he pick the size so perfectly? I spun to look at myself from every angle. I felt beautiful. Sexy. He had exquisite taste.

The gold filigree in the dress offset the burnished undertones of my skin to a tee. I would have never picked this dress for myself. True, I loved to dress sexy, but I had to admit, the saying that 'allowing a man to dress you in what *he* thinks is sexy on you,' hits different. His choice was a 10-out-of-10 recommend, for me. And this dress—chef's kiss. He'd given me a whole attitude adjustment about going to Iya's party. However, it also had me buzzing with anxiety.

My stomach churned as I put on the finishing touches of my makeup and was ready to walk out of my bedroom. This was going to be the first time I'd ever brought a man around my family. And Okiyo was far from just any man. His presence alone commanded attention, and my family would have a field day talking about how fine he was.

Because let's face it. He was spectacular to look at. The way he carried himself with an air of prestige without being pompous made me internally drool, though I'd not be letting him know that anytime soon.

The bigger cause for Iya and my mother's whispers tonight were going to be around whether or not he was the cause for me walking funny or being sore when I've come around in the past. That and maybe the fact that he was ten years older.

I took another steadying deep breath. *Get it together, Delia! It's just a party.* Yeah. Just a party that you're showing up to with your shit talking ass mom in attendance. I took one more breath, choking as I swallowed a mouthful of the Baccarat I'd just sprayed on the pulse points of my neck.

Stifling my cough I stepped out of my room, where Okiyo was waiting. And just like that, my nerves went out the window. *Talk shit about who?* Let them talk. He looked divine in the three-piece, smoke grey suit. His calm demeanor once again steadied my nerves. I... we were about to be the center of attention tonight.

"You look stunning," he said, bending over to kiss the hand I'd held out to his once proffered arm. "Ready?"

"As ready as I'll ever be," I replied, still trying to get over the fact that he was my plus one to this party. I wanted to pinch myself as

I hid the smile that forced its way onto my lips as I turned off the light switch and followed him out the front door.

We arrived at the small venue of the party and the place was already buzzing with people and chatter. Some I knew and some I didn't because these were Iya's and Justin's friends. Okiyo must have sensed my anxiety because he placed a hand at the small of my back. I melted into his touch. I giggled inwardly at my grown ass feeling like a schoolgirl out with a boy for the first time.

As we moved deeper into the room, Okiyo leaned in and whispered, "I'll get us some drinks. Be right back."

I nodded, watching him disappear into the crowd. Just then, a man approached me, his eyes narrowing and then lighting up with recognition. I wasn't expecting the animation that he exhibited next.

"Yo! We got a celebrity in the building."

I looked over my shoulder, trying to also see who he might have been talking about. No one was behind me. I turned back, totally confused but shrugged it off as I waited for Okiyo to come back with those drinks.

The same guy who spotted the invisible celebrity, now stopped another guy in passing to pull him down to his very short level. Now he pointed at me. The two guys were now looking and pointing in my direction, as Justin walked up to them. Now, they all were looking at me. Little stubby was still pointing. The second guy's eyes grew wide as if in recognition. Justin's head reared back and his face scrunched up. He appeared just as confused as I was.

They were now moving as a group in my direction.

"Yo! That is her!" The taller guy in the bunch said. They were close enough now and there was no mistaking he was referring to me. *What the fuck?*

This was a bit weird and the hairs on the back of my neck stood up. It was something about strange men walking up on me that activated my fight or flight response. With Okiyo, it was a dark hallway and the fight in me was triggered. With these guys, even though Justin was in the group and was just as sweet as he could be, I began looking for an escape route—a pathway through the crowd to follow in the direction Okiyo had taken. I couldn't move though. The small space was a bit too crowded to make a quick enough escape.

"Hey!" The little one shouted in camaraderie with his other two friends, "We got the Viper in the building, my dude."

Fuck! It was the big question mark on Justin's face as he stared at me for understanding about what his friends were talking about that had me wanting to disappear through the floor.

I felt like a deer caught in headlights as I shrugged my shoulders at him as if not knowing what he was talking about while my eyes frantically searched for Okiyo. I was ready to get the hell up out of here. Or at least away from these three stooges.

"It is you," the other guy exclaimed, now really moving in closer to me as if to give me dap as he all but shouted, "You beat that chick's ass last week! You did your thing in that cage."

"Let me shake your hand," the other friend chimed. "Justin, you know the Black Viper?"

Justin only shrugged with a lost smile on his face when he responded, "This is my soon to be sister-in-law. Iya's sister Delia. Delia, meet these jerks, who obviously have no manners."

My heart sank. *So much for anonymity.* And here I thought having a fine ass man on my arm this evening would get the tongues wagging. Who knew this would be my ultimate fighting champion reveal.

"I, uh... Yeah nice to meet you, too." I responded as he took my hand and shook it aggressively.

The other guy now introduced as Dez, continued to give a blow by blow of the fight I had with Storm. My sister's fiancé's eyes locked on mine in total bewilderment almost if silently asking what the fuck are they talking about.

It didn't matter because friend number one, aka Big Mike, even though he may have been a whopping five feet two inches tall, but was built like a linebacker, had the whole floor's attention at this point, "The way you dodged that last punch and then got hit with that sucker punch! Man, that was brutal!"

People around us started to turn and listen. I felt heat rising in my cheeks. The last thing I needed was for everyone to know about my involvement in underground fighting, especially at a family event.

Okiyo reappeared, carrying two glasses. He took one look at my face and the man talking to me, and his eyes narrowed. He handed me my drink and leaned in close.

"Do I need to permanently silence this bloke?" He whispered.

I shook my head vehemently, though it was a turn on to know he'd threaten violence in my honor. Immediately, by body warmed at the thought of his total possession of my body with just his tongue and hands last night. I couldn't help but whisper back. "No. Your hands are deadly. Let's go."

I grabbed his hand, certain he'd missed the double meaning of my words. I mouthed a quick I'll explain later to Justin. Then followed Okiyo's lead, grateful for the escape further still into the room.

I groaned outwardly this time. Stopping abruptly behind Okiyo as he stopped to look down at me.

"Did you mean for us to go back towards the exit?" He asked, piercing my eyes with his to see what now troubled me.

His eyes followed mine as I looked over to the group of women whispering mutedly in the corner. It was my mother and Iya. I didn't have to see them to know who the loud raucous laughs and exclamations of, 'Girlllll,' while bending over trying to politely hold in a laugh, belonged to. Oh they were so into ki-keeing it up, *gossiping*, to notice me. *Yet.*

Curiosity and a devilish grin bloomed on Okiyo's face as he looked at the two of them and back to me. "Let me guess. Mom and sister?"

"Yep."

"Ahhh. Striking resemblance. I see where your beauty comes from."

He gave my hand a squeeze. Shockingly, he pulled me towards the two conspirators. One with the wine glass, my mother and the other with the champagne flute, Iya.

They'd probably had a few of them by now, by the way they were laughing it up. Couldn't lie, for a hot second I wished I were included in their bond circle of girl talk, but quickly pushed it away. Tucked my thought neatly behind the anxiety of *whatever the hell Okiyo had up his sleeve.*

My mother saw us coming before Iya did and I swear I heard her, hit Iya with a, "*Psst.* Iya, who is that fine ass man coming over here with Delia?" As Iya attempted to turn around, mom swatted her, "Don't turn around now, they—"

"Delia!" My mom exclaimed, batting her long done up eyelashes at me innocently, the whole time her eyes on Okiyo as she smashed me into a hug. "You made it, baby."

Lord this woman knew how to put it on.

"Yes, I'm here. Why are you two over here tucked away instead of out there mingling?"

"Oh you know, just over here catching up with mom," Iya said as they looked at each other and they both folded over laughing at some inside joke we'd likely caught them in. *Yeah. They'd had quite a few of those glasses of wine and champagne.*

I already knew I was going to be next on their hit list by the way mom asked, "And who is this handsome fellow whose hand you are clinging to Ms. Thang." She never stopped fluttering those eyelashes either. Not in a flirtatious way, but Shayla Aguillen had never seen me bring a man around and she was going to milk the info out of him because she knew I would not be forthcoming with my business, since they'd basically made up stories about me and my 'men friends' out of thin air. To actually have some proof tonight was going to have my mother and sister in a tizzy.

"Oh yes, big sister, do tell," Iya said, eyes batting in happy surprise as she continued, "Because he has a big 'ol Cheeto eating smile on your face."

Not waiting for me to make the introduction, Okiyo reaches for my mother's hand first and pulls it up to his lips, "I am Okiyo Bamdi," he pauses gently releasing my mother's hand and turns back towards me.

My mother damn near swooned as I caught her mouthing to Iya, "British?" Then she did a little shimmy with her shoulders, lips pursed and eyebrows raised. And Iya hit her with a shrug lipped smile and a "Yassss Bitch!" look. All of this was silent sister girl sign language Okiyo may or may not have been able to interpret had his eyes been anywhere on them.

But they weren't, they were on me when he responded to my mother. "I am a... close friend of Delia's." And I almost forgot we were talking to them too because the way he looked at me with total respect, admiration and a hint of lust, made me forget to make myself small in their big presences.

His look made me feel wanted, cared for and seen all at once and I relaxed and openly smiled at him as if we were the only two people in the room. And without taking my eyes off of him, I said, "Okiyo, this is my mother Shayla Aguillen and my younger sister, Iya. Iya's getting married soon and this is her anniversary party to Justin, one of the guys we just encountered when we first got here."

He broke eye contact first, then turned again to nod in greeting to my mother and then to my sister. "It is a pleasure to meet you, ladies. I see where Delia gets her beauty from. Congratulations, Iya. Lucky fellow you got there."

He was such a gentleman and I almost wanted to laugh out loud in thinking of what the conversation between my mom and Iya would be when we gave them their privacy back.

And it needed to be soon, because what I did not want was to be back here with them when or if word of my fight made it back to this part of the room. Justin would be spilling the news to Iya soon enough, probably over pillow talk tonight, and she could surely do the honor of telling my mom. I tugged at Okiyo's arm, breaking up the small talk he was having with both my mother and sister then whispered in his ear, "I'm ready to go."

He winked and bade both my mother and sister good night. "Delia and I have some catching up to do." Was his parting remarks.

And when he stirred me away, I looked back over my shoulder and sure enough the two of them were bursting to talk about this juicy little story of me and Okiyo.

I heard my mom whisper horribly just before we were out of earshot, "Lord for a minute, I thought the girl was into women."

And Iya's retort in a mock British accent made me smile on the inside. "Absolutely not. That man is a man's man and my big sister picked a proper good one in that fellow."

Of course her accent was horrible but the fact she claimed me as her big sister as though she were indeed proud of it is what made coming to this party worth it. Okiyo, and the naughty things I wanted to do to him to return all the favors he'd given yesterday was going to make leaving this party worth it.

But, as we made our way to the exit, both of our phones buzzed simultaneously. I glanced down at my screen and saw a message from Rudy.

Oh no.

Okiyo looked at his phone, then at me. "Just got that message too huh?" I nodded my head, "Rudy just messaged me. Looks like I got 48 hours to respond."

I was in Okiyo's lap, undoing his tie before the hired car could pull away from the party. The partition was up and the driver was taking us back to Okiyo's condo. We had about a thirty minute ride and though we had just crossed the line into intimacy less than 24-hours ago. The anxiety of the message we'd received about taking the title fight in Mexico mixed with the lingering heat from the way Okiyo brazenly looked at me as if he fully possessed me had me wanting to strip completely and fuck him in the back of this car.

Adrenaline coursed through my body and I needed to release it now. Funny how I'd gone several months at a time without sex but I'd wanted this man since our first touch and now I'd felt the precursor to what it may feel like to have his full body on top of mine, in me. I wanted it even more.

I kissed him longingly as he grabbed the fleshy skin of my hips and ass and pulled me into him. The tiny thong I wore under this dress was the only thing keeping my wetness from soaking through the fabric of his trousers.

When he sucked in my bottom lip deeply then released it to trail kisses across my cheek to settle his lips just behind my earlobe to suckle the pulse point of my neck there, my pussy clenched. I wanted something to grip, but we were fully dressed. Between thinking of ways to get his pants down to slide his dick out and sink onto it before we reached our destination and the fact my next fight could quite possibly be in Mexico sent shivers up my spine.

Passion and fear was a heady mix. I panted as he continued to kiss and suckle my neck as I sucked on his earlobe.

His hand reached between us. He slid my thong to the side and again found my slick wet folds and slid two fingers inside me while he cupped my mound in the palm of his hand.

He simultaneously pumped his fingers inside me while rolling his thumb over my swollen clitoris. I rode his hand.

Between moans I whispered, "If I take this fight... Ahhh," I whimpered, "It will be more than just a match."

He began a slow rhythmic rubbing and stroking with his hands causing my body to slow a bit from my frenzied pace. "Keep going love." Okiyo coaxed, with double meaning. Keep talking but also keep riding his hand.

My body obeyed in one way, my mind the other. I rolled my hips slowly. "Mmm, sssss," I hissed with a slow silky intake of air through my teeth, "It will be a homecoming. A return to my roots of sorts, but for the first time."

"Yes, love," was all he said in response before beginning to pummel my pussy hard and quickly between us. His other hand was on my hip coaxing me to ride his fingers harder and faster.

My breath came out in quick pants as my body tensed in pleasure. I barely heard him when he whispered, "This fight will be dangerous, luv." I was too close to the edge of coming undone in his lap, but he was communicating out loud the concern I'd seen in his eyes. I came so hard. So completely. *I came way too fast.* A similar thought I had about making a decision to take this fight or not... This is happening way too fast.

Chapter 23 – Okiyo

I watched intently as Delia paced back and forth in the gym. Hands on her hips, shaking out her legs from the intense jump rope routine, I'd put her on. Her skill was already top notch but she'd made up her mind that she was taking the fight in Mexico. Her eyes intense with focus.

I had my own feelings about her accepting this fight. But I would never exert my will on her or hinder her need for the release she could only find in the cage.

No. I wouldn't exert my will on her decision to fight just like I wouldn't exert my will on her body even though my body was quite literally fighting to be inside of her. It wasn't time. I'd not penetrated her. Even though she'd nearly begged me to after we'd gotten notice the fight in Mexico had officially been announced.

Instead, I allowed her to take out her anxiety on my face and hands. Taking her body in the way I wanted too could add a layer of complexity to this thing we had. She needed to be focused on this fight not on me fucking her senseless.

The fight. What we knew was it would be within the next three weeks. After I was expected to be back in Kenya. That was a challenge I'd have to take on with Delia being none the wiser. I didn't yet know the how of it all but I needed to figure that out soon because Rudy had just left to go enter Delia's name in the bout officially. I was going to need King to help devise the plan.

In the interim, Delia had accepted a short turn fight. It was last night and she'd won. I no longer had to goad her into getting in the cage and turning up. She crushed it—flawless victory. And today? She was right back in the gym, pushing harder than ever.

Skill-wise, she was there. She'd tasted victory and now the beast inside of her was raging, ready to tear through anything in her way. At this point, it was all about endurance, resilience—staying power. That's where I came in.

"Let's talk," I said, catching her mid punch. She stopped smiling and wiped sweat from her brow.

"About what? I stopped playing small." She said, mocking my accent. "Plus, I just won another fight last night." She leaned in, pecking me on my lips before continuing, "Don't tell me you're losing confidence in me already." She rolled her eyes.

"Nope. I'm absolutely confident you'll get in that ring and do everything you are supposed to do. Keep punching," I demanded holding up the sparring gloves so she could continue doing the combos we'd been practicing. "Mexico's a different beast." I raised my hands up high signaling to her to do a Roundhouse kick. And she did it effortlessly.

She continued a series of combo punches, kicks and blocks as she breathlessly responded, "I never thought I'd say this, but I'm ready for whatever comes my way, Okiyo. I wanna win."

"I know," I said, trying to keep my voice steady. Changing up my tactics a bit to see if I could get her to falter on her desire to go to Mexico. *Not a chance.*

"They fight dirty there, Viper. The underground scene is notorious for being ruthless. We need to prepare for anything and everything."

She dropped her gloves and searched my eyes to see what the meaning was behind my statements. She nodded; her expression serious. "What do you suggest?"

I folded my arms considering her question. "We're going to have to change up our training strategy. First, we need to work on your defensive skills. You need to be able to block and counter any attack. And we need to train with the assumption weapons might be involved." Delia's eyes widened slightly, but she nodded. "OK. I've used the sticks and nunchucks before."

"We'll start with those. The other thing we need to consider is the climate difference between Atlanta and Tulum. The coast of Mexico is tropical rainforest. If you're not acclimated properly, you're going to be susceptible to dehydration, fatigue, and increased physical strain."

I watched Delia closely now. The determination in her eyes was unmistakable. Her focus was sharp, and I could see she was already thinking ahead, likely preparing herself for the championship bout in Tulum, Mexico. She mentioned her father grew up just outside Tulum, though she'd never been.

"Well I guess I'll have to start practicing Bikram yoga to get acclimated. I'm going to Mexico for this fight. And despite the fact my dad never took us to his hometown—I never understood why — This is a homecoming. I'm going and I'm going to win."

No. Sweetheart. We are going.

"Go hit the bag," I told her, satisfied with her training in the ring.

Without question, she moved to the bag and started her drills again. I silently chuckled.

I could also guess why her father never returned or took his family to visit before his passing. He'd likely fled with his mother as a youth because of the escalating violence there. It still simmered beneath the beauty of Tulum today. Another reason why she'd not be taking this trip alone and why I needed help from King to plan this properly. Not because I didn't believe in her but because we'd be stepping into the belly of the beast.

And though I was due to be back in Kenya before the fight was likely to commence. I'd make the necessary arrangements to see this through by her side. And she was determined—too determined—to show what she was made of there. I didn't like it. But I respected it and praised the change I'd seen in her in such a short time. It was my duty to ensure she stayed safe by training her for whatever happened in the cage and protect her from anything outside of it.

After leaving the gym, Delia and I headed to the 3W office wrap up the final updates to the security and architectural plans for the Gastrafrique developments. She had thrown herself into work with newfound vigor.

Her boss, Rhiyan, was back from Hawaii and was extremely impressed with the security revamp we'd all but completed. The one most notable was the Rue d'Orleans Paris project. During the update to Rhiyan, I stopped in front of the blueprint on the screen, glancing at Delia before speaking.

"I think you'll find the security updates on most of the projects pretty straightforward," I said with a grin, "But this one... this one took some real creativity to get right. And it wasn't me. Delia cracked it."

Rhiyan's eyebrows shot up. "Really? Isn't this the project we nearly scrapped because no one could create a design that accounted for the open waterway security issue along the Seine." She turned to Delia, surprise and a healthy dose of pride flickering in her expression. "You solved it?"

Delia stepped forward, standing tall as she moved to the screen, gesturing smoothly at the blueprint. "It took some research, but yes," she said confidently. "We wanted to keep the site open and free flowing, especially with the shopper and guest access, without compromising security. So with the help of our civil and structural engineers, I designed a barrier system that blends into the architecture, here and here." Her finger moved expertly across the screen, showing the strategic points. "Plus, we integrated the surveillance monitoring system Mr. Bamdi has originally planned around the buildings to also span the waterway —discreet, but comprehensive. The design is seamless, but if there's an actual security threat at this site once it's built, this system allows them to lock it down fast without disrupting the site's function."

Rhiyan blinked, clearly impressed. "Damn, Delia. Here I am about to fuss at you once again for not having gotten your license to practice yet, but now I'm thinking you might need to get licensed in security planning—civil and structural design too." Her surprise softened into a smile. "You've got one hell of a brain on you, you know that?"

"She's definitely got what it takes." I nodded at Rhiyan before turning my attention to Delia. I winked, causing her to blush and quickly lower her eyes. "Once she got in her zone, she reworked the whole south-side access like it was nothing. She has proven to be as capable as you said she was, Mrs. Kekoa."

Rhiyan nodded her head, wholeheartedly agreeing. "Go get your damn architectural license, Delia. You've been outsmarting half the team here without it."

Delia blushed slightly, but looked absolutely sincere when she shook *her* head in agreement with Rhiyan's demand.

As Delia continued explaining her revisions, Rhiyan couldn't stop praising her. Every nod, every approving smile from Rhiyan confirmed what I already knew—the security revamp and architectural design she updated were exceptional. The firm was likely on track to win another award, all thanks to her.

I leaned back slightly, watching Delia in her element. The confidence radiating off her was sexy as hell. There she was, commanding the room, pointing out solutions with ease, her voice steady and sure. She was owning her space.

She was balancing everything so well; work, her training, even facing some of her demons head-on. And damn, did it show. That self-assurance, the way she moved, the fire in her eyes when she talked about her work... I couldn't help but be drawn in.

But the truth was the beast wasn't just coming out in the ring anymore. It was showing up here, too, in the office, in the way she approached every challenge thrown her way. She was fierce, a rock star in every sense of the word.

The shift in her was undeniable. The doubts and hesitation were giving way to something stronger—something unbreakable. She was finally realizing what I'd seen in her all along. And that... She... was something to be reckoned with.

Chapter 24 – Delia

The small café buzzed with a low murmur of conversation and the clinking of coffee cups. Despite the warmth inside, a cold knot of dread twisted in my stomach. My fingers tapped restlessly against the smooth wooden table, barely noticing the comforting scent of fresh pastries and rich espresso.

I should've felt at ease in the cozy atmosphere, but I didn't. Today, I was coming clean with my family. The cat was already out of the bag after Justin's friend recognized me at his and Aya's party, and I couldn't hide the truth any longer. Didn't want to.

After my mom and sister met Okiyo at the anniversary party, I wouldn't be able to avoid explaining him away either. And though they hadn't heard the news about my fighting at the time Okiyo and I walked up on them laughing and gossiping in the back of the party, the truth wouldn't stay buried for much longer. Iya's fiancé, Justin, was bound to spill what really happened after his friends recognized me. And Iya was sure to spill it to my mother.

And just like that, within 24 hours, Iya was lighting up my phone, furiously texting we *had* to do brunch this weekend. The sudden urgency? Clearly, it wasn't because they missed me or cared about what was actually going on in my life. No, it was because I'd shown up to the party with a man. The irony was enough to make me roll my eyes. They hadn't been this eager to meet up in months.

But, honestly, I was ready for it. Okiyo had pushed me to stop hiding, and maybe he was right. The weight of keeping it all bottled up was exhausting. I was ready to come clean about the fighting—and maybe brunch with a side of mimosas would make it easier.

As I sat there, mindlessly perusing the menu, the words blurred together as my thoughts drifted. Then, through the window, I spotted Iya walking in. She saw me right away, a wide smile spreading across her flawless face as she waved. As always, she looked effortlessly put-together—tall, svelte, makeup perfectly on point, and her hair pulled into a cute, messy bun only she could make look intentional.

We were sisters, but aside from the shape of our eyes—thanks to our mother—there wasn't much else that physically tied us together. Our mixed Afro-Latina heritage gave us both deep brown skin, but mine was like smoked cinnamon compared to her warm, toasted amber. And while we both had wild crowns of hair, she kept hers bone-straight and polished, while I let mine grow as wild and unruly as I felt inside.

"Hey, sis," Iya greeted as she sat down, her massive Gucci bag immediately taking up a whole chair beside her. Her eyes narrowed slightly, scanning me as if she was assessing whether I was hiding something. "You look tense. What's going on with you?"

I rolled my eyes, the sisterly love strong but undeniably strained.

Iya always had a way of getting right to the point, though I could tell by the way her fingers fidgeted with her napkin that she was debating whether to dive right into the real conversation or let things simmer with some small talk first.

"Why don't you tell me?" I shot back, crossing my arms in a half-playful, half-defensive stance.

She smirked, but it didn't quite reach her eyes. "Oh, don't play coy with me. You know why we're here."

There it was the impatience under the surface. Iya was ready to get answers, and I could already sense the questions about Okiyo and the fight hovering on the tip of her tongue.

"I figured Justin told you about the conversation with his friends at your anniversary party and your nosy ass wants answers." I said, leaning back in my chair. "So, are we gonna do this over mimosas or what?" After putting it at least partially out there. I scanned the room looking for a waiter. Never around when you need them.

I turned back to Iya, taking a moment to look expectantly at my sister, knowing she was barely able to contain herself. She probably already knew most of it, but I wasn't about to give her the satisfaction of prying it all out of me. Why let her dig when I could just lay it out and beat her to the punch?

The way I'd been handling things—keeping my head down, acting like I didn't have the right to take up space—you'd think Iya was the older, stern sister. But no. I was the older sister, and it was damn well time I started acting like it.

"Uh-huh, I see you over there, sitting like you don't know any-thing, but you're literally about to burst at the seams wanting to ask," I said, folding my arms. "So yes, I fight. Not street fighting *per se*, but MMA. Mixed martial arts, you know, like that."

I cringed internally for a second. Sure, some of those fights were in underground circles, barely legal, but the last thing I wanted was to give Iya more reasons to stress. Telling her outright that my matches were sometimes just one step away from back-alley brawls wasn't the move.

Iya raised a brow, her smirk deepening. "Well, I wasn't about to burst at the seams, but now that you're sharing... say more." She waved her hand in a 'get on with it' motion, clearly savoring this.

I leaned back, deciding to give her just enough to satisfy her cu-riosity. "I'll talk about the fighting, but if you're expecting details about anything else—like Okiyo—that's off limits."

Iya's eyes widened slightly, and she opened her mouth to protest, but I cut her off before she could start. "Nope. Don't even try it. This conversation is about me, not him."

Sitting back and folding her arms, Iya arched a perfectly shaped brow and pursed her lips. "Off limits? Hmm. We'll see *what'cho* mama got to say about that."

I ignored Iya's poke about Mom and kept going. "So, I've been doing it now for about ten years. You guys always thought I was into something, and I didn't exactly correct you because I wasn't sure what I wanted it to become. But I'm really good at it."

Iya's eyes widened before that slick grin of hers spread across her face. "Wait," she paused, holding back a laugh. "So all these years, we thought you were getting it in hardcore style," she said, rolling her torso in a slow seat twerk, "but you're out here letting chicks punch on you in a cage? That's what's been giving you all those bruises and making you walk funny?"

"Girl, stop," I shot back, rolling my eyes. "You are *so* exaggerating. I wasn't around y'all acting loose, and I sure as hell have never been walking funny. I just let y'all run with it."

Iya leaned in, her voice dropping to a level that caught me off guard. "Um, girl, do you not remember the night Justin proposed? You had a bruise covering half your neck and shoulder. You tried to hide it with makeup, like you always do, but Delia... I know you. I might not act like it all the time, but you're my big sister."

She paused, her eyes softening, and for the first time in a long time, I could feel her heart in her words. "Nobody said anything because you've been so closed off. No... you weren't always like this. But ever since... *that*, you've shut down, and we didn't know how to help. None of us did."

Her face crumbled just a little, her bravado slipping as sadness threaded through her expression. Seeing her like that, vulnerable, cracked something open in me. All this time, I'd been blind to the fact she was feeling it too—missing me, the way I missed her. How could I have been so selfish? So consumed by my own guilt, I never stopped to think maybe I wasn't the only one suffering. I was too busy dimming myself, shrinking so no one would think I was forgetting, or worse, I didn't care.

Even in therapy, I hadn't let go. I couldn't see beyond my own pain, couldn't see how shutting myself down meant leaving Iya to deal with everything on her own. That's exactly what I had been punishing myself for all these years, wasn't it? Not being there when she needed me. And all along, I was making the same mistake—pulling away, trying to carry this guilt alone.

I swallowed hard, the lump in my throat growing unbearable. Fighting... it was supposed to be a release. A way to escape.

I opened my mouth, the words heavy, reluctant, but needing to be said. "Fighting... it's been a way to cope. With everything."

My voice cracked, and I hated how exposed I felt, but I couldn't stop now. "I thought... I thought maybe if I just hit something hard enough, or if I let someone hit me, maybe it'd all make sense. Maybe I'd feel less broken. But it never does."

Iya's eyes softened even more, her tough exterior melting. For the first time in years, I felt like she wasn't just my sister. She was *my person* again—the one who knew me, even when I didn't know myself.

Iya's expression shifted, growing more serious. "Coping with what, Delia?"

My throat tightened, and I could feel the sting of tears threatening to fall. I glanced down at my hands, twisting my fingers together, unsure if I was really ready to open up like this. But she deserved to know. After all this time, she deserved the truth.

Taking a deep breath, I kept my eyes on my hands and tried to steady my voice. "I've been carrying so much guilt... about what happened to you. I thought... maybe if I punished myself enough, it would make things right. Let people see how sorry I was. I thought if I took the blows, it would mean something."

I laughed softly, bitterly, still staring at the table. "And we both went through counseling... and look at you, Iya. It worked for you. You're getting married. You're beautiful, successful—you have it all. But me? I didn't know how to get over it. Everyone kept telling me, 'It's not your fault, it's not your fault,' but that didn't make it easier to apologize to you. It didn't make the guilt go away. And then dad died. I didn't have anyone. You had mom and I was left figure shit out on my own. That's not on you, but it's what led me to *this*," I paused, risking a glance at her, then looked away again.

"So I went to the gym, just to blow off some steam at first, and ended up sparring with this guy. He didn't care I was half his size. Didn't care I was a woman. His punches just kept coming. He knocked me on my ass more times than I can count. And the pain... God, the pain. It hurt like hell, but it was the first time I felt like I was releasing all the shame and guilt I'd been bottling up inside."

I forced myself to meet her eyes, the words tumbling out more urgently now. "Fighting became my escape. My way out. And I got good. Really fucking good. But it wasn't the fighting I was addicted to—it was the pain. It made me feel... something. A little less invisible. A little less numb. And when I didn't have anyone to ask for help... *it* became my help."

Iya reached across the table and squeezed my hand. "Delia, what happened to me wasn't your fault. You were a kid too—you can't keep doing this to yourself. I get it, you want to fight. You want to let it all out in the ring. But do you really need to keep competing? Does it have to be that brutal? Why not just train hard and leave it at that?"

I swallowed, forcing the lump in my throat down. "Those words sound oddly familiar," I muttered, my mind immediately flashing to Okiyo's constant pushing and prodding.

Iya's face tilted down slightly, her eyes peeking up at mine with a mischievous glint. "Familiar words coming from a *goodt* looking British guy, perhaps?" she teased, her smile widening as she clearly opened the door to talk about him.

Of course, she'd find a way to drag him into this. I would love to say I was saved by the bell, but before I could answer Iya's question about Okiyo, our mother strolled in, right on cue.

Mine and Iya's conversation was much needed and I was able to release some of the guilt I'd been harboring. But with the release of the guilt came anger that had been simmering for years boiled up at the site of my mother.

Mom slid into the chair, completely oblivious to the storm brewing between us.

"Hey, my girls," she greeted, sliding into the seat with the elegance of a queen. "Y'all care to share what's got you two over here all huddled up like Bonnie and Clyde?"

Her voice was light, like this was just another brunch, just another day. Meanwhile, I was fighting to keep from breaking down right there in front of her. But that was the story, wasn't it? I'd been breaking for years, and she hadn't noticed.

Iya must've sensed it. She spoke up first, her hand finding my shoulder in comfort, squeezing lightly.

"I think you and Delia need to talk," she said softly. Then, she grabbed her phone and stood, giving me one last reassuring look before walking out to the patio, leaving us alone at the table.

Mom's eyes flickered from Iya to me, confusion etched into her features. "Talk about what? Iya said you were going to tell us something about a fight. This wouldn't have anything to do with that fine man you brought to the party would it?" She chuckled nervously, picking up the menu, yet to actually look at me.

She sat across from me, still as elegant as ever, her perfume clouding the space between us.

"Wow," I sighed. "Iya said..." I let that sit there between us for a moment and just looked at her.

Mom blinked, a hint of confusion crossing her face when she finally registered the tears running down mine.

"Are you serious? Iya tells you that we need to talk. You and *Delia*—" I said, my voice trembling with disbelief. "And you start off with *Iya said*? Wow!"

She blinked, clearly taken aback by my tone. "Well, I—"

"You don't get it, do you?" The words burst out of me, quick and sharp, the anger laced through every syllable. "You haven't gotten it for years. You haven't asked how I've been in *years*."

Her mouth opened as if to say something, but no words came out. For once, she seemed to realize that she couldn't smooth this over with a dismissive laugh and a change of subject.

"All this time, you've put everything into Iya," I continued, my voice rising. "After what happened to her—after she was assaulted—you threw me into therapy and never checked in again. It's like I didn't exist anymore."

"That's not true," she said, but there was no strength in her voice.

"Oh, isn't it? What about the jokes you made when you saw the bruises after my fights? Or the fact that you didn't even know I stopped going to therapy until a year after I quit? Or when I got my degree, the one I busted my ass for? You never even asked why I became someone's assistant instead of an architect, did you?"

Her face softened, confusion turning to pain, but it wasn't enough. Not yet.

"I needed you too, Mom." I could hear the crack in my voice now. "But it was always about Iya. You protected her, and I get it. She needed you. But I needed you too."

Mom's face registered understanding of what I was trying to say, her lips parting slightly, but no words came out. For once, she just actually listened.

"You sent me to therapy for a while," I continued, my voice growing stronger. "And thought that was all I needed after finding my sister with blood on her thighs. You left me to be *handled* by a stranger. It was a full year later before you even realized I wasn't going anymore. You threw me in there to keep me busy, to keep me out of the way while you focused on Iya. And I don't blame you for wanting to protect her, but damn it, I needed you too!"

Her hand moved instinctively toward mine, but I pulled back.

"You know why I never brought anyone home to meet you? Because I didn't know how to let anyone in. I didn't know how to *let* anyone care for me because I didn't feel like I was worth it. You only cared about what I looked like on the outside—" I paused needing to catch my breath.

Her eyes filled with tears. "Delia, I didn't realize... I was so focused on keeping Iya safe after—" she broke off, her voice trembling, "after what happened. And then, losing your father..."

I felt a fresh wave of emotion crash over me at the mention of my dad. His absence had left a gaping hole in all our lives, and it only compounded everything I went through. I had never had the space to grieve him properly, not with everything happening with Iya.

"We all lost him," I said quietly, my voice breaking. "But I lost you too. You shut me out after Iya was assaulted. You stopped seeing me. You stopped being my mother after Dad died. I thought it was my fault. I thought you stopped loving me. That I wasn't worth loving."

Tears spilled down her cheeks now, and she reached for me again, her hand trembling. This time, I didn't pull away.

"I'm sorry, Delia," she whispered, her voice raw with regret. "I didn't mean to make you feel that way. I thought... I thought you were okay."

I shook my head, finally meeting her eyes. "I wasn't okay, Mom. I'm still not okay."

The silence between us stretched long and thick, punctuated by the quiet sobs of my mother.

"I'm sorry," she whispered again, gripping my hand. "I didn't know how to be there for both of you. And it's no excuse Delia, but when your father died, I thought I was doing what he needed me to do, protect his baby."

"I was your baby, too." I said. I could feel the weight of my anger beginning to lift, just a little, as I watched my mothers body racked with tears.

I squeezed her hand, feeling my own tears slip down my face. "We can figure it out. But you have to start seeing me. I need you to see me."

Her head dipped, her shoulders shaking as she nodded. "Baby, I am so, so sorry, Delia. Please forgive me. I love you and I want to be there for you. I'm just please asking you to let me in. You've been so closed off. And that's not on me. As your mother, I should have checked on you. Did more to check in with you. I just... How can I fix this?"

I looked at her for a long moment, searching her face for sincerity. And for the first time in years, I felt the support of my mom.

"Well first we can talk about my upcoming fight," I said, my eyes softening on her before I looked out the window raising my hand to wave Iya back inside.

Iya threw me a wink before settling back into her chair. She grabbed both mine and mom's hand and squeezed. I looked around the table. It actually felt like for the first time in a long time, everything was going to be ok. That we were ok. I began telling them about my upcoming match in Tulum.

"MMA?" My mom raised a brow, tears now dried from the napkin she still had clutched in her hand. She had the classic *'I know my babies, but I don't know this ugly ass baby'* look on her face when I explained I'd started MMA training years ago. "Like... Kimbo Slice MMA?" She said almost in disbelief.

Iya chuckled, never missing a beat. "Now, *Ma*, you know that man's been dead for some time now, but... yeah, something like that."

Mom's face twisted in a mix of confusion and disbelief. She shot me a look while simultaneously flagging down the nearest waiter, her finger circling in the air. "Oh, no. I need a drink *neow* before we go any further. Waiter! Three mimosas, please—and *make'em* strong, baby!"

She turned back to me, shaking her head like she just couldn't fathom it. "Now, why in the world would you wanna go and do that? You're too pretty to be getting punched on?"

"It's... complicated. It started out as a way to cope, I hesitated, catching Iya's eye, "But I've gotten really good at it. So good, that I have a title fight in Mexico coming up."

"Oh no, Delia," my mom protested, "You can't do this—"

I cut her off short. "Yes. I *can* do this. I appreciate your concern, but you don't get to interject in my life after one conversation and one apology."

Iya nodded her head accepting that my decision was made. Our mom sighed, her eyes full of that special blend of motherly concern and weariness. "Ok. You're right, but Delia, please be careful."

My phone buzzed, just as my mom launched into another round of questions about MMA. I glanced at the screen—Rhiyan. *Perfect timing.*

I sent her a message late Friday night, asking for some time off for a "trip," but I hadn't exactly explained the real reason. The fight? Well, that part I hadn't quite worked up the nerve to share with her even knowing I'd be spilling the beans to Iya and my mom today.

I excused myself from the table with a quick, "I'll be right back. Work call."

"Girl, you don't ever stop working, huh?" Iya teased, already swirling her strawberry garnish in the remaining swig of Mimosa in her glass.

"Order me a Long Island Iced Tea—top shelf," I called over my shoulder with a grin. "I'm gonna need more than a Mimosa."

I walked out to the patio, taking a deep breath before answering. "Hey, Rhiyan. You got my message, I see."

"I did and just wanted to follow up on your request for time off. You mentioned needing some days away and I just wanted to make sure everything was ok."

"Yes. Everything is fine. I'm not exactly sure how long but I'm taking a trip down to Mexico and just wanted to let you know before I book the trip. I can fill you in on the details as I get them. Is that Ok?"

"Heck yeah it's ok. You and Okiyo have been working really hard on the security planning. You deserve some time off. Just fill out the leave request. I'll approve it."

"Ok. I will. Thanks Rhiyan."

"Take care of yourself. And if you need anything while you're out, just holler."

Heading back to the table, I spotted my drink waiting for me—tall, cold, and exactly what I needed.

The rest of brunch flowed much easier. We laughed, shared stories, and for the first time in ages, I felt that old, easy rhythm with Mom and Iya come back.

As we were getting ready to leave, Mom leaned in close for a hug, lowering her voice. "Let's talk again real soon, Delia. I will be checking in on you more. And if you're up to it, maybe you can tell me about that fine Okiyo from the other night. I can tell he's really into you."

I chuckled, squeezing her tighter. "I'd like that."

Chapter 25 – Okiyo

I STOOD OVER THE dining room table, maps of Tulum laid out in front of me like pieces of a puzzle waiting to be solved. King had just wrapped up the logistics, and everything was in place. Secluded villa, ruins tucked away from prying eyes, perfect for training, and just enough off the radar to keep Delia safe. But something about this trip had my mind spinning, more than just the fight ahead.

"That's perfect," I said, already thinking ahead. "Charter a flight for us. I don't want anyone on the ground knowing we're there until it's too late."

"You got it, boss," King replied, but then, as usual, he couldn't help himself. "But man, three weeks alone with that woman? In a villa by the ocean? You sure you're there for security, or are you planning to finally lose that cool of yours?"

I rolled my eyes, but a faint smirk tugged at my lips. "Focus, King."

He laughed, that low southern drawl. "I am focused. You're the one who's gonna have a hard time focusing—if you know what I mean."

"Delia's my priority," I said, knowing there was more weight to those words than I intended. I didn't want to admit it, not even to myself. But King wasn't wrong—three weeks with Delia, alone in Tulum, was bound to stir something up.

"You say that now," King replied, still chuckling. "But a woman like her, in a place like that? Shit, Okiyo, the storm's comin' and you're already standing in the eye of it."

King's words had a way of sticking. There was truth to them, even if I wasn't ready to acknowledge it fully. "Just make sure the villa is secure and the ruins are ready for what we need."

"The ruins are perfect for training," King said, switching gears like the pro he was. "Old Mayan structures, abandoned in parts, with enough rugged terrain to put her through hell and back. Secluded enough for privacy, close enough to the villa so she can rest in between sessions."

"And the villa?" I asked, even though I already knew the answer.

"Exclusive. Private beach. Ocean views that'll make you forget why you're there in the first place. You know the deal—it's paradise, man. And it's all yours... well, hers too. But I know you're smart enough not to mix business and pleasure, right?"

Before I could respond, my phone buzzed again. Delia. I glanced at the clock, guessing she'd just wrapped up brunch with Iya and their mom.

"Send me the details as soon as they're final, King. Need to take this call."

I swiped to answer. "Hey."

"Hey," she replied, her voice lighter than I expected, but I could still sense a little weariness beneath the surface. "Just finished brunch. Survived."

"Barely, I'm guessing."

She laughed, and damn if that sound didn't do something to me. "Yeah, barely. It got pretty ugly, but I think we're going to be ok. All of us."

"Glad to hear it. You ready for the trip down to Mexico?"

"Yeah. I talked with Rhiyan. Told her I needed some time off. That I would share the details once I had a clearer understanding of the date. Of course I didn't say fight date. But just let her know I'd request the days once I had more details."

"Well I got some dates for you. We'll leave soon—details are coming your way."

There was a pause on her end. "Soon, huh? Just like that?"

I chuckled, low. "Just like that."

And as I hung up, my mind spun again. Three weeks alone with Delia, on an island that was as beautiful as it was dangerous. I'd told myself it was all about the fight, all about making sure she was ready for whatever came next in that ring. But I knew better.

The ruins in Tulum would break her down and build her back up. And me? Well, I had my own storm brewing. A tempest named Delia and I was at the center of it.

I was falling for her, though I kept trying to pretend I wasn't. Three weeks. I just needed to keep my head straight for three weeks.

But I knew better. This wasn't just about training anymore, or even about keeping her safe.

"I cannot believe you did all of this," she did a three hundred sixty degree turn in mid stride as we walked across the tarmac to the waiting private jet. "When—*how* did you even book this?"

"Enough Delia. I'll explain on the plane." I grabbed her hand and tugged her swiftly towards the steps that we'd ascend to board.

She only hesitated for a moment more as she took it all in, much like she'd done when we entered the private terminal at Hartsfeld Jackon International with its own TSA and chauffeured BMW that drove us as close to our plane as it could legally get. She then held her hat to her head so not to lose it to the gust of air from the spinning propellors and moved as fast as she could in the heels on her feet to catch up to me.

I'd told Delia about my plans for her training and the need to get to Mexico sooner rather than waiting until the fight. She needed enough time to acclimate. And yes, even the private flight was a necessary safety precaution.

The flight had been smooth. But the air between us carried the weight of everything that was coming. As the coastline of Mexico began to come into view, I could see her whole body lean toward the window, mesmerized by the stretch of azure waters below. The beaches were ribbons of white sand, framed by the vibrant green of the jungle spilling toward the ocean. The waves glistened under the sun, a postcard from paradise.

Delia's lips parted slightly, her breath caught in the awe of the scene. "I finally get to see the place my father was born," she said to herself as her eyes glossed over at the sight. I could feel the emotional pull it had on her.

"It's beautiful isn't it?"

"Yes." She nodded, swiping at her tears before turning from the window to look at me. "This swanky ass plane is great and all," she said with an approving once over at its luxury. Her eyes still shimmered with tears but a smile broke through as she continued, "But I cannot wait for us to land."

"Me too. You're gonna love the villa," I said, keeping my tone light. She was about to step into a place of beauty, but she had no idea the hell I was about to put her through in that same villa.

Training would be excruciating. I was going to push her to her limits.

She nodded, her eyes back on the coastline, the ruins of ancient temples barely visible through the intermittent cloud cover. The sun danced on the water's surface, casting everything in gold.

When we arrived, Delia's eyes indeed widened in surprise.

"*Oh my God.* This place is breathtaking." She said of the villa perched on the edge of the jungle with a view of the Tulum ruins in the distance. It indeed was a decadent monument to paradise. King had shared the images of the compound prior to me agreeing on the location. It was indeed opulent, but I settled on it more for its isolation. The perfect blend of luxury and seclusion.

The single story structure was wrapped in floor-to-ceiling windows that invited in the vibrant greens of the jungle and the deep blues of the Caribbean from almost every room. Every inch of the place screamed indulgence, from the intricate stonework to the private infinity pool glistening below.

The lush outdoor terraces were impressive, but what really caught my eye was the dojo-style room at the back, overlooking the pool—perfect for the intense training I had planned for Delia. King had even arranged for gear to be shipped in from a local contact—everything we needed to train and spar with.

Four bedrooms, each more succulent than the next. The kind of places where you'd sink into the bed and forget the world existed.

Plush linens, marble floors, and warm golden light pouring in from the oversized windows. I couldn't help but imagine... No. This wasn't the time for that. Delia and I would be sleeping in separate rooms—I'd made sure of that. Still, as I glanced at each bedroom, a familiar heat stirred low in my gut, harder to ignore than I'd like to admit.

Her voice cut through my thoughts. "I knew Tulum was a tourist's paradise and had some great resorts, but I never imagined this. All I ever really heard about Mexico was from my father's stories," she said softly, her voice tinged with nostalgia. "He used to tell me about growing up in the barrio... nothing like this, though."

I nodded, trying to refocus. "This isn't about luxury, Viper," I reminded her, keeping my tone steady. "This is about preparing you for the fight of your life."

Undaunted, a slow smile crept across her lips. "Well, you sure know how to pick a nice place for," she paused, biting her lip before allowing her eyes to sensually caress my face, "sparring." Her eyes were filled with mischief. "If I didn't know any better, I'd think you were trying to impress me."

That damn mouth of hers. Her words and the lip biting caused me to shake my head. If she only knew what both did to me. If she knew the thoughts racing through my head, the tension pulling tight in my groin, she wouldn't torture me so. I shook my head again, chuckling this time. She absolutely *would* torture me. Of course, my face betrayed none of these thoughts.

Delia twisted her lips and simply nodded at my deflection.

"Well, I see *your* wall is back up." Her expression hardened. She walked away presumably to continue her exploration of the house. Her confident stride pulled my gaze after her. I couldn't tear my eyes away from her retreating back. Determination was set on her face when she tossed a curt, "I'll be ready to *spar*," over her shoulder. Bloody hell. The real question was would I be? How was I supposed to stay focused on anything other than the sway of her hips?

I was here to protect her, train her. But all I could think about was the storm brewing between us. This wasn't just a villa in paradise. It was the stage for something much bigger. And as she disappeared into the hallway released an audible groan.

We arrived early in the morning, but it was already a warm 85 degrees outside. I'd been staring out at the pool when Delia made her way back over after exploring the remaining parts of the house. The slight irritation she'd exhibited earlier had seemingly dissipated.

Delia stood beside me; her eyes locked on the view as well. The coastline stretched out beyond the pool's edge. I could feel the awe in her silence, the quiet admiration as she took it all in.

She let out a slow breath.

"How are you feeling," I asked, sensing her mood.

"Okay, I guess. This just all feels like paradise." Her eyes looked out over the pool and at the beauty of the tropical horizon beyond. "But you basically said it earlier. We're here to get ready for this fight."

I smirked. Glad her mood had lightened. "Well we're not starting today. Rest up and enjoy this," I said, following her gaze before moving to step away, "while you can. I'll be in the study. Need to get a few things done."

"Work?" she asked, finally breaking her gaze from the view to look at me. "But we pretty much finished the security revisions."

I nodded, my tone serious. "We're here for training, Viper, remember? There's a lot to be done before we even get started."

She didn't respond immediately. Instead, she glanced down at the pool, her brow furrowing as if deep in thought. I turned away, already plotting out the logistics in my head. But just as I took my first step toward the villa, the sharp splash of cold water hit my back.

I stopped in my tracks, frozen.

Delia's laughter rang out behind me, light and teasing, but I didn't turn around.

"You didn't just do that," I muttered under my breath.

"I did indeed," she mimicked my accent as was becoming her go to way of getting under my skin.

Her laughter grew louder, and I could hear her shuffling behind me, like she was getting ready for round two. I turned slowly, my eyes locking on hers. She had already kicked off her shoes and pants. The last button of her shirt was now free.

"I think you need to relax, O," she said, peeling off the shirt and tossing it onto a nearby chair. She stood before me in a simple black bra and matching panties, her skin glowing in the soft mid-morning light.

"Delia," I warned, keeping my voice steady, "I've got work—"

"Tomorrow," she interrupted. She moved toward the pool, dipping a foot into the water. "We start tomorrow. Right now, we're here, and it's beautiful." She descended the steps into the pool backwards, sinking into the water, her eyes still locked on mine.

I shook my head, trying to fight the pull of her energy. "You enjoy yourself. I've got things to—"

She didn't wait for me to finish. With a sudden, purposeful splash, she sent another wave of water directly at me, soaking my shirt and pants. I stood there, stunned for a moment, before narrowing my eyes at her. She floated there, grinning like she'd won some kind of battle.

"Delia..." I started, but she was already backing away in the pool, her arms floating lazily on the surface as she smirked.

I sighed, knowing full well I had lost this round. There was no use trying to fight it. Not here. Not with her.

Without a word, I pulled my shirt over my head, dropping it onto the chair beside hers, then kicked off my shoes and stripped down to my boxers. My focus was solely on her, floating there, her confidence and playfulness radiating from every inch of her.

"Happy now?" I asked, stepping into the pool.

Her smirk deepened. "Maybe."

I waded toward her, the water lapping gently at my waist as I closed the distance between us. She didn't back away, didn't flinch. She was testing me, I could tell. The tension between us shifted—this wasn't just playful anymore.

But I kept it together. I kept my focus.

Tomorrow, we'll start training, and it would be brutal. But right now? Right now, I picked her up as high over my head as I could and dunked her completely under the water.

She came up sputtering the salty water of the natural pool and pulling the curtain of curls out of her face. She was a sight. I quite literally howled in laughter. *Payback.*

Chapter 26 – Delia

DAY ONE OF TRAINING, and Okiyo did not come to fucking play. No pool time. No rest. Just heat, mosquitoes, and these dusty ass ruins staring me down as I ran up and down the ancient stone steps. My lungs were burning by the fourth lap, and sweat was dripping into places I didn't even know could sweat. It was at least a billion degrees outside.

"Damn, Okiyo!" I gasped, my breath coming in ragged bursts as I dragged myself up another set of stairs. "I thought we'd at least get breakfast before you threw me into the fire. Are you even gonna let a girl eat?"

"Move your ass, Delia," he snapped back, all military authority. "You're running like you've got a stick up your ass or like you're a 90-year-old woman."

I rolled my eyes, muttering a quiet "shut up" under my breath before picking up the pace. It wasn't like I didn't know what to expect. He'd been dead serious ever since he got out of that pool yesterday. No intimate time, no lingering looks, just a clear-as-day order: *Be up by 5 a.m.*

Jerk didn't even give me a chance to charm him into my bed last night. Like, how he was ok with pleasuring me with his fingers but hadn't allowed me to ride his juicy dick was beyond me. Nope. Instead, Mr. *Dutiful* made sure I had a decent meal last night, ensured I was comfortable—then left me alone to prep for *this*. I thought we'd wake up and ease into the training. But no. I woke up to this *hell*.

Hell, at this point, were we ever going to cross the deep stroke bridge? Even in the midst of these drills, with my sweat glands running like a river, I wanted him bad. He'd taken off his damn shirt and those abs had my river running *there* too.

But fine. If he wanted to play hard to get and a tough guy, I could play the game too. I pushed harder, determined not to let him see how much I was struggling in this heat. Every lap, every step, I dug deeper. I knew what was at stake. Even if he wouldn't ease up on the training or the dick, I had a point to prove.

Out of the corner of my eye, I saw him smirking at me, like he knew exactly what buttons he was pressing. He might've been tough, but I was getting to him too. Yesterday's playful water fight showed me that much.

"This is where your endurance gets tested," he called out as I finally reached the top again, my legs feeling like jelly. "You need to outlast your opponent. The fight's gonna be brutal, Delia. You need to be tougher."

I gritted my teeth, ignoring the way my body screamed in protest, and forced myself to keep going. Four more rounds of this hell, up and down, up and down, until my legs just gave out. I was done. Spent.

"All right," Okiyo finally said, that smug tone making me want to punch him. "We're done here. Sprint back to the villa."

"What?" I blinked at him like he'd lost his damn mind. "You dragged me through the jungle, made me run these death stairs, and now you want me to sprint back to the villa? I don't even know where the villa is, Okiyo!"

He just looked at me, completely unfazed. "Well, you better get moving and find it before it gets dark. You don't wanna be out here by yourself."

And with that, he took off, his long strides quickly eating up the distance. He didn't even look back. That bastard was really gonna leave me out here if I didn't get my ass in gear.

I cursed under my breath and started running, each step feeling heavier than the last. The sun was high, the air thick and humid, and the mosquitoes were relentless, but I couldn't help it. As I ran, something caught my eye—a wild patch of dahlias, growing defiantly in the midst of the jungle's chaos. Their bright, vibrant petals looked so out of place in all the green.

I slowed down, just for a second, admiring how they thrived out here, growing wild and free. Just like me.

But of course, Okiyo's voice rang in my head, reminding me of what was at stake. I shook my head, pulling myself back into the moment. No time to admire flowers. I had a fight to win.

It had taken three full days of running through the jungle with Okiyo, up and down the ancient temple steps of Tulum, before my body finally started to acclimate to the suffocating humidity. It was brutal. Okiyo was relentless, pushing me beyond my limits. But I got it.

My lungs burned less, my legs no longer felt like they were on fire, and my stamina was transforming before my very eyes. I could feel the change in myself, the way my body was adapting—getting stronger, faster. Even my reflection in the mirror showed it. My muscles were beginning to pop in ways I hadn't expected. Honestly, I was starting to look like a shorter version of Megan Thee Stallion, and let's just say... I wasn't mad about the attention. Catching those steely glances from one of the most handsome men I'd ever seen didn't hurt either.

This morning, I woke up expecting the same routine—ruins, running, and more running. I was lacing up my tennis shoes when Okiyo strolled into the great room, cool as ever.

"Go change. Put on a swimsuit," he said casually, like that was a normal request in the middle of *hell week*.

I paused mid-lace, blinking up at him. "Wait, are you serious? A day off?" I let myself relax, already thinking about which cute swimsuit I was about to put on for some long overdue beach time.

But just as quickly, Okiyo burst my bubble with a low, stiff laugh, that damn half-smirk curling at his lips.

"Nope. We're sparring." He held up two long sticks I hadn't noticed until now, and I groaned internally. "You need to learn to block, deflect, and counter with precision. They won't be playing fair with you, Delia. If someone picks up a stick, you better know how to pick up one too—and know how to use it."

I dropped my head back against the chair and sighed dramatically, but deep down, he was right. No one was going to take it easy on me, and I couldn't afford to slack. I glanced back at him, catching that intense glint in his eye that sent a shiver down my spine.

"Alright, alright," I muttered, dragging myself up. "But if I'm gonna be getting my ass kicked on a beach, I'm at least going to look good doing it." I shot him a teasing look before heading to change. He gave nothing away, just nodded like the stoic beast he was.

And just like that, he walked out the back door of the villa, leaving me standing there with my mouth wide open as I watched him disappear into the jungle. Seriously, did this man think I had a built-in GPS to find all these hidden spots? Zero cares given about leaving me in the dust. Typical Okiyo.

But I was getting used to his tactics. Slowly, I was learning to think quicker on my feet, to keep up with the way he kept me off balance. So, instead of standing there pouting for too long, I did what he asked—no, demanded—and headed upstairs to put on my swimsuit. But if he thought he could bark orders at me without consequence, he had another thing coming.

I wasn't just going to give him a swim-ready Delia. Nope. I was about to give him a distraction he wouldn't soon forget.

The two-piece I chose wasn't just a swimsuit. It was *the* swimsuit. The kind of bikini that left nothing to the imagination—the yellow scrap of fabric barely covered what it needed to in the front, and my curves weren't exactly tamed by it either. The top? Two triangles, tight and teasing. If he wanted to test my limits, I was about to test his focus.

By the time I made it to the beach, Okiyo was already into his morning capoeira. His movements were mesmerizing, fluid and controlled, every muscle in his body taut with precision. But I knew his tell. His eyes would narrow just slightly whenever something caught him off guard. And when I strolled up in that bikini, I saw it—those crinkled, narrowed eyes.

Got him.

I bent down to untie the laces of my tennis shoes, slowly, because he was watching. My back to him, I pretended like I didn't notice, like I wasn't deliberately taking my sweet time. That's when I felt it—his shin connecting with my ankles, throwing me off balance before I even had a chance to react.

I hit the sand face-first, a squeal of surprise escaping my lips. Oh, *hell* no.

Quickly, I rolled to my side and sprang back to my feet. My body moved faster now, more precise. Three days of grueling training had sharpened me up, and though he got me while I wasn't paying attention, little girl Delia was gone. Wrong bitch, wrong era.

Game on.

We moved fluidly across the sand, the sticks clashing in rhythmic patterns. I'd fought with sticks before, but it wasn't my go-to style. Still, it didn't take long for me to catch on to some of the moves Okiyo was using, and in a few instances, I was even able to match him. His strikes were deadly, but my body was smaller, quicker, more agile. I could block and deflect each blow with a flick of my wrist or a well-timed pivot of my hips.

He pushed me harder than ever, testing my reactions with each strike, but I refused to back down. The sun was relentless. Sweat dripped off of me, but I held my own. Each time our sticks met, it sent vibrations through my arms, but instead of wearing me out, it fueled me. I could feel my confidence growing with every block, every deflection, every attack I countered.

Finally, after what felt like an eternity, Okiyo's thick baritone cut through the air. "*Hyte*," he called, his signal that we were done—for now.

I dropped my guard and took a deep breath, knowing this wasn't the end of the day's training. It was just phase one. He crossed over to me, nodding his approval, the hint of a smile on his lips.

"Good job," he said, waving his hand toward the cliffs. "Let's head over there."

I looked in the direction he'd indicated and all I saw were cliffs that rose dramatically on the right side of the beach. Massive slabs of rock jutting up toward the sky. Some easily 15 to 20 feet high, standing like silent giants against the ocean backdrop. I'd seen them in the distance before, but up close, they were breathtaking. Their sheer height and rugged beauty took my breath away. My awe was short-lived.

Okiyo continued, his voice low and calm as he explained. "There's an inlet on the other side. It's about 20 feet deep, and you can dive off the cliffs safely without worrying about rocks below."

I blinked at him, then glanced up at the cliffs again, the water below glittering in the sun. A laugh escaped me before I could stop it.

"And how do you propose we get up there?"

He smirked, his eyes narrowing slightly. "We climb."

"Smart ass," I muttered, leaving him in my dust as I headed in the direction he'd pointed. The climb itself was stunning—wild vegetation creeping up the cliffs, the sun casting shimmering light off the waves below. But I knew better than to expect Okiyo would let me stop and admire the view. No, there would be no distant horizon gazing with him. This was going to be brutal, and strangely enough, I was ready for it. A part of me was even looking forward to whatever madness he had planned.

We reached a secluded spot where the cliffs stood tall and imposing over the churning sea below. My breath caught at the sight. It was beautiful, yes, but the drop? Intimidating as hell. The water below seemed miles away, dark and swirling like a challenge I wasn't sure I was ready to accept.

Okiyo came up beside me, nodding towards the edge with a look that told me all I needed to know. "You know how to swim, right?"

I nodded slowly, hesitant, knowing damn well he wasn't planning to jump first. He caught the look on my face and gave me this deadass serious nod, "Belly first."

I spun towards him. "I *know* you fucking lying."

He stood there, arms crossed, like this was some kind of joke, waiting for me to accept the insanity he'd just proposed. Belly first? From a 20-foot cliff? Into the water?

"If I hit that water belly first, it's going to hurt like a *bitch*," I protested, crossing my arms and shaking my head.

"Of course it's going to hurt, Delia," Okiyo said, as if explaining some universal truth. "That's the point. When you get out of the water, you ask yourself, 'But did I die though?' And when the answer is no, you sprint your ass right back up this hill and do it again."

I stared at him, utterly unconvinced. My face must have screamed it because he kept going, spouting off more of that intense MI6-level logic that I couldn't even argue against.

"You need to be able to absorb pain and keep going. This," he gestured toward the cliff, "is training your mind to overcome that fear. You get why I'm doing this?"

I wanted to argue, to call him out for being insane, but even as the words were forming on my tongue, I felt the sharp push against my back. Suddenly, the world was rushing toward me—no, *I* was rushing toward the water. The next thing I knew, I was midair, my arms flailing as I plummeted towards the cold, blue expanse below.

My body hit the water with a stinging force, pain exploding across my chest, stomach, and thighs. It was like being slapped across every inch of my front, and I gasped involuntarily as I sank into the cold embrace of the water.

And then... nothing.

I floated in that brief, weightless silence beneath the surface. My body was humming from the impact, but beneath the water, it was peaceful. The pain started to ebb away as I drifted, weightless and free. I opened my eyes and found myself in a blue oasis, an underwater world that was almost too beautiful for words.

I kicked toward the surface, and as I broke through, sunlight hit my face. The sound of the waves and the world rushed back in, and I felt *alive*. More alive than I had in years.

Above me, Okiyo stood at the cliff's edge, clapping slowly, his eyes glinting with approval. Something clicked at that moment. I felt invincible, like I could conquer anything.

Without even needing his command, I took off. I sprinted back up the hill, feet pounding against the rocky ground, heart pumping with adrenaline. When I reached the top, I didn't hesitate. I dove again.

And again.

Chapter 27 – Okiyo

DELIA'S BODY HAD BEEN pushed to the limit. I could see it in the way she moved, every step labored, her muscles screaming from the cliff dives and endless cardio sessions through the ruins. But beneath her fatigue, there was a glimmer of pride in her eyes.

We walked back to the villa in silence, the sun dipping low on the horizon. For once, I wasn't forcing her to sprint through the jungle or barking orders to keep her on her toes. No, today I let her walk beside me, her pace slower but steady. She'd earned that.

"I must say," I finally broke the silence, my tone light with genuine admiration, "I'm impressed. You've done more today than most could handle." I meant every word. Watching her push past the pain, past the mental barriers had been something to see.

Delia's eyebrows raised slightly as her eyes flicked to mine. Her smile was soft, sheepish even, as if my words had caught her off guard. She glanced down, eyebrows raised in disbelief. Despite the exhaustion weighing on her limbs, I could see the energy radiating off her, the spark in her words.

"I didn't think I could do half of what we did today. But now..." She paused, her eyes gleaming with excitement. "I feel like I'm ready to take on whoever the hell they throw in the ring with me."

A smile tugged at my lips, but a shadow of concern lingered. "And what if," I said, my tone more serious, "it's not a woman they throw at you?"

I watched her closely, searching for any sign of hesitation. She met my gaze, her confidence unwavering. Delia wasn't naive. She knew the possibilities, the dangers. The way I'd adjusted her training, made her fight harder than ever before, it was all in preparation for that potential reality.

With a light smile, she answered. "I know you've been thinking about that. It's in the way you've trained me—preparing me for anything. So if they throw a man at me, let him come. I'm ready. You know I'm ready." She winked and gave me a playful bow. "Do not fret, my good English Sir."

I chuckled at her little display, though the thought of her facing a male opponent still gnawed at me. "Hold on to that good feeling," I said, my voice softening. "You say that now, but remember—you're going to be sore as hell tomorrow. Don't get too high on that horse just yet."

We approached the villa, and I guided her inside, her steps heavy but determined. I drew her an ice bath, knowing she would need it to soothe the bruises and stiffness that were bound to hit hard once her adrenaline wore off. She was holding up well, but the physical toll was undeniable.

I opened the door to the bathroom. The warm air met the frigid water in the tub causing steam to rise off the surface. "Go ahead, soak," I said, my tone stern against the wide-eyed look of apprehension she was giving. "Go ahead. You need this, Viper."

Surprisingly, she didn't argue. Just shot me a tired, resigned look and eased herself into the icy water with a wince. I'd given her brief instruction on how to approach the ice bath. Three to five minutes in, three-minute break, repeat until she hit thirty minutes total.

As I closed the door behind me, I caught one last glimpse of her, eyes closed, a faint smile on her lips despite the cold. She was tough. Tougher than anyone I knew.

I left her there and went to the kitchen to start dinner, giving her some space to unwind. But even with busying myself with preparing our meal, I couldn't stop thinking about the fire I'd seen in her today. Damn if I didn't find her even more appealing.

My phone buzzed as I was chopping vegetables. It was King with an update on some supplies I'd requested. I exchanged a few quick messages, my mind half on the conversation and half on Delia.

By the time I returned to check on her, she was no longer in the bath. I frowned. Thirty minutes had not gone by. The villa was quiet, but I had a sense of where she'd be. My feet carried me toward the dojo, and as I entered the hallway, the sound of wood clashing against wood confirmed my suspicion.

She was there, in the dojo, moving through the stick forms I'd taught her earlier. The skylights cast a soft glow on her, illuminating the sheen of sweat that glistened on her skin. She was lost in the rhythm, each motion precise and deliberate, her body flowing with a confidence that was intoxicating to watch.

I leaned against the doorframe, arms crossed, observing her. There was something about the way she moved—graceful, yet powerful. I watched her without intruding. It gave me a chance to see her as she truly was, unguarded and focused.

When she finally noticed me, she didn't stop. She simply raised one hand, beckoning me to join her. A slow smile tugged at the corner of my mouth. She was getting bold. I liked that. Without a word, I crossed the room and grabbed another stick, falling into stance opposite her.

"Keep up," I said, my voice low and challenging.

Her grin widened as she responded, "Bring it."

We began to spar, the energy between us electric. I didn't hold back—I never did. My strikes were hard, my movements fast and unrelenting. But she was keeping up, blocking, deflecting, countering with a skill that impressed me. She was learning fast, and that only fueled the intensity between us. Each movement was charged with something more than just training. It was primal, raw. Lust.

The memory of our kiss—the way I'd taken her that night, the way she'd melted against me—flashed in my mind. As our sticks clashed in rapid succession, I couldn't shake the thought of her soft lips, the taste of her skin, the way she'd trembled beneath my touch. I could see the same fire in her eyes now as we sparred, the same hunger. It mirrored my own.

She moved with purpose, her strikes gaining confidence, her body fluid and fierce. Then, in a flash, she found an opening. I barely saw it coming. She ducked under one of my strikes, twisting her body with a speed I hadn't anticipated. Before I could react, she wrapped her legs around my waist, pulling me off balance and bringing me down to the mat with her body pinning mine.

The shock of it hit me as we landed, her chest pressed against mine, her breath hot against my skin. My hands instinctively went to her hips, gripping her tightly, unsure whether to push her off or pull her closer. The air between us was thick with tension, and for a moment, everything else disappeared. It was just her and me, the heat of our bodies, the weight of our desire hanging between us.

Her eyes locked with mine. I saw a flicker of emotion in them. She didn't attempt to hide it. I held her gaze as the possibility of how this moment would play out ran through my mind.

"What are you waiting for?" she whispered. Her voice was barely audible but it cut through my musings and the pounding of my heart.

I didn't answer with words. I didn't need to. My grip on her hips tightened, and in one swift motion, I rolled us over, reversing our positions so I was the one on top. The sticks clattered to the floor, forgotten. My lips crashed against hers, the kiss fierce and demanding, mirroring the intensity of our sparring.

Her legs wrapped around my waist, pulling me closer, and I could feel the heat of her body through the thin fabric of her shorts. My hand slipped between us, pulling the waistband of her shorts down, finding the slick center of her arousal. She was so wet and ready. This time, I didn't hesitate. Couldn't control my need for her any longer. I quickly pulled the drawstring of my pants and freed my aching knob, positioning the tip at her entrance. I paused only to meet her gaze for her permission.

Her eyes were half-closed, her lips parted as she nodded, giving me all the permission I needed. With a deep groan, I sank into her, her body welcoming me in a way that left no space between us. I roughly yanked her spandex shorts the rest of the way down to her knees. She wiggled her legs the rest of the way out of them and opened for me. I sank deeper into the slippery, throbbing wetness of her pussy. Her back arched and she pressed her hips up to meet mine as a sensuous moan escaped her lips.

We moved together, the dojo floor hard beneath us. I took care not to crush her under my weight. The only thing that mattered was the way her body responded to mine, the way our movements were synchronized in a dance that was both a battle and a surrender. Her nails dug into my back, pulling me deeper. I gave her all of me, burying my rigidness to the hilt in her.

Everything else fell away. The fight, the training, the looming threat of what was to come. It all disappeared, leaving just the two of us, and raw need. The storm between us was raging with a force that neither of us could stop.

And I didn't want to.

We lay there on the dojo floor for a while, clinging to each other. I didn't want to let go for fear of us losing the moment. The silence between us was heavy but comforting. As I held her, skin warm against mine, one thing was certain—I'd never get my fill of her. Not now. Not ever.

After a while, I slipped from beneath her and padded on bare feet to the bath. This time in the ensuite bath where Delia slept. I began to run her a hot bath. The water filled the tub slowly, the steam curling up to meet the cool air in the room. It was the kind of warmth that would soothe her muscles and ease the tension without negating the effects of the ice bath earlier.

I called her and she lazily made her way to the room, a look of satiety on her languid face. She was pliable and acquiescent in her post coital glow.

While Delia was preparing for the bath, I slipped into the kitchen and plated the food I'd prepared earlier onto smaller saucers. I added Fresh fruits, a bit of grilled chicken, nothing heavy. The truth was, I needed to clear my head. I'd planned to leave her in the bath with her food settled on the side of the tub so she could dine on it and fully relax, while I took my plate back to my own chambers.

When I came back to the bathroom, she was already sinking into the water, the soft light of candles she'd lit dancing off her skin. The steam rose around her, enveloping her in a delicate veil. She looked peaceful for the first time all day, her eyes closed, her lips parted in a soft sigh.

I placed her plate on the edge of the tub. "I'll leave you to it," I murmured, rising, about to head for the door with my own plate.

Before I could move to leave, I felt her hand wrap around mine. The touch was gentle but firm, stopping me in my tracks. I turned to face her, and her eyes were soft, pleading in a way that sent a wave of warmth through my chest.

"Join me," she whispered, her voice fragile, but the need behind it was undeniable.

For a moment, I hesitated. But the way she looked at me... how could I deny her? Hell, how could I deny myself?

I set my plate down and untied the loose pants allowing them to fall to my feet before stepping out of them completely naked. Her eyes never left mine, her gaze lingering in a way that made my pulse quicken. The water lapped gently at her shoulders as I slid into the tub behind her. She shifted slightly, allowing me to slip in, her back resting against my chest. My arms naturally wrapped around her, pulling her close, the warmth of the water mingling with the heat of her skin.

We sat there in silence, the crackle of the candles and the soft hum of music filling the space. I could feel her muscles beginning to relax against me, her breathing slowing as the tension melted away. I rested my chin lightly on her shoulder, taking in the scent of her hair.

After a few moments, she spoke, her voice barely above a whisper.

"What were you dreaming about that night?" She asked.

"Hmm?" I murmured, unsure of what she meant.

"The night of the fight with Storm. You were having a fitful dream. It's why I ended up on the floor with you. I wanted to cover you with the blanket from the bed and you grabbed me."

"Mmm. Yes. I remember," I said quietly, contemplating whether to share the dream with her.

My muscles involuntarily tightened as the memories of that night flooded back.

I hadn't ever wanted to talk about it. Had never talked about the recurring dream with anyone. I forced the tension from my shoulders. Not exactly sure where I should begin.

"It wasn't just a dream, Delia," I said softly, my voice low and rough. "It was a memory."

She turned slightly in my arms, her eyes wide with concern.

"It was about my parents." I continued, feeling the familiar tightness in my chest as I spoke. "And my brother."

I could feel her body still. Her hand reached for mine under the water, our fingers intertwining. The gesture encouraged me to continue.

"We were kids, running from the violence that surrounded us. Genocide. My father sent us down the river, told us to hide in the thicket. But..." My voice faltered, the image of my brother's last moments flashing vividly in my mind. "My brother didn't make it. I later learned that my parents didn't either and after some time in an refugee camp. I was adopted by a family in the UK."

The silence between us was thick, heavy with the weight of my words. She stayed quiet, but her grip on my hand tightened, grounding me in the present.

"I became who I am because of that day. I joined MI6 to make sure I'd never be that weak again. I needed control. Over my life, over everything."

She shifted again, turning more fully towards me, her eyes locked on mine. She didn't say anything just gave me her silent comfort. A silent decree that I wasn't alone and it was ok to not want to relive the memory.

I'd wrapped myself in her silence. The walls I'd built around my heart began to crumble, piece by piece, and for the first time in a long time, I let someone see the vulnerable parts of me.

"Why was that memory triggered on that night?" she asked softly.

The silence wore on for a bit. The only other sound the gentle splash of water.

I closed my eyes, the memory of it still so vivid. "That night, when Storm issued that illegal blow... I saw it happening in slow motion. Then you fell face forward to the mat, it mirrored my brother's body falling to the ground when he was shot down."

She stiffened again, a soft gasp escaped her lips but she didn't pull away. Instead, she pressed closer, her breath warm against my skin. "My God," she whispered, her voice trembling.

I held her tighter, resting my cheek against the top of her head, feeling the weight of the years of holding on to my own grief. The world around us faded into the background, leaving just the two of us, wrapped in warmth and understanding.

Chapter 28 – Delia

T HE STEAM FROM LAST night's bath still clung to my skin, the weight of Okiyo's traumatic childhood pressed against my chest. We hadn't spoken much since then, but it wasn't the heavy silence of before. He'd let me in and something between us had shifted.

Over breakfast, Okiyo suggested we step away from the villa, from the intensity of our training. *Take a break,* he'd said. Hell yes. I needed a break and wasn't asking any questions in case he changed his mind. And now, here we were, walking hand in hand through the heart of Tulum.

The vibrant streets felt like they were pulling me in. The hum of laughter, the quick flick of conversations I couldn't fully understand, as my Spanish was elementary at best. The scent of fresh tortillas frying nearby wafted up into the air and surrounded us—it was alive, more alive than I had ever imagined. I smiled up at Okiyo in pure heaven as we wandered past a row of colorful stalls. He caught my eye and gave my hand a squeeze, his thumb brushing softly over mine.

"How does it feel to finally be here amongst your father's people?" he asked, his voice low, a soft rumble in the background of the bustling street.

I looked around, trying to capture it all in a single breath. "It feels like... like stepping into one of his stories," I admitted. "Everything he used to say about this place, about the people, the streets... it's surreal." I took a sip of the juice from a street vendor, the tartness waking up my senses even more. "But he never told me it would smell this good." I smirked up at him, grabbing my midsection being extra to emphasize my desire to at least taste something from each of the stalls of food we passed by. letting a bit of the tension slip away.

Okiyo chuckled softly, his hand settling on the small of my back. "You're just greedy."

"No. I'm fucking starving," I said playfully, reaching up to fist the collar and lapel of his button down to pull him to me. I nipped at his lower lip before suckling it between my teeth.

"Mmm..." he moaned, tasting my lips before pulling away with a peck. "Like I said. Greedy." We strolled deeper into the town center.

We ducked into a shaded alley, the heat from the sun finally easing off. Okiyo stopped, pulling me gently into his arms. His fingers curled at my waist as he looked down at me, his eyes lingered on my lips once again as he dipped down to press his forehead against mine. It was sweet. A side of him I'd relish because it was very rare coming from him. Passionate. Protective. Yes. Sweet was not a word to describe Okiyo.

I pulled back, slightly scanning his face. "You good?" I asked, feeling the light tension in his body. "Last night... after everything you shared..." I stammered through my words, not wanting to make the moment awkward.

He let out a breath. "I'm good. Better, actually. I've never shared that with anyone." There was a look of peace that crossed his face.

"I'm glad you did. I feel like I understand you. Helped me understand *us*." I smiled up at him, feeling that warmth again—the kind that made me forget everything except how safe I felt when he was near.

We walked for a while longer, winding our way through the bustling market streets. I could feel the warmth of the sun on my skin, the energy of Tulum seeping into me. The sounds of street vendors calling out, the chatter of locals, and the distant rhythm of a mariachi band playing off in the square—it was almost overwhelming, but in the best way possible.

At one stall, I reached for a woven bracelet, the intricate design catching my eye. Okiyo leaned over my shoulder, his breath warm against my neck. "You should get it," he said, his voice low and soft.

I laughed lightly, running my fingers over the delicate threads. "You trying to buy me trinkets now?"

He smirked, his hand slipping around my waist again, pulling me close. "Nah. I just like seeing you happy."

I glanced up at him, a teasing grin on my lips. "Keep talking like that, and I might start to think you're soft."

Okiyo gave a low chuckle, his eyes locking onto mine with that same intensity that always sent a thrill down my spine. "Don't push it, Viper. I'm giving you one day off. That's all."

I raised a brow, feeling possessive, snaking a hand around his waist this time to press my body into his. "Then I'll make the most of it."

The rest of our afternoon was full of stolen moments; kisses, hands lingering just a little longer each time we touched. Everything felt lighter today. The weight of our pasts, of the training and the looming fight—it all faded into the background. For the first time in a long while, I let myself just *be*. And for a while it seemed that Okiyo had too.

Everything about this place was all a comforting reminder of the stories my dad used to tell. I could almost hear his voice now, weaving tales of the vibrant streets, the colorful markets, and the way the world here always felt alive.

And now, for the first time, I was here, walking those same streets, feeling the pulse of the city under my feet. It was everything I'd imagined—maybe even more.

Okiyo's hand tightened around mine as we moved through the crowd, his thumb brushing lightly against my palm. His touch was steady, grounding me in the present moment, even though I couldn't help but feel a bit overwhelmed by the sights and sounds. There was a sense of freedom in this break, a moment to breathe and soak in the beauty of this place. But beneath that, I couldn't shake the feeling that something was always pulling his attention elsewhere.

It wasn't anything he said. Okiyo didn't need to voice his thoughts for me to know that he was scanning our surroundings, always aware. It was in the way his gaze lingered just a little too long on certain faces, the way his body seemed tense even when he was beside me, his arm brushing against mine.

I squeezed his hand, trying to draw him back into the moment. "It's beautiful, isn't it?" I said, smiling as I looked up at him.

He met my gaze, his eyes softening for just a second before they flickered back to the crowd. "It is," he said quietly, but there was something else in his tone. Like he saw a different side of this place than I did.

"You know," I said, glancing at a vendor who was selling fresh fruit from a wooden cart, "I get why my dad loved this place so much. It feels... alive."

Okiyo's lips quirked into a small smile, and I could feel him relax just a little as we stopped by the cart. "I can see that."

The vendor, an older woman with a wide smile, handed me a slice of mango, and I took it gratefully, the sweetness exploding in my mouth as I took a bite. I offered a piece to Okiyo, and for a moment, the tension in his face eased as he accepted it, his fingers brushing mine.

As we wandered deeper into the market, I could feel the atmosphere shift. The laughter of children echoed through the narrow alleyways, the vibrant sounds of street musicians mingling with the chatter of tourists and locals alike. Every one of my senses were engaged—the smell of grilled meats, the feel of the sun on my skin, the sound of the waves crashing faintly in the distance.

Tulum was everything I'd hoped it would be. Us being out in the heart of the city felt like a world apart from the intense training we'd been doing. It was the reprieve I hadn't realized I needed.

But there it was again. I could sense it in the way Okiyo's grip tightened around my hand, the way his eyes kept scanning our surroundings, never resting in one place for too long. He wasn't saying anything, but I knew him well enough by now to recognize when he was on high alert.

"You okay?" I asked softly, glancing up at him.

He didn't answer right away, his gaze flicking to the side before turning back to me, his expression carefully controlled. "We need to move. Stay close to me."

"What's going on?" I asked, feeling a knot of tension in my stomach tighten.

He pulled me closer, his voice low and calm, but there was an edge to it. "We're being followed."

I felt a chill run down my spine, the festive atmosphere around us suddenly feeling distant and disconnected. I hadn't noticed anyone, but if Okiyo said we were being followed, I trusted him. My heart began to pound in my chest, but I forced myself to stay calm.

"Following us why? For how long?"

"Last few blocks," he said, his eyes sweeping over the crowd. I glanced around, trying not to be obvious, as he tugged me along. "Keep up, Love."

The market was crowded, and there were so many faces. It could've been anyone.

"What do we do?" I whispered. My voice was barely audible over the buzz of the market.

Without answering, Okiyo pulled me toward a narrow alley between two stalls. It was dim and shadowed, the vibrant noise of the market fading as we slipped further inside. He moved quickly, guiding me behind a large stack of crates, positioning himself between me and the open end of the alley. His body blocked me from view, and his hand came up to cup my face gently, his voice calm but firm.

"Stay right here," he murmured. "Don't move unless I say."

The shift in his demeanor was sudden. I nodded, my back pressed against the cool wall of the stall as I watched him step forward slightly, his eyes trained on the entrance. I felt the air shift—Okiyo's entire body tensed, his focus razor-sharp. Every instinct in me told me to run, to do something, but I stayed rooted to the spot, forcing myself to stay still.

It wasn't long before I saw a figure appear at the edge of the alley—a man, his face partially hidden by a baseball cap pulled low over his eyes. He was tall, stocky, his gait purposeful as he moved toward us.

I felt my breath catch, my heart hammered in my chest as the man got closer, his eyes scanning the alley. He didn't see Okiyo standing in the shadows, waiting for him.

Okiyo moved. In a blur of motion, his hand snapped out to grab the man by the front of his shirt. In one swift move, Okiyo slammed his head into the wall of the stall.

"Why the bloody hell are you following us?" Okiyo growled, his voice low and deadly.

The man struggled, but Okiyo had him pinned, his forearm pressed against the guy's throat. I watched, frozen, as the man's face turned red, his eyes widening in panic. He tried to mutter something, but it was garbled. Okiyo pressed harder.

"I'm going to ask you one more time?" Okiyo demanded, his eyes flashing with a dangerous intensity.

The man tried to shake his head, but Okiyo wasn't having it. In one smooth motion, he brought his knee up and knocked the guy's legs out from under him. The man crumpled to the ground, gasping for air.

Okiyo cocked his fist back to strike the man, but he rushed out, "I was just sent to shake the girl fighter up, *cabron*. That's it!" He croaked in a deep Spanish accent before cowering further under Okiyo's stare.

Okiyo pushed the guy forcibly down to the ground then turned back to me, his face calm, controlled—dangerous. "We're leaving. Now."

Without waiting for me to respond, he grabbed my hand and pulled me out of the stall, his body tense and alert as we weaved through the market, moving quickly but without drawing attention. My pulse raced, my mind trying to catch up with what had just happened.

"What the hell?" I asked breathlessly as we made our way toward the edge of the market.

"It's a warning," Okiyo said, his voice low as we slipped through the crowd. "They know you're here now. They're trying to scare you. Perhaps get you to back out of the fight."

"Who knows I'm here? Who would even care?" I asked questions in rapid fire, totally confused.

"Gambling is a big deal here. Lots of money exchanges hands on fights. Cock fights. Street fights. It doesn't matter." Okiyo looked at me for a long moment, as if considering how much more to share with me. "Where there is money to be made in Mexico, you can best believe the cartels are going to be in on it. A win or a loss by you stands the risk of two things; One. Somebody winning or losing a lot of money," he paused to make sure I was following.

"Whoever sent a goon to shake you up, probably has already placed a bet against you and wants you to lose. The other thing at play. You're a virtual nobody here on the fight scene in Mexico. Lots of egos and butt sore locals if you end up beating their champion."

I swallowed hard, the weight of his words settling over me like a cold blanket. It was starting to make sense now—the tension, the unease I had felt from the moment we arrived in Mexico. There were other players involved, and they weren't playing fair.

We finally broke through the crowd and onto the street. Okiyo was still holding my hand, his grip tight but steady as he led me back toward the villa. My mind was racing, but I tried to stay calm, focusing on the warmth of his hand, the steady rhythm of our steps.

"Is this why you've been on edge?" I asked softly, glancing up at him.

He didn't answer right away, but I could see the truth in his eyes. "It's certainly why I came with you here to Mexico. And kept your training secluded," he said after a moment. "I needed you to be ready for whatever, down here. The climate, the terrain. I needed us here to get better intel on ground to make sure I could keep you safe."

His words hit me like a punch to the gut, and I felt my heart sink.

Almost apologetically and as if he read my mind, he continued softly. "This place isn't what it seems, Delia. There's a lot more going on than what you see on the surface. Your father knew that. It's likely why he never came back or brought you and your sister here."

The Tulum my dad had described was a paradise, a place of beauty and warmth. But now, standing here in the fading light, I could see the cracks in that image. The danger had been there all along, lurking beneath the surface, waiting to show itself.

The villa came into view, the once-comforting sight now tinged with unease. Okiyo slowed as we approached the entrance, his eyes scanning the street one last time before we slipped inside.

Once we were behind the compound's gates, Okiyo finally allowed his shoulders to relax as he turned to me. "We're safe here," he said.

He guided me inside the villa. The weight of what had just happened hung heavy in the air between us, but I knew better than to press him for answers now. He was always two steps ahead, always protecting me, and I trusted him.

As we stepped into the cool interior of the villa, my phone buzzed in my pocket. I pulled it out, glancing at the screen, and felt my stomach drop.

"What is it?" Okiyo asked, his voice immediately sharp.

I held up the phone, showing him the message. It was from Rudy.

"Your bout's in 48 hours."

The room felt like it had tilted on its axis, and I struggled to catch my breath. The fight was happening. It was real. And it was coming faster than I had expected.

Okiyo's eyes darkened as he read the message. "Get some rest," he said quietly, his voice steady but firm. "We have work to do."

And just like that, the reprieve was over.

Chapter 29 – Delia

THE LAST TIME WE'D left the compound was only two days ago, but felt like a distant memory. The hired car waited outside, its engine humming softly as Okiyo and I made our way toward it. The fight came a few days earlier than we'd expected. There was a weight to us leaving that I couldn't explain.

Okiyo opened the door for me, his eyes meeting mine briefly before I climbed inside.

The driver gave him a polite nod as he slipped into the seat beside me. The car rolled forward, and I watched through the window as the villa disappeared behind us, replaced by the dense jungle and winding roads.

"Alright. this is it. Time to show and prove, Viper." His gaze was intense, eyes penetrating mine deeply as if seeking any hesitation I may have.

This wasn't just a fight. It was a culmination of everything I had been training for, everything I had been running from and toward at the same time.

"Indeed it is," I responded. Funny how when you're around someone for a time, you start sounding like them, mimicking their mannerisms and small ticks. In this case, I mirrored Okiyo's typical use of minimal words. He wasn't having it today. He stared at me, waiting for me to say more. "I'm fucking terrified, if that's what you want me to say. My heart feels like it's about to beat out of my chest."

"That's actually a good thing. It means your sympathetic nervous system is working. Your fight or flight mechanism is kicking in." He paused for a second. A seductive smile broke through the tension in his jaw as he flicked his eyes up at the rearview then back to me, pointing both thumbs over his shoulder. "You know you can choose flight and we can turn this vehicle around."

I shot a furtive glance at him—his posture was relaxed. But he looked to be only half joking.

"After the hell you put me through? Damn if I quit now."

He pulled me into him, pressing a kiss to my forehead. "That's my girl."

We stayed this way for the remainder of the ride.

There had been a dark energy that had hung over us since the market the other day. All of that was pushed to the side when I was in his arms. He was *safety,* my calm before the storm. Plus, I wasn't going to let anybody intimidate me. Fuck the cartels. Fuck anyone who thought they could scare me into backing down.

With Okiyo's help, I was ready for this. Every ounce of pain, every exhausting day, every bruise and blister—it was all for tonight. I wasn't stupid; he had pushed me so hard, had drilled me on fighting with weapons. This wasn't going to be some organized match with rules. This was going to be a no holds barred battle.

The road twisted, and I could feel the car slowing as we approached our destination. The lights of the venue glowed in the distance—flickering torches casting long, eerie shadows across the weathered stone walls.

The car pulled to a stop, and Okiyo looked over at me, his hand resting gently on my knee. His eyes softened, and he gave me a small nod. "Let's go get this done."

I nodded, a deep breath filling my lungs as I steeled myself to go kick some ass.

The entrance was guarded by men with hard eyes and scarred faces. Similar to places I'd fought at in Atlanta, this place was a shit hole. It appeared to be an abandoned theater house. It was huge, but it was rough. Very much like the men guarding the door, clearly accustomed to places like this.

Okiyo gave a brief nod to the man at the door then whispered some sort of secret code. The two men stepped aside to let us in. I should have been surprised, but at this point, nothing he did or knew surprised me.

The moment we stepped inside, the outside world disappeared. It was an old, crumbling building. The kind of place that looked like it had seen its fair share of bloodshed. The flicker of the flames illuminated dark corners, and the shadows seemed to move with a life of their own, giving the place an almost haunted feeling. It felt like I was stepping into the past, into some ancient arena where warriors fought not for glory, but for survival.

The air was hot and humid, thick with body heat, stale sweat, and the unmistakable scent of blood. The noise was deafening—a cacophony of shouts, cheers, and the sound of fists and feet meeting flesh. The rickety bleachers were packed with spectators eager for one thing—violence.

The crowd was a mix of locals and foreigners, drawn by the promise of blood and the thrill of watching fighters battle for their lives. The lighting was dim, casting long shadows over the ring in the center. The walls were covered in old posters—some advertising past fights, others showing faded images of forgotten champions. The floor was sticky with spilled beer and other, darker fluids, the stench enough to turn my stomach.

I felt the weight of their stares as we made our way through the crowd. Whispers followed us, "newcomer" repeated in hushed tones. But I kept my head high, refusing to let them see the fear gnawing at my insides.

What the fuck had I got myself into? Okiyo turned his head to look back at me as he guided us through the crowd. I was about to lose my fucking lunch. He squeezed my hand. I needed that reassurance to because anything and everything could and was popping off in his bitch..

He turned back to me and mouthed so no one could actually hear or see what he said but me. *Do not show any fear. Yeah, well, umm. Sir? The fear was showing.* He was giving me a very calm but firm warning. I tightened up and did the best I could to blank all expression from my face..

I was the newcomer and I was going to have to come in and fuck somebody up to gain the respect of this crowd. Okiyo stopped abruptly and turned, moving his mouth down to my ear. "If anything goes awry and we get separated in this crowd, get back to the vehicle."

"Oh trust and believe, we're getting up out of here even if we have to fight our way out." At that his lip curled up into quick smirk.

"We should be fine once we make it to the locker rooms just over there," he nodded then pulled me with him in that direction.

We made our way to the small, makeshift locker room in the back. The walls were bare, the only furniture an old wooden bench and a cracked mirror. I could hear the muffled sounds of the crowd outside, the occasional roar of approval or disapproval as another fight played out in the ring.

Okiyo turned to me, his eyes intense. "You got this shit."

What an icebreaker. Okiyo rarely cursed, aside from the occasional bursts of 'swear' when he was irritated or fed up with something. The always calm, polished gent letting his inner potty mouth slip, was oddly comforting.

I closed my eyes for a moment, centering myself. When I opened them, Okiyo was watching me. The look I read on his face seemed to be a mixture of pride and something else— respect maybe? Whatever it was, my heart skipped a beat.

"No matter what happens out there, know that I believe in you," he said, his voice soft but firm.

"I will make you proud," I whispered, leaning in and placing a warm kiss on his cheek, perhaps the softest thing I would do until after this fight.

He gave me a small nod before stepping back. "Show them who the Black Viper really is."

I stepped into the ring. The glaring lights blinded me for a moment as the crowd erupted in a roar of anticipation. Across from me stood El Diablo—no, *La Diabla*. My opponent's name referred to the male instance of the devil. Thank God that I was fighting a she-devil. *Small mercy.* She was on the far side of the ring, her features obscured by the distance, but her eyes, even from afar, were cold and calculating.

Before the referee even finished giving the rundown of the so-called rules—guidelines at best—El Diablo lunged forward, a quick fist flying straight at my face. The bell hadn't even rung yet. The crowd erupted, half cheering, half gasping at the blatant disrespect. Her knuckles connected with my cheek, sending a shock of pain radiating across my face.

I stumbled back, shaking off the haze that settled in from the unexpected blow. She grinned, a mocking curl of her lips that said she thought she'd already won.

Not today.

The crowd's roar grew louder, almost a physical force pressing in on me as I steadied myself. Every nerve in my body screamed in protest, but I planted my feet, my heart pounding as I squared up to her. I wasn't going to let her get the better of me that easily.

I caught sight of Okiyo at the edge of the ring, his eyes fixed on me, his calm presence grounding me even amid the chaos. His voice echoed in my mind—*Breathe, find your rhythm.*

I exhaled, settling into my stance as El Diablo came at me again, her punches sharp and fast. I blocked each one, though the force of her blows shook my bones. She was strong, and she was ruthless, but I had trained for this. I ducked under her next wild swing, twisting to the side, and used the opening to land a quick jab to her ribs.

She winced, a flicker of surprise in her eyes, and I took the moment to find my footing. The adrenaline surged through me, reminding me of why I was here.

El Diablo came at me with a ferocity that knocked the wind out of me. Her fists were like hammers, each hit a tidal wave of pain that crashed through my body. I could feel the force of every punch rattling my bones, the impact reverberating in my chest and echoing through my skull. I fought back, tried to remember everything Okiyo had drilled into me—every grueling step of our training in Mexico. *Footwork, stay light. Blocks, absorb the force. Counters, strike back when she's exposed.*

But she was relentless, her attacks coming faster, harder with each passing second. The ring blurred around me, the shouts from the crowd fading into nothing but white noise as El Diablo pressed on, her fists driving into me like pistons. I felt her knuckles crunch against my ribs, a burst of agony that nearly brought me to my knees. I could taste the metallic tang of blood in my mouth, but I couldn't stop. Quitting wasn't an option. Not here, not now.

By the end of the second round, I was bruised and battered, my vision swimming from the blows that landed too close to my temple. My breaths were ragged, each inhale burning as if my lungs were on fire.

Every muscle screamed in protest, my legs heavy, my arms aching. But I forced myself to keep moving, to stay on my feet, to keep swinging. I had to prove myself. The first round was for Okiyo. This round was for me.

One of her punches connected with the side of my head again. Everything spun—bright spots of light popped in my vision, the world turned into a dizzying blur. For a heartbeat, I lost my footing, felt my body sway as the dizziness threatened to take me down.

No. Focus, Delia. Focus. I physically shook my head, trying to clear the haze, the sharp sting of pain kept me tethered to reality.

I couldn't afford to lose focus. Not now. Not when she was circling me like a predator, her cold eyes fixed on me, waiting for any sign of weakness.

I planted my feet, my stance widening for balance. *You've been through worse.* I pushed the words into my head, forcing the mantra between each labored breath. *You can do this. You've fought harder. You've fought meaner. This is just another fight.*

Her next attack came, and I moved—dodging left, ducking under her swing, feeling the rush of air as her fist grazed past my ear. I twisted, my own fist shooting up to catch her in the side. She grunted, staggered, and that's when I saw it.

A glint of something metallic—a knife, small but deadly—appearing in her right hand, hidden behind her hip. My heart pounded, the realization hitting like a sledgehammer. This wasn't just about strength anymore. This was life or death.

She lunged at me, the blade slicing through the air where I had just been. My instincts took over, my body moving faster than my thoughts. I dodged, felt the sharp edge nick my skin, a stinging line of pain along my arm. I grabbed the closest thing to me—a stick left from the earlier rounds; the wood worn but solid.

Fight like you're on the streets, Okiyo's voice echoed in my mind. *No rules. No mercy.*

I swung the stick, the wood connecting with her wrist. The blade clattered to the ground, and I didn't hesitate. I followed through with another swing, catching her in the side, feeling the shock of impact travel up my arm. She snarled, her face twisting in anger, but I didn't stop. I couldn't afford to stop.

My body was a live wire, every nerve firing, the adrenaline burning away the exhaustion. I moved, blocked, countered, my stick meeting her every strike, every lunge. I was faster, hit harder. *Stay ahead of her.* I had to survive.

The fight raged on, every strike sending shockwaves through my body. I fought to stay present, to keep moving, to push past the pain. I couldn't stop now—not when I had fought this hard to get here. I swung the stick, each hit met with a block from El Diablo, her face twisted in fury.

Suddenly, between dodging jabs and ducking from El Diablo's relentless strikes, something in the crowd caught my eye. I threw a quick glance toward the stands, my vision flicking between the punches and the sea of faces.

First, I caught sight of Iya. She stood near the front, her eyes wide with fear, hands clenched together as if she were praying. My heart twisted at the sight of her. I never wanted her here—never wanted her to see me like this. But there she was, worry etched across her face. And Justin stood behind her arms wrapped around her flinching shoulders.

I dodged another jab, my head snapping back to the fight for a second before I glanced again. My mother stood beside Iya, one hand covering her eyes, peeking through her fingers like she couldn't bear to watch but couldn't look away either. The protective look on her face, the fear in every line—too much to process in the middle of this brutal fight.

El Diablo lunged again, and I blocked the hit, my muscles screaming.

A jab to my side jerked me back to the present, El Diablo reminding me exactly where I was. The sight of them hit me harder than any punch she had thrown, a jolt of energy shooting through my veins.

They're here. They're watching. I have to do this.

I reset my stance and turned back to El Diablo; the stick still clenched in my hand. This bitch was relentless. Her eyes narrowed. The fury in her gaze intensified. She lunged at me again, her fists swinging, and I moved to block, but the shock and distraction of seeing my family slowed me down a bit. I tried to refocus. But not before she connected with my side, the impact sending me stumbling backward, the air rushing out of my lungs.

Fuck.

I couldn't let this end here. I couldn't let them see me fall.

I straightened; adrenaline surged through me once again. 'Fight or flight?' I recalled Okiyo's words from the car. I could feel their eyes on me, my family's presence gave me the strength I needed. *I choose to fight!* My grip tightened on the stick; my gaze locked on El Diablo.

The final round began, and I gave everything I had left. My body ached, the bruises and cuts stung, but none of it mattered now. I couldn't let all of Okiyo's relentless training be for nothing. I had only one goal—ending this fight.

El Diablo charged at me, eyes blazing, fists flying with everything she had. I ducked, blocked, and swung my stick, hearing it crack hard against her side. Simultaneously I heard the snap. My stick splintered right in my hands. *Damn it.* Without thinking, I tossed the broken pieces aside. No more weapons.

The rest of the world blurred away. It was just me and her, the pounding of my heart, the ache in my muscles, and the fight right in front of me.

She lunged again, faster this time, but I was ready. I sidestepped, every move fluid, my body working on pure instinct. I executed a back kick. My heel slammed into her ribs. For a split second, I saw the pain flash across her face.

She shook it off, then El Diablo smirked, fists back up. I know that kick had to hurt but her game face was on point. I wasn't backing down though.

She came at me hard, throwing wild punches, but I blocked her, landing an elbow into her chest before throwing a solid punch into her ribs. Same place I'd landed that kick. *Got her.* She stumbled back, caught off guard, and I didn't give her a chance to recover. I kept coming at her, pushing her toward the edge of the ring.

The crowd noise? It was just a hum in the background. None of it mattered. It was all about this moment, about finishing this fight.

One more hit, and she went down. Hard. She tried to get up, arms shaking as she pushed herself off the mat, but her body just gave out. She collapsed back, done. The ref jumped in, his hand flying up to call it.

The crowd went wild, but I just stood there, my chest heaving, breath coming fast as the adrenaline started to wear off. My stick lay broken and scattered around me, but it didn't matter anymore.

I won.

I turned, searching the crowd for my family, and there they were. Iya was jumping up and down beside Justin, her face lit up with joy, while my mother had tears streaming down her cheeks, her hands clasped in front of her chest.

I stepped out of the ring, the exhaustion finally catching up to me as I made my way toward them. Iya rushed forward, wrapping her arms around me in a tight hug, her laughter echoing in my ear. My mother followed, pulling me into her embrace, her tears dampening my shoulder.

"You did it, Delia!" Iya shouted, her voice filled with pride. "You were amazing!"

I smiled, my heart swelling with a mix of emotions—relief, pride, and something else. I looked around, searching for Okiyo, wanting to share this moment with him. But he was nowhere to be seen.

"Where's Okiyo?" I asked, my eyes scanning the crowd.

Iya's smile faltered slightly. "He rushed out of the arena a few minutes ago. He was on the phone—looked pretty urgent."

I tried to hide my frown, but the knot settled in my chest. I searched the crowd again, but no sign of him. My victory felt incomplete, the joy tempered by his absence.

The driver waited by the entrance, his eyes meeting mine as he nodded, gesturing for us to follow. It was clear Okiyo had left instructions. He always thought ahead, always ensured safety for me, and now my family.

But as I took my family's hands and began to lead them out of the arena, the question lingered in my mind: *Where the fuck was he?*

The cheers of the crowd faded into the background. Something wasn't right, and as much as I tried to stay focused on the victory, one thought refused to leave my mind.

Where had he gone? And why did it feel like everything was about to change?

Chapter 30 – Okiyo

MY PHONE RANG JUST as Delia landed her final blow on El Diablo, sending her opponent crashing to the mat. The roar of the crowd erupted around me, but the ringtone cut through the noise. I pulled my phone out and checked the caller ID. It was Leboo.

I answered, stepping back from the frenzy of the arena. I could allow myself a moment to take this call. Delia's family would be the first to celebrate with her, just as they should. She deserved to have them by her side.

I'd called them as soon as we had confirmation of the fight's details. It would mean a lot to Delia and watching her fight her heart out tonight, I was satisfied that they were all here to witness her achievement. She needed this, and I was glad she had it.

"Leboo?" I spoke into the phone, stepping further away from the chaos. I kept one eye on Delia, her family already pushing through the crowd to get to her. And, as I watched her embrace her sister and mother, a smile broke across my face.

I'd be back in a moment to congratulate her myself. For now, she had everything she needed right in front of her.

"Leboo?" I said again, straining to hear over the cheering crowd. The arena buzzed with electric energy, the sound of Delia's victory echoing off the walls.

"Okiyo—it's Bishara," Leboo's voice came through, heavy with a weight I immediately recognized. My heart sank.

"What about?" I demanded, stepping further into the shadows of the corridor, away from the celebration.

"She's—gone."

World stopped. *Bishara*? The woman who had become like a mother to me when I returned to Kenya. The woman who had taken me in, who'd shown me warmth and compassion when I thought I'd forgotten what those words meant.

Gone.

My chest tightened painfully. A memory rushed through my mind—the last time I spoke to her. That raspy, persistent cough she'd had... I should have paid more attention. Should have been more insistent that she see a doctor. Instead, I'd trusted that the herbal tea one of my men had brought her would suffice. *Not for pneumonia.* I'd been too comfortable, too focused on my own life to notice the signs. Now, the price of my negligence had come due, and the guilt twisted inside me like a knife.

I closed my eyes, fighting the urge to crumble under the weight of it.

"I... I understand," I finally managed to say, my voice hoarse. "I'll make arrangements to come home immediately."

Hanging up, I turned my gaze back to the arena one last time. Delia stood there, her family now by her side. She was smiling—radiant, victorious, with the gleam of triumph in her eyes. This was her moment. I wanted so much to run to her, to wrap my arms around her and feel the warmth of her embrace. But I couldn't—not now.

The guilt, the grief, everything twisted together in a gnawing ache that demanded action. There were things I had to do.

I walked briskly out of the arena, my steps heavy. I flagged down a taxi, my thoughts swirling with plans. I had to leave, now. Bishara deserved that much from me. But I couldn't leave without ensuring Delia and her family were safe. I needed King to arrange security for them—get them back to the villa safely, and ensure their comfort for a few days.

I gave the hired driver the instructions to take Delia and her family back to the villa.. Then, as I climbed into the taxi, I dialed King.

It was nearing dawn when I made it back to the villa. The sky was still a deep indigo, that fleeting moment before the first hints of sunrise appeared. Everything was silent, still. It almost felt like a dream, the kind where you move quietly through a world that doesn't fully belong to you.

I slipped through the front door, careful to keep my steps light, not wanting to disturb anyone. The villa was dark, shadows long in the dim early morning, and I moved as silently as possible, weaving my way through the familiar rooms.

I knew exactly where I was headed. I had to see her.

I'd sorted everything out—arrangements for my departure, ensuring Delia's family would have every comfort here before making their way back home. King would take care of them now, and they'd be in good hands.

But Delia... she was different. She wasn't just someone I was responsible for. The thought of leaving her, just disappearing without a word, twisted my chest into knots. It wasn't like me, feeling this way, wanting someone like this. Wanting her.

I'd been content being the lone wolf, untouched by emotions that tied people down. Always in control. But Delia had slipped through the cracks, had found a way past every wall I'd ever built.

Quietly, I made my way to her room, my breath shallow as I approached her door. It was slightly ajar, a sliver of moonlight spilling out into the hallway. I pushed it open gently, stepping inside.

She was asleep, curled on her side, her face relaxed, soft in the glow of the lamp beside her bed. My heart clenched at the sight of her. The fierce fighter I'd watched tear through her opponent in the ring now looked so peaceful, so... vulnerable. I had to go, but leaving her like this felt wrong. I needed to make sure she knew that I wasn't disappearing—not without saying goodbye.

I crossed the room, the soft rustle of my clothes the only sound as I moved. Her breathing was steady, her chest rising and falling in a rhythm that I found myself syncing with, my pulse calming as I got closer.

I should have just left, but I couldn't. I knelt beside the bed, my hand reaching out, brushing a stray curl away from her face. Her skin was warm under my fingertips, and I felt the heat of her seep into me, grounding me in a way I couldn't quite explain.

I took a breath, my voice barely a whisper. "Delia."

She stirred, her eyelids fluttering before slowly opening, her eyes meeting mine. For a moment, there was confusion, a haze of sleep still clouding her gaze. But then she saw me, really saw me, and her eyes widened, her lips parting as she whispered my name.

"Okiyo?"

I nodded, swallowing the lump in my throat. "I have to go."

Her brows furrowed, the confusion giving way to something else—something that twisted my heart. "Go? Where?"

I didn't have the words, not the right ones, so I just looked at her, my hand still resting against her cheek. "There's something I need to take care of," I said, my voice low. "It can't wait."

She pushed herself up, her eyes searching mine. "What do you mean? Where were you after the fight? Iya said you rushed out like it was urgent. What's going on, Okiyo?"

"Hush, love," I soothed, sitting on the bed beside her. "I need to fly back to Nairobi."

More questions.

"When?" Her voice was barely audible. The crestfallen look on her face took me out. "Are you coming back?"

I hesitated, the truth catching in my throat. I didn't know if I would be back, if there would be a way for me to return to her. But I couldn't tell her that. Not now, not like this.

"I don't know," I admitted, my thumb brushing over her cheek. "But I couldn't leave without seeing you. I needed to say... goodbye."

Her eyes glistened with fresh tears. Her lips pressed into a thin line as she tried to hold back the emotion that I could see so clearly on her face. And it broke me, knowing I was the cause of her pain.

"Stay," she whispered, her voice trembling. "Please don't go," she begged sitting up swiping profusely at the tears forming. "I thought we had more time. Why are you leaving like this?"

I closed my eyes, my resolve crumbling at her words. I shouldn't have, but I couldn't help myself. I slipped off my shoes before climbing into the bed beside her. She moved closer, her body pressed against mine, and I wrapped my arms around her, holding her as if I could protect her from the world, from everything that waited beyond this room.

She tilted her head up, her lips brushed against my neck, and I felt the tension in me ease, the weight of everything lifting just a little. I looked down at her. I saw the same want, the need that mirrored my own.

Without a word, I leaned down, capturing her lips with mine. It was soft at first, a gentle meeting, but then it deepened, the intensity growing as the reality of this moment hit me. This might be the last time I'd get to feel her like this, to have her in my arms, and I poured everything into that kiss, every unspoken word, every emotion I couldn't bring myself to say.

Her hands moved to my chest, her fingers brushing over my skin, and I felt the fire ignite between us. I pulled her closer, my body pressing against hers, and I could feel the need in her, the same need that burned through me.

She shifted beneath me, her hands slipping down to the waistband of my trousers, and there was no stopping this. Not now. Not when we both needed it so badly.

I helped her, my hands moving to pull her closer, to feel every inch of her against me. And in that moment, there was nothing else—no past, no future, just the two of us, tangled together in the darkness, the world outside forgotten.

It was slow, tender, a meeting of two souls that found something they hadn't known they were searching for. And as I moved with her, as her body responded to mine, no matter what happened next, no matter where I went or what I faced, a part of me would always belong to her.

When it was over, we lay there, our breaths mingling in the quiet of the room. I held her close, fingers combing through her hair. I had to go soon. But for just a little longer, I stayed, holding her, memorizing every part of her. Because once she fell asleep and I walked out that door, I wasn't sure if I'd ever be able to come back to this. To her.

Chapter 31 – Delia

THE AIR IN THE villa never felt so cold. I'd won both the championship and the respect of those who doubted me, including myself. Yet as I stood in the quietness of the Dojo, the open space echoing every step I took, an emptiness lingered.

Okiyo was gone. I knew that day was coming, but not like this. He'd left so suddenly, and though It wasn't personal, a hollow ache settled in my chest. I missed him already, terribly.

I walked out of the Dojo and into the main living area. Iya and Justin were totally engrossed in an episode of Your Honor on Netflix and didn't even notice me enter.. Mom sat by the infinity pool, sunglasses perched on her head, her legs dipped into the clear blue water.

I joined her.

She looked over, her expression softening as she took me in. "You okay?"

I shrugged, leaning back on my hands as I dipped my toes into the water beside hers. The coolness of the pool was a relief against the heat of the day, and I stared at the ripples my feet created.

"You've got the same expression on your face that you used to wear when you were a kid," she finally said, her voice gentle but cutting through the silence.

I glanced over at her, a little startled. "Oh, yeah? What face is that?"

She turned slightly, pulling her sunglasses down to look at me fully. "The one you had whenever you lost something important to you." She tilted her head, studying me for a moment. "I know I haven't been there for you like I should've been, but it hurts me to see you hurt. Want to talk about it, baby?"

Her words washed over me like the heat of the sun—unexpected and overwhelming. I blinked hard, looking back out at the water, my throat tight. I didn't know where to start, but her question had cracked something open inside me.

"I don't know, Mom. I thought I'd feel complete after winning this fight... but it's like there's still this piece missing."

She shifted closer, her hand landing lightly on my back. "Okiyo?"

I nodded, trying to swallow the lump in my throat. "I thought we'd have more time," I finally whispered, my voice catching on the words.

"He said goodbye. But it… it wasn't supposed to happen like this. We didn't even get to have the infamous talk about what's next, about what we are." My chest tightened, the words spilling out before I could stop them. "I thought we'd at least have a little more time before he left. I didn't think it would be like… *this*," I said, lacking the words to express how bad this hurt.

The warmth of her hand on my back was steady.

"I miss him," I said softly, my voice breaking. "And I don't even know if we were anything to begin with. What if… I never see him again?"

Mom was quiet for a moment, and then, without saying anything, she pulled me into a hug. The simple act broke me. I hadn't felt this kind of closeness with her in so long—maybe not since everything with Iya. My defenses crumbled as I leaned into her, letting the tears spill over.

"Ahh, baby," she whispered into my hair, her voice filled with a tenderness I hadn't felt in years.

Her arms tightened around me, and the flood of emotions I'd been holding back for so long rushed to the surface. I hadn't realized how much I needed this, how much I needed her.

"I thought I was fine," I choked out, my face buried in her shoulder. "But it hurts so much. I didn't even realize how much I cared about him until he was gone."

She held me, stroking my hair gently, as if trying to soothe away the pain. "It's okay to care. And it's okay to hurt. But you know what? He didn't leave because of you, Delia. He had to go, but that doesn't mean it wasn't real."

I shook my head, wiping at my face as I pulled back slightly, my voice trembling. "But what if he doesn't come back?"

She cupped my face, her thumb brushing away the tears. "If it's real, he'll come back. And if not... you'll be okay, baby. I promise."

Her words were soft, but there was a strength behind them that anchored me. For the first time in a long time, I felt like maybe I didn't have to carry everything alone.

We sat there like that for a while, my head resting on her shoulder, our feet still in the water. The heat pressed down on us, but I felt lighter, like the weight of everything I'd been holding in was finally starting to lift.

"Thank you," I whispered, my voice raw.

She smiled softly, squeezing my hand. "Always."

On our last evening at the villa, Mom, Iya, Justin and I decided to make the most of the luxury that surrounded us. Mom was lounging on one of the chaise lounges by the pool, her face tilted up towards the setting sun. Justin was trying to mix cocktails using the bar setup we'd discovered in the kitchen.

"Mom, I can't believe you didn't faint when you saw Delia in that ring," Iya teased, handing her a bright pink concoction. "You're tougher than I thought."

Mom raised an eyebrow, taking a sip of her drink. "Oh, please. You think I'm going to let my girls think I can't handle a little excitement? Besides," she looked over at me, her eyes softening, "She could handle it. She's always been the strongest of us all."

I smiled, warmth flooding me. "Thanks, Mom. But I'm pretty sure you could have taken on El Diablo if you had to."

She laughed, a rich sound that filled the villa. "Maybe. But I think I'll leave the fighting to you, sweetheart. I'm more of a cocktail and lounging type these days."

We all laughed, raising our glasses in cheers..

Chapter 32 — Okiyo

THE ACHE IN MY chest intensified as my plane touched down in Nairobi. The familiar sights and smells of Kenya—the red earth, the acacia trees swaying in the breeze, the scent of rain hanging heavy in the air—should have brought me comfort. It did not. The place that once was my refuge, that healed me after years of wandering, felt stripped of its warmth. Bishara was gone. Home was gone, an empty shell left behind.

I headed straight to the Baijan estate after landing to lay Bishara to rest. Three days later my heart was even more weighed down with grief. She was the cornerstone of this place, not just for me, but for everyone who worked and lived here. She had a way of making everyone feel as though they belonged, like family. I wondered if I'd ever feel that warmth of true belonging again.

The estate was eerily quiet this morning. The staff moved about their duties with downcast eyes, their usual chatter replaced by silence. I made my way to her office, as I had been doing every day since she passed, drawn by a need to be near her essence. The small room, tucked away near the kitchen, was empty—her things had already been carefully packed away by the staff. Yet, it was here where she had spent most of her time taking care of the family she cherished. Her spirit lingered.

I sat on the cot in the corner, the one she'd used on nights when she was too tired to walk the quarter mile to her house. God forbid anyone offered her a ride. I could still hear her laugh as she waved us off. "Pshh, Mrs. Bishara *nuh'* that old, child. *Ma' feet* still *wuhk* just fine." Her voice echoed in my memory, bringing a faint smile to my lips even as my chest tightened.

The silence cocooned me, the weight of it pressing on my shoulders. It was the same feeling I had the first night I spent at the orphanage—gnawing emptiness. The unbearable ache of abandonment. I felt it again when I was adopted.

Whisked away to a foreign place by a wealthy British family. No one looked like me. I was expected to assimilate whilst they never cared to understand me or the trauma I'd endured, losing the three people who were my world. I felt just as alone now without Bishara.

This was a kind of solitude that had defined most of my life, an emptiness that seemed to follow me no matter where I went.

I lay on the cot to be close to Bishara. I closed my eyes and the carousel images of my time with her slowly morphed to a vision in red—*Delia. Fierce, beautiful Delia.* An image of her taking a hard punch in the first fight I'd been there to witness her in. Her fiery eyes during our sparring sessions. The tenderness of our last night together. Each memory replayed in vivid detail, refusing to fade.

For so long, I believed solitude was my shield, the key to my existence. But lying here, haunted by Bishara's warmth and Delia's eyes, I knew the truth—I had lost everything. I missed them both with an intensity that took my breath away, I felt empty.

This was the price of caring. It was too much to bear.

My feelings for Delia had grown rapidly—*uncontrollably*. I tried to stop the inevitable—tried to derail the freight train barreling towards us. No matter what I did, leaving her hadn't erased the depth of my emotions. It wouldn't undo what was already written in my heart.

I would have to force myself to forget the way she felt in my arms, make peace with the distance between us. Perhaps it was better that it ended this way. To be torn apart by circumstances before either of us had to make the choice.

The cruel irony of it all was that Bishara had always pushed me to settle down, to find someone to share my life with. And now, her passing had become the very thing that pulled me away from the only woman who could have made that dream a reality.

Days bled into weeks, and I found myself sinking deeper into a depression. I wasn't someone who allowed my emotions to take control. Discipline and focus—those were the tenets I lived by. I had faced loss more times than I could count and survived. *But this...* this was different. Grief wrapped around me like a suffocating fog, refusing to let go.

I missed Delia. The other day while out with Leboo, I could swear I saw her in a crowded shop. I stopped short of reaching for the woman until she turned around at the call of her apparent lover. Thoughts of her crept in at the most inopportune times. Like during the daily security briefs from my men.

"Boss? Are you okay?" Gin asked, just this morning as I continued to sit, long after the short meeting was over.

I was too busy wondering how she was coping after the fight, whether she had healed from the physical toll it took on her when I felt his hand on my shoulder. Shaken, I could only utter a quick, "Yeah. I'm good man."

I had thought to reach out to her the other day. Picked up the phone to dial her cell and froze. Almost answered her call but couldn't bring myself to risk intensifying the pain of not being near her. She called every day for the first three weeks after I'd left.

She deserved answers. But too caught up in my own pain of loss, I didn't have any to give.

I was trapped in this endless cycle of grief, guilt, and longing, and I didn't know how to break free. I convinced myself that it was better for her, that my silence would allow her to move on. I wanted her to move on.

The estate became a self-inflicted prison of sorts. I understood perfectly why Delia sought the pain of punishment in the cage.

I tried to distract myself by throwing all my energy into the security firm. I was either locked in the security control rooms for hours or in my quarters. I pushed my men to their limits—early morning drills, late-night exercises, relentless evaluations of their capabilities. I was on them constantly, finding flaws in their performance that I would have normally let slide.

"Again," I'd bark, watching as they ran a tactical scenario. No matter how many times they got it right, I was there, pointing out something else. "You think the people coming for us are going to let you breathe? Faster, move!"

I could see it in their eyes—my men were growing weary of me. They were professionals, and I was being harder on them than usual, but I couldn't help it. I needed to stay busy, to keep my mind from drifting back to thoughts of Delia, to the empty ache that settled in my chest whenever I pictured her smile.

It was late one night, long after the drills were over, when Leboo found me in the command center. Most of the estate was asleep. The glow of the monitors was the only light in the room.

I was going over the surveillance footage of the perimeter of the estate for what had to be the third time tonight. I heard Leboo clear his throat, and I glanced up, meeting his gaze.

He leaned against the doorframe, tossing his head up at the monitors.

"You're still at it." Leboo stated rather than asking, his voice low with concern. "Okiyo, your men have checked the perimeter several times today, I'm sure."

"I know," I muttered, looking back at the monitors, my fingers tapping restlessly against the console. "Doesn't hurt to be thorough."

Leboo walked into the room, pulling up a chair next to mine. He didn't say anything for a long time, just watched as I scrolled through the footage. Eventually, he sighed, leaning back with a shake of his head.

"I've known you for a while now, Okiyo," he said, his tone gentle but firm. "I've never seen you like this though my friend."

I clenched my jaw, refusing to look at him. "Like what?"

"Like a man whose heart needs mending," he said, gesturing to the monitors, to the tension that seemed to hang around me like a shroud. "Like a man who's running from something he knows is for him but is afraid if he gives into it he may be lost forever."

I didn't respond. I couldn't. Because he was right. I was running. I was running from the pain of losing Bishara, from the ache of missing Delia, from the realization that I might have let go of something I could never get back.

Leboo sighed deeply, his hand landing on my shoulder, heavy with the weight of experience. "Okiyo, I've walked that road before. Leaving Evelyn? That was the hardest thing I've ever done, man. I thought I had to. Out of some misplaced sense of duty to my father and his debts, I let go of the love of my life. Andra grew up without me because of it. I missed her first steps, her first words—all the things a father should be there for. Yes, I erased my father's debt, built a fortune that outlived him, but none of that filled the gap where love should've been."

He paused, his eyes searching mine with a quiet intensity, as if trying to pass on the lessons carved into him by time and regret.

"Son, don't make that same mistake. You've been a constant for me and my family—a solid rock when we needed it. Men like you don't come around often. But being strong for everyone else doesn't mean you should neglect your own heart. Loss is inevitable in life, but it's love that makes it bearable, that makes life worth living."

His voice softened, almost a plea now. "You've given so much of yourself, Okiyo. But now... maybe it's time you let someone love you back. Take care of you for a while, son. Don't let the fear of loss keep you from what's in front of you."

I closed my eyes, the weight of his words settling over me. He was right, and I hated it. I hated that I couldn't control this, couldn't just shut the feelings off and move on like I had with everything else in my life. Delia had become the exception—the one person I couldn't forget, no matter how hard I tried.

But I still didn't say anything. I just nodded, a small, almost imperceptible movement, and Leboo gave my shoulder a squeeze before standing up.

"I'll be here if you need me," he said quietly before he left, the door clicking softly shut behind him.

I stared at the monitors for a long time after that, the screens blurring in front of me. The silence of the room pressed in on me.

I received a very strange visitor this morning. Mackena showed up, knocking at the door to my quarters. She and I had never been particularly close. If anything, we clashed more often than not. Mackena was fiery, opinionated, spoiled as hell, and had a knack for getting under my skin like no one else. So when I opened the door to find her standing there, I wasn't quite sure what to expect.

"Mackena." I gave her a stiff nod, stepping aside to let her in. She strolled past me, her head held high, that same air of entitlement she always carried trailing behind her.

She turned, a sly smile tugging at her lips. "I've been chatting with my big sis," she said casually, as if she had just dropped by for a social visit. I knew better. She always had an agenda.

I narrowed my eyes at her, already wary. "And?"

She strolled over to the chair across from my desk, her eyes gleaming with mischief as she sat down, leaning back with a knowing grin. "In our girl talk, she mentioned a Delia."

I stiffened at the mention of Delia's name, the air around me growing thick. "What about her?" I managed, keeping my tone as neutral as possible.

Mackena shrugged, but there was curiosity dancing in her eyes. "Andra thinks you're in love with her."

The breath was knocked clean out of my chest. I stared at Mackena, my throat tight as I struggled to find the right words to respond. She leaned back further, her perfectly manicured fingers tapping gently on the armrest of the chair, her gaze never leaving mine.

I opened my mouth to deny it, to brush her off, but she cut me off before I could even get the words out. "I was gonna ask if it was true, but I've never seen you speechless before, Okiyo. I don't need to ask." She gave me a pointed look. "It's true whether you admit it or not."

I turned away, looking towards the window, the Nairobi sunlight streaming in through the curtains. I didn't want to admit it—to Mackena, to myself, to anyone.

But she wasn't letting me off that easy. "Look, Okiyo, I know we haven't always been the best of friends. Hell, I know I get on your nerves. But I also know what loss does to a person. It makes you think you need to push people away to protect yourself. But that's a lie."

Twice in less than twenty four hours a Baijan was telling me about me.

She leaned forward, her eyes boring into mine with a strange sort of determination. "You care about Delia."

My heart began a quicker pace at the sound of her name.

"I don't know her, but Andra does and when I told her you'd been moping around here for weeks now, she said no doubt it was because of her. So this Delia must be something else to have the great Okiyo Bamdi pressed, *aye*?" The sound of her laughter sounded like brittle glass.

My expression must have changed because Mackena pounced.

"Wow! He even shifts at the sound of her name."

Mackena stood up then, smoothing her hands down her skirt, her voice breaking the silence. "You know, Andra also mentioned something else I thought you'd find interesting." She paused, watching me for a reaction.

I raised a brow, my heart thundering in my chest. "Oh?" I tried to keep my voice steady.

A smirk played at the corners of her mouth. She raised an innocent single shoulder shrug before adding, "Something about a wedding in Atlanta. Guess who's the maid of honor? Oh, and Gastrafrique is catering the event."

I felt my pulse quicken; the implication clear. Mackena's eyes glinted, satisfied that she had gotten her point across.

Chapter 33 – Delia

WEEKS HAD GONE BY since the fight in Mexico, and I was back in Atlanta—back at work, back to my life. The bruises and aches had slowly faded, but it was Okiyo's absence that left a lasting mark.

After the fight, I had been surrounded by my family, their love and support filling the void Okiyo left behind when he disappeared. Even with them by my side, though, I couldn't shake the feeling that something vital was missing.

I tried calling him several times, texting, reaching out in every way . I even went to Gastrafrique, hoping to see Andra, trying not to sound desperate as I casually inquired about his well-being. Andra had been kind, but I could tell she was holding something back.

"There's been a death in the family," she mentioned softly, her voice tinged with sadness. I could see her eyes glisten as she spoke. It made me feel bad for prying. Whatever was happening, I respected their space, no matter how much it hurt not knowing.

Weeks passed with no word from Okiyo—no returned calls, no messages. I buried myself in my work. Since I'd returned from Mexico, the one thing that kept me sane— well two things, but mainly my passion for architecture was renewed.

Rhiyan didn't even have to push. Determined to no longer be a victim of circumstance, I enrolled in a prep course for my licensing exam almost immediately upon arriving back home.

The long hours of studying and life in general left very little time to train at the gym. I worked out when I could, but had stopped fighting, at least for now. Rudy had won so much money on my fight in Mexico that he wasn't even hounding me to take another bout.

I passed the NCARB exam with flying colors. The reward was worth the sacrifice. I was promoted shortly after—now officially a junior architect. A title Rhiyan assured me was temporary until I got my first project under my belt.

Surprisingly enough, that first project turned out to be an opportunity to work with the team who'd designed the original plans for the Rue d'Orleans Paris, the very same site where Okiyo allowed me to solve the Seine waterway challenge. I was given the opportunity to design a portion of a boutique hotel on the site.

After Iya's wedding, I'd be relocating to Paris— for an indefinite amount of time. It was everything I had ever dreamed of. To be a world-renowned architect. Ok, maybe not yet, but I was on my way.

Despite all the success, despite the positive changes, there was still an emptiness.

The second thing that helped me stay sane and work through this was my return to therapy. I still missed Okiyo terribly. After about a month of not hearing from him, I decided to seek help. She came highly recommended by Iya of all people and was the very same therapist she saw years ago after her assault. As I'd recently discovered, she still saw from time to time now.

Dr. Subitha Vadlamani helped me process a lot of the feelings of guilt and shame that I still dealt with, but also my relationship with Okiyo—the intensity, the passion, and the sudden end. She constantly reminded me that people sometimes come into your life just temporarily, but their impact could be lasting.

She talked a lot about Gary Zukav's definition of soulmates, and I found comfort in that.

"Delia, tell me... what is it that still ties you to him?" Subitha's voice was gentle, but it carried a weight that made me pause. She looked at me with those dark, knowing eyes, the ones that seemed to see through every layer I had put up.

I swallowed, feeling my throat tighten.

"I don't know," I whispered, trying to steady my voice. "He just, *uhhh*... he saw me, you know? The parts of me I tried to hide. Even when I could no longer hide my hurt and shame around not being able to fight for —protect Iya, he didn't flinch. He never looked away from the wounded parts of me. Challenged me to be more. And now he's gone, and I—"

My voice broke, and I looked away, blinking back tears that threatened to spill. My eyes darted around the room, trying to find something to anchor myself to, settling on staring at the small gold clock on the table beside her chair. It reminded me of him and that damn pocket watch he'd wear.

"I miss him," I finally said, finally able to smile rather than cry at the thought of him. My voice only trembled slightly when I continued. "A long time ago, someone who was my idol told me that It was rare to find someone who truly sees what lies beneath the surface so clearly. Thinking about those words now? They truly embody how Okiyo saw me as more than what I presented on the surface. Now he's gone and I feel like I'm missing a piece of me."

Subitha was quiet for a moment, and then she leaned forward, handing me a tissue. Her presence as steady as the floor beneath my feet.

"Delia, do you believe in soulmates?"

"I don't know." I laughed softly, wiping a tear away with the tissue she'd given me. "I guess I've always thought that a soulmate is supposed to stay forever. Someone who's meant to be with you, always."

She smiled, the corners of her eyes crinkling. "Soulmates aren't always meant to stay forever. Sometimes they come into your life to help you grow, to change you in ways you didn't think possible. And then they leave, but their impact indelibly remains imprinted on *your* soul. They help shape you into the person you are meant to be."

Her words comforted me, cutting through the pain that had lodged itself in my chest since Okiyo left. I looked down at my hands, twisting my fingers together as I thought about what she said.

"So... you're saying Okiyo was my soulmate, even if he's gone?" I asked, my voice barely a whisper.

"Yes, I believe so," she said, her voice filled with warmth. "From everything you've told me, it sounds like he helped you heal in ways you didn't know you needed. He pushed you, challenged you, helped you grow. And look at you. You're stronger for it. That's what a soulmate does, Delia. They come into your life to help your soul grow."

I took a shaky breath, the tears slipping down my cheeks before I could stop them. My chest felt tight, like there was a weight pressing down on it, but there was also a flicker of something else—something like understanding.

"But why does it still hurt so much?" I asked, my voice breaking. "Why does it feel like... like there's this emptiness inside me?"

Subitha leaned back slightly, her gaze never leaving mine. "Because growth is painful, Delia. Letting go is hard. And just because he's gone doesn't mean the love, the connection, didn't matter. It mattered. And it always will."

I closed my eyes, the tears falling freely now. I could see Okiyo in my mind—the way he looked at me, the way his voice softened when he said my name, the way he held me like he was trying to protect me from the world. He had been my rock, my strength, and now he was gone. But he'd also given me the strength to be my own rock.

"You don't have to let go of him entirely," Subitha continued, her voice a steady anchor. "You can carry him with you. Carry the love, the lessons, the strength he helped you find. Let that be your closure."

I opened my eyes, looking at her through the blur of my tears. "But I don't know how to move on without him."

"You're already doing it," she said, her voice gentle but unwavering. "You're here, you're showing up, you're working through the pain. Moving forward doesn't mean forgetting him, Delia.

It means honoring what he gave you by continuing to grow." I instinctively touched my stomach as her words poured over me.

I nodded, the weight on my chest starting to lift, just a little. It wasn't going to be easy. There would still be days when the ache of his absence felt like too much to bear. But maybe... maybe I could find a way to carry him with me, without letting the pain consume me.

"Thank you, Subitha," I whispered at the end of our session, my voice barely audible.

She smiled, her eyes softening. "You're stronger than you think, Delia. And you're not alone. You have your family, your friends, and most importantly, you have yourself."

It had only been six sessions in and I did indeed feel stronger, more capable than ever to take on the challenge of creating the life I wanted.

The guilt I had carried over what happened to Iya still lingered, but I was finally beginning to let it go. The blame I had carried for so long wasn't mine to bear. The therapy sessions were tough, peeling back memories and emotions I had buried for years, but it was all necessary. I wouldn't keep punishing myself—not in the ring, not in life.

After my therapy session, I met Iya at the florists shop doing the arrangements for the wedding. I'd also thrown myself headfirst into my duties as her maid of honor, reveling in the joy and excitement that filled the air. Life was definitely moving forward.

"What do you think of this bouquet?" Iya's voice broke through my thoughts as she waved a beautiful arrangement of pink and white roses in front of my face.

I smiled, taking in the soft, romantic colors. "It's perfect, Iya. You're going to look absolutely stunning."

"I hope so!" She said excitedly, a mischievous grin spreading on her face giving me a sidelong glance. "I also want to make sure my big sis and maid of honor looks just as stunning. *You know?* In case there are any handsome potentials in the wedding party. You know Dez, Justin's best man is single... *annnnd* he's escorting you down the aisle."

I rolled my eyes. Had just finished crying on my therapists shoulder about a man I hadn't seen or heard from in nearly nine weeks.. "Iya, please. I'm not looking for a man right now. I've got enough on my plate."

She nudged me playfully. "Oh, come on. It doesn't hurt to keep an eye out. You never know who might be around the corner looking at that ass" She playfully swatted me on my rear. "And girl, that *thang is thangin'* right now!"

"Shut up, Iya," I playfully pushed her towards the register to take care of the remaining payment on all the damn flowers for her wedding and to get her attention off my spreading hips and ass.

Chapter 34 – Delia

THE ORCHESTRAL VERSION OF Outkast's "SpottieOt-tieDopaliscious" blended seamlessly with the sounds of nature, making me smile. Classical hip-hop infused the air as a string quartet played soft notes in the background. The entrance to the garden offered a bird's-eye view of the guests gathered for Iya's wedding.

It was a beautiful day for a wedding—autumn leaves rustled, birds chirped, and a gentle breeze carried the scent of jasmine, dahlias and roses, Iya's flowers of choice.

The setting was something out of a dream. It was a fairytale garden wedding, just like Iya always wanted. Though I'd been late to help my mom set it up, I was incredibly proud of the vision she'd put together, and I was grateful to have gathered myself enough to assist in the final touches.

For so long, I carried the weight of guilt on my shoulders, letting it define me. But not today. Standing here as my sister's maid of honor, watching her take this incredible step forward in her life, I felt a sense of real, honest peace. I worked hard to get here—just under three months of therapy helped me unpack years of guilt. For the first time, I was truly happy for my sister. I was happy for myself too.

I adjusted my dress, a sleek, elegant gown with rouching in the front and hugged my curves everywhere else. One thing was certain—the women in the McGee family were going to show out when it came to fashion. I smiled, thinking back to the fuss my mom made as she chose all our dresses. The champagne color she'd chosen for me complimented my skin tone perfectly. I smoothed the dress over my stomach then turned to look at my sideview in the mirror to admiring how the low back dip em emphasized the curve of my ass. I did indeed feel beautiful.

I only stepped out briefly to walk around the gardens, making sure everything was in place, but now I was quickly making my way to the bridal suite, where Iya was getting the final touches of her makeup and hair done before the big moment.

I knocked lightly to announce my arrival, cracking the door open just a bit. I didn't want her husband-to-be's prying eyes catching a glimpse of her before she walked down the aisle. We definitely couldn't break that tradition.

Iya turned around, and as our eyes met, I almost teared up. She was glowing—positively radiant in her gown, her dark curls spilling over her shoulders, her smile as bright as the sun. I couldn't help but smile too.

"You ready?" I asked, raising my eyebrows playfully.

She let out a nervous but excited sigh. "More than ready," she said, rolling her eyes up to stop tears from forming. She quickly chuckled to lighten the mood. "I'm ready to jump this man's bones. You know he's forced us to be celibate the past couple of months, right?"

Before I could respond, my mom piped in from across the room, "Damn, he put your hot ass on ice, didn't he?"

The room erupted into laughter, and I almost couldn't resist yelling out, *sounds like we'll be celebrating a baby in nine months*, but caught myself.

We all laughed again, and as the makeup artist finished up the last touch-ups on Iya, we circled around her in a tight sister circle—me, my mom, and her two other bridesmaids, friends she had been close with for years. I grabbed Iya's hand, giving it a gentle squeeze.

"You look beautiful, sis," I said sincerely, my voice thick with emotion.

She grinned, her eyes glistening with unshed tears. "Thank you, Delia. I'm so glad you're here with me as my maid of honor." Then she turned to the group and faux whispered, "She's older than me, so technically she should be my matron of honor."

I rolled my eyes, and the other girls giggled. I sobered a little as Iya continued, her voice softer, "I really couldn't have done any of this without you." She looked over at Mom, who nodded in full agreement.

A lump formed in my throat, and this time I swallowed it down. This wasn't the time for tears—this was a celebration. "You're going to be an amazing wife, Iya. And don't worry, I've got your back today. Maid of honor duties in full effect," I said with a grin.

She laughed, and the sound was pure joy.

The ceremony was ready to begin. I walked down the aisle ahead of the other bridesmaids and groomsmen, hand in hand with the best man—Dez, Justin's closest friend. If I didn't admit that Dez was fine as hell, I'd be lying, even though he was very much taken. Not to mention, he was also the one who'd busted me out to my family about my fight against Storm, which led to all of this—my family knowing, supporting, and being a part of my life again. I guess I owed him some gratitude for that, even if it wasn't the easiest way for them to find out.

The aisle was perfectly adorned, a dream brought to life with rose petals in shades of pink and cream. It all led to an altar where vines, flowers, and fairy lights intertwined to form a stunning arch that shimmered in the afternoon sun. It felt like a place where anything was possible—a place where love was celebrated, and hope was renewed.

As I reached my spot at the end of the altar, I turned, joining the rest of the guests as we all rose from our seats. Iya was about to enter, her moment arriving at last. The Bridgerton-esque quartet swelled, playing an orchestral version of a melody that felt both timeless and modern, their stringed instruments and piano weaving magic in the air.

And there she was. My little sister, glowing from the inside out. I only wish my dad could be here to walk her down the aisle. I felt a swell of pride in my chest that almost took my breath away.

This was the same little girl who used to run after me in the yard, demanding to do everything I did, and now she was the vision of beauty, walking towards her future with grace and strength. I longed for the day that I'd be able to do the same. My vision blurred for a second, but I blinked the tears away, determined to keep it together.

Their vows... *God*, their vows were everything. There wasn't a dry eye in the garden. The love between Iya and Justin could be felt reverberating through everyone present. As they exchanged rings and kissed, sealing their union, the crowd erupted in applause. I joined in, clapping and cheering along with everyone else, my heart feeling light and full.

This was love. I'd had a taste of it for a brief time. Seeing the love exchanged between Iya and Justin brought hope that it would be possible for me again.

And then I sensed something—something that made me scan the audience and the entire garden. I couldn't quite place where that tingling sensation, the feeling of being watched, was coming from.

Maybe it was the swell of emotions for my sister, the joy I felt for her and Justin. But it felt like something else, as if a missing piece of me had suddenly clicked into place. It was an eerie feeling, yet somehow, it felt like the world was finally in its proper orbit.

The reception was held under a sprawling tent, draped in soft, flowing fabric that billowed gently in the breeze. The same fairy lights from the wedding altar now hung from the ceiling, casting a warm, inviting glow over the tables.

The entire scene was like a dream, a perfect fusion of all the cultures that defined our families—Mexican, African, and American. The decor leaned towards a Mexican theme, while Gastrafrique—Andra and Kobe's restaurant—had brought the African flavors to life, and it all blended seamlessly.

When Iya mentioned wanting her wedding and reception to reflect our dual heritage, I immediately thought of Gastrafrique. They had done an incredible job, and I couldn't have been more proud of the way it all came together.

As I scanned the room, I spotted Andra across the tent, her seven-month baby bump prominent beneath her fitted dress. She looked radiant despite all the hustle, overseeing everything to make sure it was perfect. Kobe was by her side in his chef's attire, grinning from ear to ear, clearly proud of his wife and their growing family.

I made my way over to greet them, wanting to thank them for the incredible spread. Though I didn't know them very well, I'd formed a connection with Andra ever since I first stepped into Gastrafrique with Okiyo months ago.

"Delia!" Andra called out as she saw me approaching. "You look amazing, girl!"

I laughed, pulling her into a careful hug. "Look who's talking! You're glowing, Andra. How are you feeling?"

"Tired as hell," she admitted with a chuckle. "but this man here has been pampering me nonstop—rubbing my feet and making sure I'm comfortable. I'm not gonna stop him either!" She laughed again, nodding towards Kobe. "The baby starts kicking up a storm every time he does, but I'm just happy everything's going smoothly today."

She looked out across the room, her gaze settling on the guests who were either in the process of fixing plates or coming back for seconds. "The food's a hit, just like we thought!" she said, grinning, her laughter filled with love as she looked up at Kobe, pride evident in her eyes.

"Of course," I echoed, smiling at Kobe as he joined us. "You two have outdone yourselves. This is incredible. And I have to thank you for lending the camera crew and photographers from the TV show to capture Iya's big day."

"It only made sense," Kobe replied with a warm smile. "We're always looking for content for the Gastrafrique TV show and our Instagram, so when you all said you were cool with filming, it was the perfect opportunity. We're out here telling the story of love through African food too."

"Yeah, what he said." Andra laughed, her gaze never leaving her handsome husband. "We're happy to be a part of it. I'm just here barking orders while Kobe handles everything like the boss he is." She slipped her arm around his waist, and they shared a tender look.

They were so damn cute together.

Love was definitely in the air tonight. I could feel its energy radiating from Andra and Kobe, warming me as I stood there watching them.

Just like earlier today, that same tingling sensation swept over my skin, a sense of anticipation that felt almost palpable. I smiled at them, ready to bid my farewells and make my way to speak to other guests, when something caught my eye.

A sudden wisp of red.

I paused, my heart skipping a beat. It was the vibrant red of a pocket square, peeking out from a dark vest. My eyes widened, and for a moment, I held my breath. There was only one person who wore pocket squares, vests, and even pocket watches that I knew.

I turned fully, my breath catching in my throat.

Okiyo.

He stood near the entrance of the tent, dressed in a perfectly tailored suit that hugged his frame in all the right ways. The crimson square, that tiny splash of color, seemed to burn its way into my memory, making my heart clench.

He was impossibly handsome, his silhouette somehow more captivating than I remembered. His eyes locked onto mine, and for a brief moment, the world seemed to fall away. Everything else—the music, the laughter, the clinking of glasses—faded into the background as my heart pounded in my chest.

He began walking toward me, his gaze never wavering. Each step he took seemed to bring with it a tidal wave of emotions I thought I had buried.

Andra leaned in, her voice barely above a whisper. "Go get your man, Delia."

I didn't need any more encouragement. I took a deep breath, my heart thundering in my chest, and moved. My feet seemed to carry me of their own accord, meeting him halfway. The world melted away until it was just the two of us, and with every step, my pulse quickened, my emotions running wild.

When I finally reached him, I fought back tears that I hadn't even realized were forming. There he was—the man who had occupied my every thought for months, standing right in front of me, close enough to touch.

When we finally stood face to face, I found myself unable to speak. But I didn't need words—the look in his eyes said it all. He reached out, gently cupping my cheek, and I leaned into his touch, the warmth of his hand grounding me in the moment.

"I'm sorry," he said softly, his voice thick with emotion. "I should never have left you."

I shook my head, tears welling in my eyes. "You had to go. I understood."

"No, Delia," he said, his thumb brushing away the tear that had escaped down my cheek. "I should've told you how I felt. I care for you... deeply. And I won't bore you with the fact that I've never felt this way for anyone. I can't even describe what these feelings are, because, truth be told, I don't know what love is. So I won't lie to you and throw that bloody word around like it sums it all up. It's too small a word for what you make me feel."

His hand shifted slightly, cupping my face fully, his touch warm and grounding.

"*Swear,* Delia, I want the best for you, but more than that... I want to be better for you. And what I do know, without a doubt, is that my life's empty without you in it. I can't lose you again, Delia. Not now, not ever."

The way he spoke, the British timber of his voice, made his words sound like pure poetry. My heart swelled with emotion, and another tear slipped down my cheek. He quickly brushed it away with his thumb.

"I've been waiting for you," I whispered, my voice trembling. "And I didn't even know it. I sensed you before I saw you, as if the universe was telling me, even earlier today, that my world was going to be alright. And here you are."

I reached up, my hand brushing the lone tear that trickled down his cheek. "And I'm not going anywhere. Not today, not ever, so long as you shall have me, Okiyo Bamdi."

Without another word, he pulled me into his arms, his lips finding mine in a kiss that was filled with everything I hadn't said—love, longing, and the promise of a future together. The world around us melted away, leaving just the two of us in our own little bubble of happiness. Every corner of my heart that felt incomplete suddenly felt whole.

When we finally pulled apart, I rested my forehead against his, a smile tugging at my lips. "You're stuck with me now, Okiyo."

His hands rested against my waist, but something about the way his touch lingered there made me pause. His brow furrowed slightly, his fingers drifting down, brushing over my abdomen with the lightest touch. Slowly, he pulled back just enough to look down, his eyes scanning the curve of my belly.

"Delia...?" His voice was softer now, filled with an unspoken question. His hand stayed there, gentle, yet firm, as if he was trying to understand what his instincts were telling him.

I swallowed hard, the emotions bubbling up in my chest—fear, hope, excitement. "*Umm*" I began, my voice barely above a whisper, "Yes." I placed my hand over his, pressing it gently against my belly.

His eyes widened, flicking back up to mine, and for the first time since I'd known him, Okiyo looked genuinely stunned.

"*Bloody hell*," he whispered, his voice cracking slightly. He looked at me, his usually sharp, analytical gaze softened by something more vulnerable. "We're having a baby?" The words hung in the air, full of disbelief and wonder.

I nodded, tears welling in my eyes. "Yes. In about seven months." I scrunched up my face, "It's kind of what happens when you screw a girls brains out on a dojo floor, I guess." I smiled at the bigger smile spread across his face and placed my other hand over his.

For a long moment, he just stared, his hand trembling slightly as he absorbed the news. Then, with a deep breath, he pulled me back into his arms, holding me so tightly I could feel the weight of all the emotions he hadn't spoken.

"You and our child…" he whispered against my ear, his voice thick with emotion. "You are my world. I swear it, Delia. Nothing else matters." He pulled back just enough to cup my face, his eyes burning with a promise. "I'll be here. Always."

I let out a small laugh, wiping the tears from my eyes. "Well, you better be, because things are about to get even more complicated." I took a deep breath, the reality of everything hitting me at once. "I'm leaving for Paris after Iya's wedding… for work. I'll be there for a while."

His expression shifted, a mix of surprise and understanding flashing across his face. "Paris, huh?" he said, his eyes lighting up slightly. "Overseeing the security upgrades we worked on together?"

"Yes," I said, nodding. "And… helping design a new hotel for 3W."

His eyes widened in realization, a proud grin slowly spreading across his face. "Designing a hotel?" He raised an eyebrow, his voice filled with excitement. "That means you've got your license. You're an official architect now."

I nodded, my own smile widening as the weight of his words hit me. "Yes, I am."

He let out a joyful laugh, his hand cupping the back of my neck as he pulled me into another kiss, this one filled with pure pride.

"Bloody brilliant," he murmured against my lips. "Even more to celebrate, love."

I looked up at him, my heart swelling with gratitude and love. "Paris may be far, but it's nothing compared to the distance we've already crossed."

He grinned, leaning down to kiss me again, slower this time, as if savoring the moment. "I'll follow you anywhere, love."

The End

Thanks for reading *Tempest In Tulum*. Please consider leaving an honest review about this work on the store where you bought or on Amazon at the link below.

Click or Scan to leave
an honest review.

About the Author

CHER TERAIS IS THE ultimate Renaissance woman! With a passion for travel and an eye for gorgeous interior design and architecture, she's crafted beautiful stories centered around black love and its complexities.

Take a journey with her from busy street markets to distant escapes in her books that will take you around the world.

Originally from Warner Robins, Georgia, Cher spent time in the Army before moving to the Middle East as a Program Manager. Her travels allowed her to dive into diverse cultures as well as serve as a springboard for more trips around Asia, the Caribbean and Europe. Proud mother of two daughters and one grandson, Cher encourages them to pursue their dreams of no limits!

Follow her on social media (@cher_terais (all major platforms) @cher_terais_author on TikTok) to learn more about this amazing author who calls the suburbs of Atlanta home!

Don't forget to checkout other books in the Wanderlust Romance series!

Bali Blue

Mess on the Mara

Stay even more connected by scanning the QR Code below to get bonus content for Cher Terais's books. Discover the fun things like:

The soundtrack to this book and the others

Inspiration boards and visuals for each book;

Free downloadables, short stories and more!

https://linktr.ee/Cher_Terais

The trip doesn't stop here! *The Booked Club* community and podcast are COMING SOON!

Sign up for my mailing list for more details!